# ESCAPING DENVER

# BOOKS BY TEAGUE BOHLEN

STANDALONE NOVELS

*Escaping Denver*

*The Pull of the Earth*

SHORT STORIES

*Flatland*

NONFICTION

*The Snarktastic Guide to College Success*

(with Sandra Mizumoto Posey)

# ESCAPING DENVER

TEAGUE BOHLEN

BLACK
STONE
PUBLISHING

Published in 2025 by Blackstone Publishing
Cover and book design by Sarah Riedlinger



Printed in the United States of America

First edition: 2025
ISBN 979-8-228-31205-0
Fiction / Science Fiction / General

Version 1

Blackstone Publishing
31 Mistletoe Rd.
Ashland, OR 97520

www.BlackstonePublishing.com

*For Stephanie,*
*who squares off against all monsters*
*and looks damn fine doing it.*

Whoever fights monsters should see to it that in the process he does not become a monster. And if you gaze long enough into an abyss, the abyss will gaze back into you.

—Friedrich Nietzsche

We have met the enemy and he is us.

—The more succinct Pogo,
by way of Walt Kelly

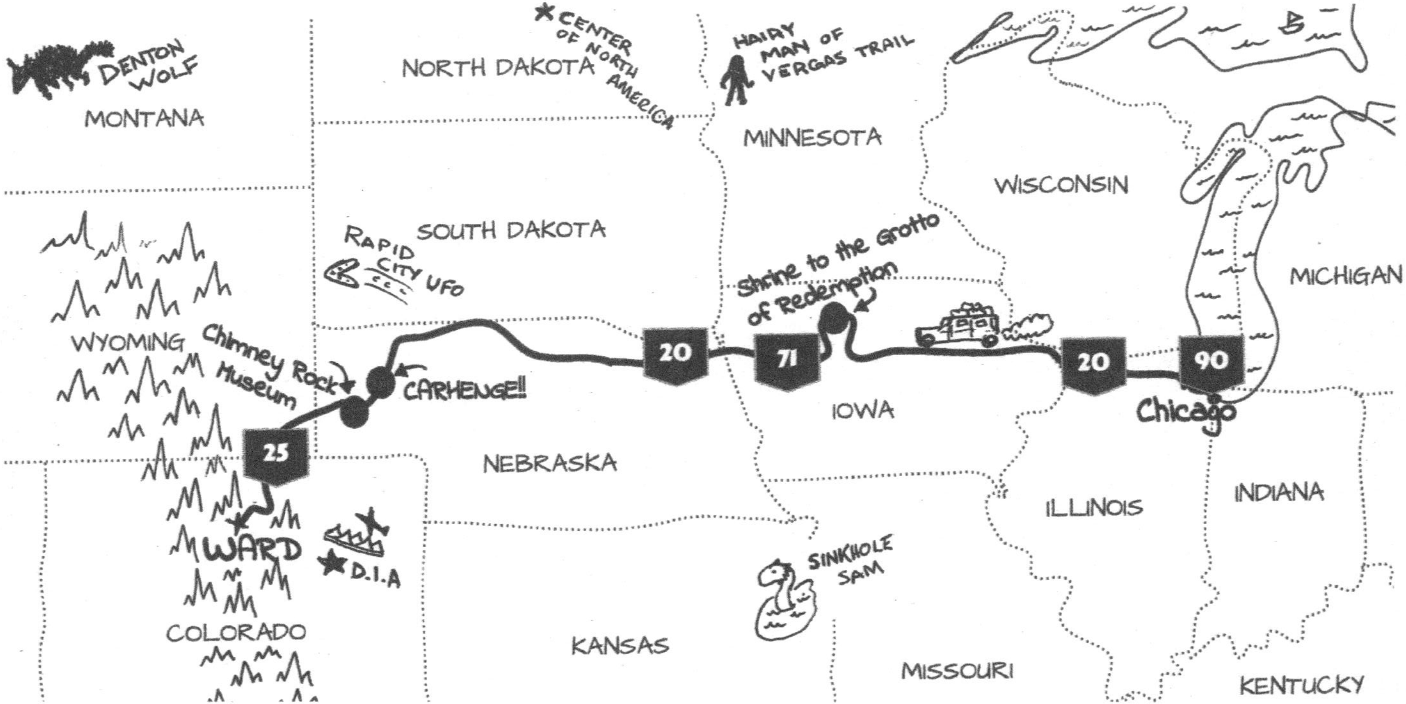
DENTON WOLF
MONTANA
NORTH DAKOTA
CENTER OF NORTH AMERICA
HAIRY MAN OF VERGAS TRAIL
MINNESOTA
WISCONSIN
MICHIGAN
SOUTH DAKOTA
RAPID CITY UFO
WYOMING
Chimney Rock Museum
CARHENGE!!
Shrine to the Grotto of Redemption
20
71
20
90
Chicago
25
IOWA
NEBRASKA
ILLINOIS
INDIANA
WARD
D.I.A
SINKHOLE SAM
COLORADO
KANSAS
MISSOURI
KENTUCKY

# PROLOGUE

SOMEWHERE BENEATH DENVER INTERNATIONAL AIRPORT

If anyone were there to witness it, they would hear the man's footsteps first. Door after indistinguishable door, floor tile after floor tile after beige floor tile veined in black. Walls eggshell white. The doors are wooden, or veneered to look that way. Institutional, some might say. Built by the lowest bidder, others might counter.

But not the doors at the end of the hallway, where the man pauses. These doors are most definitely wood. Quartersawn oak, from the look of it. Heavy. Built to withstand. He opens the door with an unsteady hand—in the other, he holds a Pelican case covered in stickers from far-off places that are most decidedly not here. They are colorful, announce excitement, pleasing. The only things that are, in this hallway.

When the man opens the door, he sees only the back of the woman's chair, facing the back wall as though there were something there to see. "What the fuck happened?" she asks in a clipped voice.

"We don't know," the man stammers out. "We don't know how many are dead. How many got out. We have people on it, examining the footage."

"Double their efforts," she responds, calm. Too calm. "Triple it. Whatever you have to do."

"I assure you," the man says with forced conviction, "we'll get to the bottom of it." He holds out the Pelican case, opening it to show off its contents—a foam shell filled with memory cards, like butterflies pinned to a collector's board.

The woman turns her chair to look. The light from the desk glints off the memory cards, and illuminates one more thing adorning the interior of the case: are those spots . . . blood?

Or so might be the question. If anyone was there to witness it.

# CHAPTER ONE

CHICAGO, ILLINOIS

Jessica Boyer heard the scream come from right above her. She was under the Brown Line stop on Damen, out on a run for the second time that day because her brain wouldn't stop working, and her feet always seemed to quiet it. The scream was almost a cry for help, she thought, something uncontrolled from the belly. Had someone been hit by the train? Mugged? She considered the options as she clambered up the steps, taking them two at a time without even thinking. It was the voice, or rather the timbre of it, that made her react. It sounded like a kid.

Jessie had been right about the kid part, but not the cause—there was a girl somewhere on the cusp between tween and teen, purple hair spilling over earbuds and eyes alike, on her knees next to a woman in business clothes—a woman twitching in a way Jessie recognized only too well.

It was a grand mal seizure, something Jessie had experienced herself, but never seen up close and personal. This showed all the signs: the woman was jerking uncontrollably, her eyes shut tight, her skin slightly blue. She'd peed herself and had bit the shit out of her tongue or cheek, based on the little bit of blood in one corner of her mouth. She was letting out little whines with every twitch, like a dog that had been hit by a car and didn't understand why it couldn't get up.

The girl was understandably apoplectic, and Jessie knelt down next to her. "It's okay," she said, "it's okay."

"It's *not* okay!" the girl screamed, tears tracing thick mascara trails down her cheek. "What the fuck is happening?"

"She's having a seizure," Jessie said, forcing calm into her voice. "Has she had one of these before?"

"I don't know," the girl said, apparently unable to lower the volume or pitch of her voice. She grabbed at her violet hair, exposing blonde roots. "I mean, we're just reconnecting. I've been living with my dad for—"

The girl was cut off by a man with a briefcase and a huge belt hanger of a belly. He held out his wallet and shoved it into the girl's hand. "Here, put this in her mouth!" he said.

"Ew," the girl said, suddenly subdued. "Here." She handed it to Jessie.

The leather wallet was still butt-warm and slightly moist. "No," said Jessie, handing the thing back to Big Belly Briefcase with two fingers. "I know you're trying to help, but that's a myth. It can actually hurt someone."

"But she'll swallow her tongue," he protested, but weakly, and put his wallet back in his slacks. "I saw it on a cop show."

"That's TV," Jessie said. She looked Purple Hair squarely in the eyes and said, "The only thing to do is to sit with her and make sure she's safe until it passes. When the shaking stops, we roll her on her side gently so she can breathe better."

"You a nurse or something?" Big Belly asked with a hint of accusation.

"Or something," Jessie said without looking up. "I'm Jessie. You're doing all right. You need to breathe too."

The girl nodded. "I'm Kira," she said. "How long does it take to stop?" And then, like a breeze passing, the woman on the L platform ceased her violent jerking and lay still, almost as if she was asleep now. They rolled her on her side gently; the woman didn't stir.

"She'll be okay," Jessie said. "That was the clonic phase. It's the worst. She'll calm down now and then slowly come to, and she won't remember a thing."

"The colonic phase?" Kira's grimace would have been comical under different circumstances.

"Clonic," Jessie repeated, shaking her head. "It just means it's the time in the seizure with convulsions. Don't worry. You'll get to know the terminology—that is, if you're going to be around your mom."

"Yeah, well," Kira said. "I don't know. I haven't seen her in like six years, and then she pops up out of nowhere and asks to meet me for lunch at Golden Nugget Pancakes. Apparently, we used to go there when I was little. Before she walked out on me and my dad."

"Stress can bring it on," Jessie offered. "So, if she was nervous about meeting with you . . ."

"Probably was," Kira admitted as EMTs came up the stairs like a rushing wave, pushing their way in. "She should have been, anyway."

Jessie stood up and got out of the way. The experts were here. She could relax. But she felt for this girl. Someone who had been abandoned by her mother. Jessie sort of knew how that felt.

"All I wanted was a fucking omelet," the girl said to no one in particular.

"Are you going to be okay?" Jessie asked the girl, who just shrugged, still gazing down at her mother.

"She'll be fine, ma'am," one of the EMTs said. "Are you related to either of these ladies?"

Jessie shook her head no.

"Then I'm going to have to ask you to leave this area," he said. "If you need to catch the next train, you'll have to walk down to the next stop. Or wait down on street level for us to reopen the platform."

Jessie walked slowly toward the stairs, listening to Big Belly Briefcase arguing about how it was a free country, and he needed to catch the next train and something about delusions of grandeur. *Look who's talking*, Jess thought as she descended the stairs back down to the street. She turned on her earbuds and cranked up the Tom Petty playlist she'd chosen for the afternoon's run.

She glanced at the time before stowing her phone back in the zipper pocket of her sweat pants. 4:30 p.m. Almost rush hour. Traffic was already thick, and so were the sidewalks. As much as she loved running—as much as it helped her maintain a certain mental balance—she hated running at this time of day. Everyone seemed so pissed off.

Not Jessie. She forced a feeling of well-being into her chest since she knew that was the goal. *Fake it till you make it*, she thought, though she didn't know where she'd learned it or if she actually believed it.

She started running, controlling her pace, straight up Damen Avenue.

Jessie felt as though she'd been running all her life, but it had really started that summer after she had her first seizure. It had been Easter when the seizure hit, a Sunday at the Methodist church her grandmother attended and taught Sunday school to a room full of four- and five-year-olds. Jessie was thirteen. She was sitting in one of their undersized chairs, helping her grandmother by cutting Jesuses out of green felt so the kids could glue googly eyes and halos on them.

Jessie didn't remember freezing all of a sudden, mid-scissor-cut. Didn't remember dropping the felt Jesus and safety scissors or clattering to the floor from the foot-high chair, sending art supplies across the floor. Didn't remember convulsing and drooling, or her grandmother screaming, and some of the children following suit, or wetting herself in her new pastel sundress, or church services stopping cold, or the ambulance arriving and being carted away to the hospital where she'd wake up with maybe a dozen little googly eyes that should have belonged to Jesus still stuck to her back.

"You always did like all eyes on you," her mother said when recounting what had happened. Jessie had to admit, all these years later, that it wasn't a bad joke.

But in that moment in the hospital, Jessie hated her mother—and not for the first time. Or the last.

Jessie would have another seizure in May, and another right on schedule in June before they declared it was officially a "seizure condition," though they wouldn't otherwise give it a name. Jess had heard the word "epilepsy" before and wondered why it didn't apply to her. She was too afraid to ask.

She had a neurologist who told her that she'd have to monitor herself carefully, whatever that meant. He didn't elaborate—he just prescribed a medicine that would essentially make her forget anything she might have learned in first period geometry that fall. But that summer before—that was when Jessie started running.

She began running around the block, and adding another block every day if she could. By the time school started, she was no longer measuring her runs by blocks, but rather by time, running as far as she could before turning around halfway through and running back.

It was the cadence that helped her. The metronomic pace of one foot after the other, over and over, propelling her forward. It was like meditation, in a way. She got lost in it sometimes. Every day, without fail, rain or sun, no matter how her left knee shrieked or that stitch in her right side kept making a reappearance. She bought new running shoes every month, just in case. They were on automatic shipping. Also just in case.

Jessie took a deep breath as she passed Winnemac Park on her left. Someone was out cutting the grass—it was one of those smells she loved, craved even. Especially when she found herself spending too much time indoors. Jessie realized she'd slowed down to take in more of the cut lawn in the air, so she picked up her pace, that familiar heaviness starting to rise up her legs.

*Ain't no hill for a stepper*, Jessie remembered her grandmother saying. She'd died later the same year the seizures started, but had lived long enough to tell Jessie how proud she was for all the running. She'd said Jessie's grandfather was a runner too. What kind, Jessie didn't know, but always wished that she'd asked.

What Jessie had asked her grandmother was what that phrase meant: *Ain't no hill for a stepper.* It meant perseverance, her grandmother explained, and winked in a way that made Jessie feel like she should understand it better than perhaps she did at that moment. Now, over a decade later, she felt like she knew—well enough, at least—to keep going.

But the mystery of her condition, thick like nighttime summer air, heavy and portentous. Why her? Why seizures? Why was their source so inexplicable? Why was she on phenobarbital for half a year, and then taken off any sort of treatment? Why had she had no seizures since, except for that one time when she was home from college to visit her mother?

Though she figured that the stress inherent in seeing her mother might have been all the answer needed for that question.

Why was she allowed to go untreated, but not allowed to get a driver's license? Why didn't she care more that she couldn't? She didn't want to drive—not really, since it would make her more nervous than she cared to admit—but she wanted to want to drive. Which made very little sense, she realized.

She'd told a boyfriend that once when he expressed annoyance that she couldn't ever take a turn at being the designated driver, especially since she didn't like to drink. He shook his head, scoffing, and she broke up with him a few days later.

The running was part of the way Jessie dealt with the mysteries in her life—keeping a tight grip on her body and what it could do. It released some of the pressure for what her body might do, without any real warning. It had been nearly a decade since her last seizure, and Jessie was determined to keep that particular streak going.

But she also kept her head busy with other mysteries. She'd always been interested in solving puzzles, and those kid-safe stories that always ended with cracking the case. But she moved on to mysteries of the unsolved variety, delving into everything Hans Holzer ever wrote about real ghosts and mysterious disappearances. The *Mary Celeste*. The Dyatlov Pass nine. Jack the Ripper, Atlantis, the Loch Ness Monster, Bigfoot, and the Voynich manuscript. And so much more. It was dizzying. Beautifully so. There was so much more mystery to the world than people thought, so much going on around them that they didn't bother to notice, consider, or investigate.

Jessie was thinking about all this as she jogged through the southern gates of Rosehill Cemetery, one of her favorite places to run. There was such quietude here, this sprawling garden of ended lives right in the heart of the city. She ran a somewhat random loop around the grounds, eventually aiming to exit the gates on Western Avenue where it intersected with Bryn Mawr and head home.

Jessie shared a small bungalow in the North Mayfair neighborhood with her best friend Toby. They'd somehow lucked into a beautiful little house with a brick front porch that had a view of Gompers Park up the street if you craned your neck a little. To say it was affordable was an understatement. In a part of town in which monthlies could be ridiculously high even for run-down rentals, they paid almost a quarter of what their neighbors did. And they split that half-and-half, even though Jessie had the larger of the two bedrooms. It was the only way they could have stayed in the city. Toby stocked shelves at a local Osco while working on a fantasy novel he wouldn't talk about. Jessie was a paralegal, or did the work of one anyway, which was only barely connected to her double major in sociology and anthropology.

Left on Pulaski from Bryn Mawr, heading south.

Jessie realized she had to kick it into high gear if she was going to have time to shower before her Zoom meeting. She'd taken too long on the L platform, not that she regretted a minute of it. She wondered if that girl Kira would make up with her mom. Meet her for more pancakes. Come to learn terms like tonic-clonic and ictal and the adopted French of grand mal and petit mal. Or maybe hers would be a one-and-done seizure. Some people were lucky like that. Both in terms of seizures and in the ability to connect with their mother in a significant way.

Jessie's head started feeling fuzzy, which often happened when she was thinking too much about seizures. Probably just a panic attack of sorts, but it was bad enough that it made her want to get home even more and stand in a hot shower for a bit. That usually calmed her down, made her a little more able to focus, let her catch a thought, and hold on. Jessie closed her eyes for a moment as she ran, breathing purposefully and forcefully, trying to find her center.

Which is probably, as she crossed Foster on Pulaski heading for the park, what made her completely oblivious to the black sedan bearing down on her.

# CHAPTER TWO

ALBANY PARK, CHICAGO

"What the fuck, Jessie?"

Toby's voice came from behind her as she felt a sharp tug on the back of her sports top—one that literally pulled her back to the curb and off her feet. She landed hard on the concrete as the car sped by, seemingly oblivious to what had almost happened.

"Watch it, you asshat!" Toby yelled at the sedan as it continued down the street and away.

Jessie took a deep breath from where she remained sitting on the curb, her feet on a storm drain. She looked down into its depths, momentarily grateful for her continued ability to marvel at what mysteries might lay below. She closed her eyes as she felt Toby grunt down next to her, settling his bulk so her shoulder touched his bicep.

Not for the first time, Jessie was reminded that her longtime friend was not only big, but pretty strong too, even if those muscles were wrapped under some chub. But Toby carried it well, Jessie had always thought, even back when she'd first met him in college in the University of Illinois dorms. She'd initially thought he was hitting on her when he asked her if she'd ever played Dungeons & Dragons. Turns out he wasn't—he was just part of a group that desperately needed a cleric. That gaming group didn't last long, but her friendship with Toby did. They stayed close throughout college, even when Jessie dated some guy or another. Toby never seemed to date, and didn't even seem like he wanted to. He was satisfied to be Jessie's bestie—or so he claimed—and he never gave Jessie occasion to doubt his sincerity.

"Thanks," Jessie said weakly.

Toby shook his head and pulled absently at an earlobe. "If I hadn't just got off my shift, that could have been really bad."

"I blame the earbuds," Jessie said, taking them out and putting them away in their case. "That and just thinking too much."

"That tracks." Toby shot her a grudgingly amused look. "Just fucking be careful, okay?"

"Yeah, yeah," Jessie said. "Thanks, Dad."

"*Walk right side, safe. Walk left side, safe,*" Toby said in his best Mr. Miyagi. "*Walk middle, sooner or later, get squish, just like grape.*"

"Is it worse to get *squish like grape*?" Jessie asked. "Or to quote old movies that had some terrible racial stereotypes?"

"Is it wrong that your near-death experience has made me want to stream every single Karate Kid movie again?" Toby mused.

"Well, I have a Zoom to get to," Jessie said, getting up and brushing herself off. "So you can watch anything you want."

"Oh, right," Toby said, standing too, and they started to cross the street with the light this time. "Today's the final meeting of your little Scooby gang before the big face-to-face. Aren't you afraid of meeting these people? I mean, they could be anyone."

"I've seen them on Zoom a bunch of times," Jessie said.

"And I've done my due diligence, you know that. It's the one benefit to working this stupid law office job. They have access to all sorts of databases."

"That you illegally access," Toby pointed out.

"Small crimes in the pursuit of larger truths are, in essence, no crime at all," Jessie countered.

"Who said that?" Toby asked.

"I did," Jessie said. "Just now. Can you run with me the rest of the way? I'm going to be late even without the shower."

---

Toby declined her invitation to run the rest of the way, which Jessie found satisfactory if only because she made better time running home alone. She beat him home by about ten minutes, but those were well spent with a quick rinse off and change of clothes.

Jessie sat at the big desk in the living room to the right of the picture window looking out onto the street. It was her favorite seat in the house, an oversized executive chair with *Real Artificial Leathers* according to the tag on the underside. And the desk was an old professorial piece from the Northwestern surplus sales the campus would sometimes have. The price was right, but it nearly gave Jessie and Toby twin hernias getting the thing off Toby's pickup truck, up the front steps, and into the house. They weren't planning on putting it in the living room, but they both agreed it was fine right where it was. In the end, it made the two of them closer, if that was even possible—Jessie would work there while Toby watched his movies.

When Toby came through the door, he was dripping with sweat.

"How are you that sweaty?" Jessie laughed.

"Humidity is a bitch," was all he said before disappearing upstairs.

Jessie took a pull on her ginormous water bottle that held all the $H_2O$ she was supposed to consume throughout the day. She accomplished it most days by sipping diligently and then downing what remained before bedtime like a cartoon drunkard. She was looking forward to seeing everyone—her friends, now, she supposed she should call them, if only online.

They'd met in a subreddit created by followers—okay, maybe superfans—of the *Escaping Denver* podcast. Jessie had heard about it through a friend of a friend, this truth-is-stranger-than-fiction podcast about something very weird and very real happening in the subterranean depths beneath Denver International Airport. That there was a sort of world-dominating cabal called the Collective running everything from their secret lair that was likewise full of horrors and secrets and undiscovered power. Like Illuminati-level stuff, only bigger. And *true*. Jessie didn't understand why it wasn't a bigger story nationally, internationally even, but she suspected that they might be just in Schopenhauer's first stage of truth: that first, things are ridiculed, and then violently opposed, and only going through those first two stages is something accepted as self-evident.

Even more fascinating—the piecemeal story came directly from the two people, Noah and Sara, who woke up trapped down there, told through audio files emailed to a random stranger on the surface. He, in turn, posted them in some semblance of narrative order to the internet. It touched on what seemed to be all the mysteries of the world, while also being a story of escape and discovery. Jessie had immediately become obsessed.

She wasn't alone. Others gathered online, through all sorts of platforms, to dissect the posted recordings and the analysis from the show's accidental narrator—the dude who'd been selected by the fates to receive the transmissions in the first place. Jessie had found her group, all of whom seemed serious about finding out more in a boots-on-the-ground fashion. Actually going to Colorado to see what was what. Maybe—just maybe—to help answer the many questions that came from the information that Noah and Sara had managed to send out into the world. It was madness, and it was delicious, and Jessie wanted—needed?—more. She checked her hair in the video feed, adjusted the camera angle, and logged into Zoom to start the chat, right on time.

As usual, Walt was already there, messing around with his settings. "Jessie!" he cried, his dad energy evident in the sonorous chime of his voice. "I'm here. Just can't figure out the video settings, but I'll get it, don't you worry."

"Take your time, Walt," Jessie said. "No one's waiting on you."

"Yet!" he chuckled. "I don't want to be tardy."

Walt said things like that unironically. He was in his mid-fifties, a high school geography teacher somewhere in Nebraska. Jessie had only heard his voice. In the few times they'd all gotten together on Zoom, he'd never been able to start his video. Jessie imagined him tall and paunchy, bald with horn-rimmed glasses that looked modern but, in reality, were just the same model he'd been wearing since he'd been a kid. When he heard Jessie's proposal to turn interest into action—to actually try to breach the considerable defenses of the depths under Denver International Airport—he was all in. It wasn't even much of a drive for him, Walt had said several times just before telling everyone the exact route he'd take south and west to the airport.

Otomi popped up in another window. She was as taciturn as always, and only gave a quick affirmative nod to Jessie before turning off her video and typing BRB in the chat. Jessie didn't know what to make of Otomi. Crazy quiet, and intense at the same time. Jessie didn't think she'd ever seen the woman smile. Everyone else in the group was friendly and fairly outgoing—even Jace, whose personality was tinged with so much bombast and ego that it was tough to take him seriously. And it wasn't even that Otomi was unfriendly; she was just all business all of the time, and didn't seem to condone anyone else acting otherwise.

Carla's video came into view, and she smiled at Jessie as if to make up for Otomi's lack of congeniality. "Hey, girl!" Carla beamed. She was a bodybuilder and part-time bodyguard, and had been in some magazines, all oiled up, teeth gleaming. Jessie always thought those magazine covers were photoshopped—but Carla . . . well, she proved it was possible with enough meticulous attention to the physical form and the unguents required to keep it looking the same on the page as it did in real life. Jessie had liked her from the start—she was the kind of person who clearly took no shit from anyone, even back when the sum total of what Jessie knew about her was a bunch of words in an online forum.

"Carla!" Jessie said, taking another drink from her considerable water bottle. "Good to see you. Looking good, Mama."

"Hi, Carla!" Walt said, still audio only.

"Hey Walt! And I'm like three years older than you, *chiquita*," Carla chastened, her Puerto Rican-by-way-of-the-Bronx accent coming to the fore. "You better watch yourself."

"Why can you call me a little girl, and I can't call you Mama?" Jessie laughed.

"Because you can't pull that shit off, sweetie," Carla replied, but she was laughing too. She was also sweating.

"You just come from working out?" Jessie asked.

Carla shook her head and wiped her forehead with a workout towel from some local boxing gym. "I wish," she said. "The super was supposed to come up here today and look at the AC, but I just got a text from him saying it was too hot. Can you believe that shit? I mean, I'm like, yeah man, it's fucking hot. That's why I need you up here. I'm going to go light his ass on fire once I'm off this call."

"Good luck," Jessie said.

"You know what you can do to cool down," Walt interjected, "is wet that towel in some cold water and hang it over a table fan."

"Way ahead of you, Walt," Carla said, moving the camera over to show that exact setup behind her on the right. "But thanks. Get your video on, so we can see you."

"Working on it!" he exclaimed.

"Does he even have a camera?" came a sudden voice, and Jessie realized that both Jace and Alton had finally shown. That was all of them, at least if Otomi came back. Jessie suspected she was there, and just didn't want to be seen.

"Yes, I have a camera," deadpanned Walt. "But thank you, *Jacinto*." It was a minor challenge from Walt, using Jace's full name, but from him, significant.

"Jace," the younger man said with a scowl. His face was thin, like a bird's, Jessie thought, and his devil's fork goatee wasn't helping matters either. He was the youngest of the crew by at least a few years. The facial hair was supposed to age him, but instead just made him look more like a high school kid auditioning for a stage play.

"Why you gotta go with a name that sounds like some white dude in a bad action movie?" Carla rolled her eyes.

"It's a nickname," Jace said. "It's not like I'm doing it to diss my *abuelita*."

"You should ask your abuelita if it bothers her," Carla said. "I bet she doesn't call you no fucking Jace."

"Hey Alton," Jessie said. "You want to chime in on this name debate?"

"Nope," Alton said, overpronouncing the P. Alton had been a surprise—the only one of the five others in the group that Jessie considered not to fit his voice, or the way he described himself. When he'd introduced himself in the chats, he'd said he was a doctor, an ER guy without much in the way of family. Too busy, he said. He spent most of his time working, and what downtime he had, he tended to sleep and listen to the podcast. He was also a collector of Americana—tin toys, old signage, mechanical banks, lamps, and knickknacks, which Jessie found odd. He said he was from Connecticut, and now lived in Boston, but he had no accent at all, and his skin was nearly as tan as Carla's. He had thick and wavy dark hair that he kept long on top and short on the sides, which set off some very green eyes. The man could have posed for romance novels. Not that Jessie read those. Much.

"We're all here," Jace said. "Can we just get started? I have a repair gig across town that I need to get to when we're done."

Jessie smiled patiently at Jace's short fuse—as abrasive as he could be at times, the team needed someone as tech-savvy as he was. Jessie had made sure they had a techie for what they were about to do—plunder the depths of DIA, even if it were only for information, for confirmation, for . . . well, whatever they would find.

Carla, meanwhile, was the muscle. Otomi worked as a pilot for some private air service, and had some survival training from a stint in some military service—exactly which one, she wasn't saying. Alton was the medical resource, and Walt—well, he was just someone who wanted in, and who Jessie didn't really have the heart to turn down. It didn't hurt that he knew his stuff. *Who knows?* Jessie thought. *Maybe Walt is an untapped resource waiting to spill.*

Jessie thought of herself as the brains of the outfit, even though that was embarrassing to admit, even just to herself. She sat under a wall of framed academic awards and a master of philosophy from the University of Chicago that only served to remind her that she had an as-yet-unfinished PhD in social thought and an effectively abandoned fellowship with the Pozen Family Center for Human Rights. She knew the podcast and all its mysteries had taken too much of her attention, along with affecting her financially. But this wasn't a distraction, she reminded herself. This was an alternate path forward down a unique path to a PhD. In short, delving into the depths of DIA might just end up being the best doctoral thesis ever written.

Jessie had been the one to do the research, the one to tie data points together, to tease out this detail here and this detail there, and to connect the dots to suggest one of the hidden entrances to the massive underground complex rumored—more than rumored, Jessie reminded herself—to be under the most mysterious airport smack in the middle of America and the biggest travel hub for more than a thousand miles in every direction.

"We can absolutely get started," Jessie said. "Walt, you okay if we start while you're futzing with the video?"

"Please do," Walt sighed.

Jessie shared her screen with the group. It was a map of Colorado and the surrounding states, with different locales marked. DIA, of course. The air force base down in the Springs, the FBI offices in the suburbs of Denver—the neighborhood nestled within the upscale community built on the former grounds of Stapleton Airport. Coincidence? Jessie wasn't sure those existed anymore. And then there was a pin to the north and west of Denver, up in the Rocky Mountains. "Okay, gang," Jessie said. "Here's our destination: Ward, Colorado."

"I still maintain that the name is someone's joke," Alton said.

"Maybe, but it's not mine," Jessie said. "If you triangulate all the different site references from different parts of the podcast, you end up with at least one access point, and this is it."

"Wait, joke?" Jace looked confused. "What's the joke?"

"Ward," Otomi said, suddenly clicking her video back on. "It's an old term for guard. A symbol for protection."

"Like guarding an entryway into a vast underground complex," Carla added, just in case Jace was still slow on the uptake.

"Okay, okay," Jace said sullenly.

"Didn't do the reading, I see," Walt teased.

"I did," Jace countered. "I'm just not a word nerd. And anyway, I said before that it seems too far away from DIA to be connected to it. It's the other side of Denver, and way up there."

"Not that far, especially as the crow flies," Walt said, and they could hear his keyboard clicking. "Just west on 36 through Boulder and up 119 through the canyon to some town called Nederland, and then another half hour north on 72 . . . which is the Peak to Peak. Maybe ninety minutes from DIA, less from Denver proper."

"And we know the underground complex is said to cover miles and miles of area," Jessie said. "Who's to say how many miles? When you're digging it all out of the earth, there are no real natural boundaries to recognize."

"Water?" Alton offered.

"Sure, if it was deep enough," Jessie responded. "But there's none between DIA and Ward so sufficient that it would make it impossible to dig either under or around." There was a silence as they all took it in. "And like I said, this isn't me throwing a dart at the map and trying to argue that it's the place. I found Ward by following the evidence. It was all in the email I sent you. But I promise—something is there."

"Here's my question," Otomi said. "Why are you so certain that no one else has already found this?"

"I'm not," Jessie said. "Hell, it could be common knowledge for locals who don't know what it really is. We won't know until we go up there."

"Have you figured out how we're getting there?" Alton asked.

"I found someone, yeah," Jessie said. "Or rather, Toby did. He has some friends who know some guys who know this woman—she's a guide, I guess you'd call it. She takes people where they need to go."

"Like a chauffeur?" Carla asked.

"More like a coyote," Jace said. "That's what this person is, right?"

"Probably, yeah," Jessie replied. "I didn't ask for her full résumé, and having spoken with her over the phone, I doubt she'd offer one. I'm not even sure she gave me her real name."

"What did she say it was?" Alton asked.

"Patsy," Jessie said. "Patsy Klein."

"That could be her real name," Walt reasoned.

"And she might get caught walking after midnight," Jace said. "Whatever. If she's able to get us to the location, I don't care what she wants to be called."

"Agreed," Otomi said. "But what makes you think she knows enough about the area to get us to a place most people don't know exists?"

"She says she does," Jessie said. "I told her what we were looking for, and she immediately knew what I was talking about."

"You don't find that at all suspicious?" Alton asked.

"I would have if she found me," Jessie said. "And she didn't know what I was talking about in terms of a hidden entrance into a top secret underground complex. She knew where there was a shaft in the ground that seemed to have no bottom and that no one could explain what it was or had even gone into it."

"Or did, but didn't come back," said Alton.

"True," Jessie nodded.

"So, we could be heading out and finding nothing," Jace said. "Or just an old mine shaft or something?"

"That's the risk of all exploration, isn't it?" Jessie asked.

There was a pause in the group that Alton finally broke. "We all knew what we were signing up for, right? I'm ready to give it a shot."

"This is why I wanted to meet over Zoom," Jessie said. "I want to look into each of your eyes and trust that we're all about to do this thing. Jace is right; it might just be a hole in the ground. But there are signs . . . like real signs . . . that it's potentially a whole lot more. I need to know that we're all in. Like no shit, we're doing it."

"No shit," Alton said. "We're doing it."

"No shit," Walt echoed.

"No shit, I guess," Jace said.

"No shit, chiquita," Carla agreed.

"In," Otomi said.

"Okay," Jessie pushed on. "What other details do we need to work out? Has everyone taken the time off work? Made your travel plans? We're only a couple of weeks out now."

Everyone nodded, and Walt said, "You can't see me, but I'm holding up the printouts of my itinerary."

"It sucks we can't fly," Carla said. "I mean, I get it, but damn, that's a long way to drive."

"If we fly," Jessie said, "we're exposing ourselves. Remember how the first two were taken."

"Yeah, yeah, from flights," Jace muttered. "But I agree with Carla. Maybe we fly partway and then rent a car to drive the rest?"

"Up to you," Jessie shrugged. "But I won't."

"I'm not far enough to bother," Walt said, and his video flickered for a moment, and again went black. "Hey, did you guys see that?"

"Briefly," Jessie affirmed. "Keep trying."

"The original two were taken from flights that weren't going to Denver," Alton reminded the group. "So, if you're on a plane at all? I'd say you're not safe."

"Still okay if I hitch a ride with you, chiquita?" Carla asked. "I'll drive to Chicago by myself, but it'll be more fun if we carpool along the way."

"So long as you don't mind my friend Toby doing the driving," Jessie said, and pointed the camera in his direction. "Say hi, Toby."

Toby raised his hand and waved from the couch where he was, in fact, watching *The Karate Kid*.

"Personable, isn't he?" Jessie smiled. "I promise, he's a peach."

"He looks like a peach," Carla admitted. "All big and fuzzy."

"Well, well . . ." Alton said, raising an eyebrow. "Do we have our group's first romantic entanglement?"

"Toby also looks pretty plump and juicy," offered Jace, who was the only one who laughed.

"Okay, not liking him," Toby said without looking up.

"Shut the fuck up, *Jacinto*," Carla snarled. "Or else I'll call your abuelita, and she'll whoop your ass."

"You sure you don't want to join us in the car?" Jessie asked Alton. He was the only other one coming from essentially the same direction. Jace was in California, and Otomi was from Phoenix.

"I'm sure," Alton nodded. "I might max out my shifts before hitting the road, and just drive straight through."

"It's a thirty-hour drive," Otomi said. "Impossible."

"Or at least dangerous as hell," Jessie concurred.

"I've worked triple rotations," Alton grinned. "This'll be nothing. And I'm not planning to do it; I just want the option if the shifts fall into place that way."

The screen brightened slightly as Walt's digital window shifted from black to an image—not of Walt, but of Walt as a talking potato.

"Oh Jesus," Jace said.

"Am I on?" Walt asked happily.

"You're a potato, *papi*," Carla said.

"Is that a Puerto Rican thing?" Walt the potato asked. It sounded like a sincere question.

"We can't see your face, Walt," Jessie explained as Alton and Jace were shaking with stifled laughter. Otomi and Carla just shook their heads, in disapproval and amusement, respectively. "You have some sort of filter on, and you look like a potato."

"Like a *potato* potato?" he asked.

"Yes," Jessie said, fighting back laughter.

"Like a potato you'd eat," Walt said, still hunting for confirmation.

"I don't know how else to explain this, Walt," Jessie replied.

"Well, I'm stumped," Walt said. "I just don't know how this darn thing is supposed to work."

"It's okay," Jessie said. "Let's all share our plans to meet up in Ward; I want to record all this."

---

Jace was the first to go, having that job across town to get to. Then Otomi, who said she likewise had an engagement, and then Alton. In the end, the sun was dipping below the Chicago skyline, Toby was already on *The Karate Kid Part III*, and it was just Jessie, Carla, and Walt.

"I'm sorry about the filter," Walt said. "I can assure you that I'm not really a potato."

"We believe you," Carla said.

"We'll see your real face in Colorado very soon," Jessie added.

"Sounds good," he said. "You two be careful." And then Walt the potato blipped out.

"What if he showed up and was actually a potato?" Carla grinned.

"Honestly," Jessie said, "that would be one of the scariest things I've ever seen."

"Seriously?" Carla said. "Girl, you ain't seen nothing yet."

The women agreed to text each other when it was time for Carla to start the long drive from New York City to Chicago, and they waved to each other before clicking off. There was that awkward moment at the end of every video call, that time between the goodbyes and see you laters and good seeing yous and the moment it takes to click the button to end the call.

It was in that interim, just before Carla's smiling face and fan-blown hair disappeared from the screen, that Jessie could have sworn she saw a figure—black from head to toe—looming behind Carla in the gloom.

SERVICES
EXPERIENCED MECHANIC
Well over 30 years of experience with American cars and bikes. Fair price.
**6304 Mountainside Dr**
SONG DOG SERVICES
I've been where you need going. I can get you in and I can get you out, for a price. Woman-owned since 1987.
****************
PHONE: 575 - SONG - DOG
PAGER: 575 - 766- 4365
BOOKKEEPING SERVICES
- Accounts payable
- Accounts receivable
- Flexible rates
Ask for Brenda. 303-457-6201
Bradley and
held on August
Commonly Funeral Hor
Please inquire for details.
COMMONLY
FUNERAL SERVICES
***NEEDED***
DO YOU HAVE A TRANSMISSION FOR A 1967 CHEVROLET CAMAI Z/28??? TODAY IS THE DAY TO FINALLY SELL IT. WILLING TO PAY CASH. CALL ABE
303 - 363 -14 81
CAREERS
DANCERS NEEDE
THE FUZZY PILLOW is lo
new dancers for the su
Experience with dance an
a necessity. MAKE SO
Ask for Karl-
s - Furniture - Kitchenware
icycles - Military Medals
303 - 422 - 1986
er of Main and 3rd, Salina
ROBERTS
AUTOMOTIVE
Y AND SELL
S/BOATS
ury, shared driveway.
n by: 35 Newport St, Ward

# CHAPTER THREE

EAST OF NEDERLAND, COLORADO

"Maybe she has a roommate?" Toby shrugged in the driver's seat.

He had the window down, left arm out in the sun. The air was significantly cooler up here than it had been even just an hour ago down in Denver, so much so that Jessie had to roll hers up. The breeze coming in from the sunroof of Toby's SUV was more than enough.

"I don't know," Jessie said, popping another dill pickle sunflower seed. "I did my homework. Checked them all out as much as I could. There's no one else on her lease agreement, but that doesn't mean she doesn't sublet, or even just let a friend couch surf. But dressed in all black? What were they doing, cosplaying as a ninja?"

"That's your best guess?" Toby grinned. "Ninjas?"

"Who else dresses in black from head to toe?" She spat out the shell of the sunflower seed into the empty Thirstbuster she'd bought when they stopped for gas back in Ogallala.

"Nuns. Judges. Johnny Cash," Toby ticked each one off on the fingers of his right hand. "Also, quit eating those. It's disgusting. It's like you're chewing tobacco or something."

"I was feeling snacky," Jessie protested.

"Be snacky on something that doesn't require a spittoon, maybe?"

"Fine," Jessie sulked, putting the lid back on the drink container and dropping it in the garbage bag they had going in the back seat. She fell quiet, watching the sides of the canyon rise up on either side of the swank Navigator that Toby had borrowed from a cousin. When Jessie had taken Toby up on his offer to borrow a ride and drive her out to Colorado—*Never seen the mountains before*, he'd reasoned—she was expecting a beater. But a brand-new Lincoln? Jessie reminded herself to ask Toby about this cousin at some point. "I'm just worried about Carla," she finally said softly.

"I know," Toby responded, and put his hand gently on her shoulder. "But she'll be okay."

"You don't know that."

"True. But it's also true that we don't know what we don't know, you know? And we can't, so we do what we can."

"That doesn't make any sense."

"Sure it does," Toby smiled, putting both hands back on the wheel, ten and two. "Think about it."

"Pass," Jessie said. Toby was right about one thing. She had no way of knowing exactly why Carla never showed up at the rendezvous spot in Chicago, or why Jessie's calls went straight to voicemail. Her one relief was that she'd also never gotten the text Carla had promised to send when she was leaving NYC, so she hadn't had an accident on the road. But why would she have bailed? Without any explanation? Jessie didn't know Carla well or anything, but still . . . it didn't feel like something she'd do. And then there was that figure behind her just before the video cut out . . .

Jessie took a deep breath. Centered herself. "How much longer do we have to go? Do I have time to catch a nap?"

"A catnap, maybe," Toby said. "Go ahead and give it a shot. We maybe have twenty minutes before we hit Nederland and head up to Ward. Longer, if these cars in front of us keep riding their damn brakes."

Patsy had warned them that there wasn't spit in Ward, but there was a single gas pump in front of a general store that was sometimes open and sometimes not. This was over the phone. Jessie was pretty sure she'd said "spit," anyway. But Patsy had also said there was a pretty big lot in back where they could all park for however long they'd be gone, and they'd be safe enough there. They could meet, load up what she called her War Rig, whatever that was, and go from there. Jessie imagined it as some sort of semitruck, one of the big ones, all chromed out and shiny.

Not that Jessie knew vehicles. She'd never owned one. She'd gotten her license, but never drove, which was why Toby was—generously, she thought, because fifteen-plus hours in a car is nothing to take lightly—in the driver's seat. It was also Toby who'd finally made her do it, having taken her down to the DMV in Calumet Park, south of the city. It had a reputation for being a little easier and a lot calmer than Chicago facilities—and at least a brand-new driver wouldn't be braving busy streets.

Still, Jessie hated driving. It made her nervous. She wasn't all that much more enamored with riding shotgun, either. She'd become too used to the L, and she liked someone else being in control.

If Jessie was exhausted, she knew Toby had to be even more bleary. They'd done the drive straight, stopping only for gas and fast food along the way. Maybe not the best of plans, but they'd spent hours waiting for Carla to show, giving her the benefit of the doubt until they finally had no choice but to leave without her.

Jessie fell asleep at some point, dozing for a precious few minutes, but slept hard in that short nap because she dreamed.

Dreamed, oddly enough, about her single-story childhood home downstate, a small house in a modest town where her mother had always lived and stayed when Jessie went to college. Fled to college, more like it. She rarely went to visit her mother. Most of the furnishings in that house were the same ones with which Jessie had grown up, taut white fabrics upon which no one was allowed to eat or drink—ever. The pictures on the wall were all the same, too. But still, on those rare occasions when duty would poke Jessie into a visit with her mother, it never felt like home. Her mother was never what anyone would call nurturing, but that house was a new level of disassociation. It was sterile, like no one lived there at all. When she was away for long enough, Jessie would find herself feeling sorry for her mother, living alone in every way a person can. And then she'd visit, and Jessie would be reminded exactly why she couldn't afford her mother that indulgence.

And then she'd flee again.

---

The town of Ward was falling, or so it seemed to Jessie when Toby took a hard right off the Peak to Peak and just kept turning. The road was a wide and steep switchback, heading down into Left Hand Canyon and beyond, and every building there could be accurately described as *ramshackle*, which for some of them would be a kindness. The one-pump general store was perhaps the brightest spot in town, its clapboard walls painted a clean white, offset with red trim on the eaves and corners.

"Is that them?" Toby said, squinting at the parking lot behind the store.

"Must be," Jessie said, rubbing her eyes. "Jesus, is that a Tesla?"

"Someone's fancy," Toby commented, raising an eyebrow.

"Says the guy driving a new Lincoln Navigator," Jessie countered.

Toby ignored her. "I don't see anything that could rightly be called a War Rig, though," he said, still craning his neck as he approached.

He was right, Jessie realized. There was a silver Tesla glinting in the sun next to what looked like an old blue Saturn sedan. On the other side of that was a gleaming red motorcycle with a slim figure still straddling the seat and talking to two other people. Toby pulled into the lot, and the guy on the motorcycle—a Ducati, Jessie realized—waved. It was Jace, with Alton and an older guy she assumed was—finally—Walt. Toby pulled in so that they were on Jessie's side of the Lincoln.

"You guys have some nice rides," Jessie smiled, rolling her window down and taking off her sunglasses.

"Yeah, that Saturn's gonna turn heads," Jace said, poking Walt in the shoulder.

"I hate buying cars," Walt replied, as though that were all the explanation warranted.

"That your Tesla?" Toby leaned over from the driver's side.

Alton shook his head. Jessie thought he was even more impossibly handsome in person, his wavy locks moving as if digitally enhanced. "Just a lease," he said. "And an indulgence, for sure. I was worried it wouldn't even make it on the roads out here. If we get some rain," he added, toeing the dirt lot with a sandaled—and pedicured?—foot, "this place is going to turn into a mud pit that I might need your SUV to help pull out of."

"My good ol' Saturn has all-season tires," Walt said as Toby shut off the SUV. "Just had 'em put on at Costco last fall."

When Jessie got out of the Lincoln, she did a head count. "So, we're just missing Otomi and Patsy?"

"And Carla," Walt said.

Jessie wrinkled her nose. "I don't think she's coming," she said. "She never showed up to drive out with us. I haven't even been able to get in touch with her."

"Maybe she got a security gig she couldn't pass up?" Alton suggested. "She did say her work was feast or famine, depending on who was in the city and needed some quick muscle."

"That doesn't explain why she wouldn't call though," Jessie said. She'd kept the ominous figure she saw—or thought she saw—between her and Toby. She wasn't even sure why—maybe because it was nothing? Or because she wanted to exercise some caution, at least initially, with these strangers becoming friends? "Or why she wouldn't pick up when I did."

"That's true," Alton conceded.

"Who knows the mysteries of life as a professional meat shield?" Jace laughed. "She's fine. I'll bet she shows up at some point with some kind of crazy story. But more importantly, is no one going to say anything about my bike? I mean, come on."

"It's nice," Walt said. "Red."

"I've seen too many crotch rocket accidents in the ER to not have some reticence in celebrating them," Alton said.

"It's not a crotch rocket," Jace said, and Jessie didn't know if he was putting on an offended affectation, or if the response was real. "It's a Ducati. It's a pasta rocket."

"We call them donorcycles," Alton said. "Lots of our organ donations come from people riding those things. And generally, they're otherwise young and healthy. You're a transplant team's dream."

"Well, this is all very cheerful," Jace said. "Good to meet you guys anyway." The group shook hands, and Jace turned to Toby. "You coming with?"

"Nah," Toby replied. "I'm just her ride."

"You're a big dude," Jace said. "If Carla really isn't coming, we could use a strong back on our team."

"And you're here now," Walt agreed. "What were you going to do if not come along?"

"See Rocky Mountain National Park," Toby shrugged. "Do some hiking. Camp a little. Maybe drive back down into Boulder or Denver or both, see what's there, and possibly even drive south to see Pikes Peak. I've never been out this way before."

"Eh, that's family vacation shit," Jace scoffed.

"Maybe." Toby looked sideways at Jessie, silently asking for her take.

"If you want to come, I'd love to have you," she said. "I just didn't think it was your thing. But Walt's right—you came all this way. Might as well keep on going. If you want."

"Okay." Toby looked relieved. "If Carla doesn't show, I'll tag along."

"Super," Alton said, distracted by a sound coming from the sky. They all looked up. There was a helicopter descending slowly toward the east end of the parking lot. It was a precarious landing with little room for error, but it did so safely, nonetheless.

"Holy shit," Jace said. "Is that Otomi?"

A lithe figure hopped gingerly out of the pilot's side of the copter. It was canary yellow, with a green pinstripe and the number 1138 emblazoned on the tail boom.

"Well, I gotta say," Walt said, hitching up his pants. "That's just impressive, is what that is."

Otomi sauntered over to the group with a pack slung over one shoulder. "All right," she said. "I'm here. Let's get going."

"You're not the last to arrive," said Jace, who seemed a little too happy to offer the correction. "We're still waiting on Patsy."

The late-day sun glinted off Otomi's sunglasses as though flashing Jace a frown. "Okay. What about the bodybuilder?"

"Her name is Carla," Jessie said. "And she didn't show up."

"Fantastic," Otomi said, dumping her backpack on the ground and turning back to the aircraft. "I need to lock up the Sikorsky."

"Hey," Jace said, already half off his bike, "can I come too, maybe check out your ride?"

"No," Otomi responded without looking back.

"You really have a way with the ladies," Alton said to Jace.

"Fuck off," Jace spit back. "I didn't hear her inviting you back there either."

"True," Alton replied, the ghost of a smile playing on his lips. "But I didn't ask."

---

When Patsy's War Rig pulled into the lot, the sun was already starting to sink behind the rise of the mountains to the west, casting an early shadow over Ward.

"Is that the infamous Ms. Klein?" Walt wondered out loud.

"What a piece of junk," Jace sneered. And it sort of was: an older Winnebago, from the look of it, outfitted with a heavily chromed grill that curved around its entire front chassis and windows that had been replaced by louvered metal shutters. The front windshield was completely black, the tinting was so dark. It had no side mirrors anymore, and the original headlights looked to be busted out, with heavy-duty halogens mounted right above them, behind the aftermarket megagrill.

As the tricked-out vehicle approached, it became clear that the carcass of a deer—or the front half of what used to be a deer—was woven through the crosshatching of the grill itself, one hoof still poking through the wrong way, its dried and tattered skull flopping off one side, the skin sloughing off in scraps. From somewhere within the beast came a designed cacophony of air horns in two quick blasts.

The cab door of the Winnebago opened to reveal a thin, leathered woman with short spiky gray hair and mirrored sunglasses, wearing worn blue jeans and a flannel shirt with the sleeves cut off. Her bare arms were deeply tanned, possibly scarred, and muscled in a wiry and clearly capable way. She was smoking a hand-rolled cigarette that smelled like cherry pipe tobacco, and when she grinned, her teeth were surprisingly white, but jagged and askew, as if they might try to make a break from her mouth but were too scared to move.

"Well, hello, crew," Patsy said with a voice more gravelly than the shoulders of the road through Ward. "Which one of y'all is Jessie? And by that, I mean, who's got my money?"

"That'd be me," Jessie replied with a shy half wave. She opened her pack and pulled out a bulging envelope, inches thick, and handed it over to Patsy. "It's all there."

"I trust you," Patsy said, but thumbed through the money anyway before spitting the nearly spent butt out of her mouth and scuffing it into the dirt with her boot. "We'll be together for a piece, so I doubt you'd do me wrong right up front." She turned to survey the group. "Okay, so I'm seeing the wrong six here, right off the Wells Fargo. Who we missing, and who's Tubby here?"

"Toby," he said, taken aback.

"I wasn't told of a Toby or a Tubby neither," said Patsy directly to Jessie. "Where's the big girl? Bertha, Ethel, Little Lotta . . ."

"Carla," Jessie said.

"That's her," Patsy nodded.

"We don't really know," Jessie answered, not completely sure how much she should tell Patsy at this point. "She didn't meet up with us to make the drive. Toby's coming in her place, if that's okay."

"Makes no never mind to me, Lulu," the woman said. "He's your Tubby."

Toby looked around for an audience that wasn't there to back him up. "Can we not with the casual cruelty?"

"Aw, names don't mean nothin'," Patsy grinned. "You are who you are no matter what an old bird like me wants to call you. And I don't mean anything by it except that I don't need to be bothered learning your name, you know? Not worth the time. Anyway. Everybody grab your stuff and pile into the War Rig. Main door's on the other side there."

"I'll call you Toby," Walt said, putting his hand on the younger man's shoulder. "You don't let her get to you."

"You got room in that contraption for me to bring my bike along?" Jace asked. "I'm not crazy about leaving it here with just a wheel lock."

"Not a chance, Charlie," Patsy responded, and hoisted herself back up into the driver's seat of the Winnebago.

"She's not good with names," Otomi said flatly.

"We're not her friends," Alton reminded her, picking up his two bags. "We're just her clients. It's the same reason I call every kid I see come through the ER the same thing: Tiger. Makes them feel good, and lets me not have to remember anything more than I already do."

"I do *not* feel good about this," Toby murmured, staring at the beast of a vehicle in front of them.

"Hop on the bus, Tiger," Patsy said. "This motherfucker is leaving in five, with or without ya."

In the hubbub of everyone making sure they'd loaded

everything into the Winnebago and secured their own vehicles, Jessie didn't notice the pair of gangly-looking guys until they were only a few feet away.

"You can't park all this shit here," said one in nothing but dirty overalls and expensive Tevas.

"Nice shit though," another said, this one just in jeans and Birkenstocks and a T-shirt that advertised OK Soda. "Be a damn shame if something were to happen to all of it."

"We were told we could park here," Jessie retorted, though at the same time she considered that helicopter parking probably hadn't been part of the deal.

"I don't know who told you that, ma'am," Tevas said. "But it wasn't me, and this is my store. Which means it's my lot. Which means you don't have permission from the guy you should have gotten permission from."

"The *guys* you should have gotten permission from," Birkenstocks said.

"Right," Tevas corrected himself. "The two of us."

"The two of you own this store?" Jessie asked. "Together?"

"We're entrepreneurs," said Birkenstocks, and the two laughed.

They couldn't be much older than she was, Jessie thought. She was about to ask some more pointed questions—figure out if this was a real problem or a small-town shakedown—when Patsy swung down from the driver's seat of the Winnebago and ambled up behind her.

"You fellas have a problem?" she asked. She'd lit up again while in the RV, and took a long draw.

"We don't," Tevas said. "But you all might, unless you have a way to pay for parking here for . . . how long is it?"

"It's open-ended," Jessie answered.

"We're just heading up past Brainard Lake . . ." Toby started, but was cut off by Patsy, who lightly backhanded him in the chest for emphasis.

"Shut up, Tubby," Patsy said. "Don't tell these pissants a damn thing. They don't own this place. They're just some good ol' boys whose cornbread never quite got done in the middle, ain't you?"

"You saying we're stupid?" Tevas bristled.

"Oh, certainly," Patsy drawled. "And not only that—I'm also saying you're about as tough as cotton candy in the rain."

"You better watch your mouth, lady," Birkenstocks said, but stepped back a little.

"You know who'd love to hear about this?" Patsy smiled, but not kindly. "Your uncle." She stepped forward and pulled her collar down and to one side, revealing some sort of thick burn scar—*Is that a brand?* Jessie wasn't sure—below her collarbone. "You know how I know your uncle? I think you do. You want me to tell him about the little peckerwoods who're running his shit and drawing all the wrong sorts of attention? You want me to tell him that you reneged on a deal he and I struck? You want your uncle to cloud up and start raining all over you boys?"

Jessie had no idea what any of this meant, but whatever it was, it was making these two would-be thugs turn even whiter than they already were, stuttering and starting to sweat.

"What's your name again?" Tevas sounded suddenly subdued. "Maybe I need to check our calendar inside . . ."

"Wanda," Patsy said. "Wanda Jackson. I'm just sure you're gonna find everything you need when you turn tail and run your little puppy asses back into that cute little store y'all got there."

"Yes ma'am," Birkenstocks said, putting his hands up as though there were a punch coming. "We didn't know you'd talked with our uncle."

"It'd be a damn shame if we came back and found even

a scratch on these vehicles," Patsy pushed. "If they were even fuckin' *dusty*, you know what I mean?"

"Yes, Ms. Jackson," Tevas said. "We'll not only keep them safe, but we'll even keep them clean. How long do you need to leave them here?"

Patsy took another long draw on her cherry cig. "As long as I damn well please," she said. "That good with you boys?" She peeled two hundreds off a folded stack from the front pocket of her jeans and threw them in the dirt. Tevas bent down and picked them up without taking his eyes off Patsy.

"Yes, ma'am," Birkenstocks said, and pulled on the back of Tevas's overalls toward the store. "We'd better get back in and mind the store now."

Patsy nodded, and watched them retreat with a steeled gaze. "Tell your team to double-time it," she told Jessie in a quiet voice. "We gotta rabbit."

The War Rig was smaller on the inside than Jessie had imagined; the single door on the passenger side was set behind the front bucket seat. On the left, facing the back of the RV, was a kitchenette with a single touch she might call homey: a clean hand towel emblazoned with a rooster hanging from a ring by the sink. But the sink itself held a few dirty bowls, as well as a multitude of flatware soaking in a wide-bottomed coffee mug full of suds.

On the counter to the right looked like everything required to make your own bullets: casings, a press, a small scale, and more small pieces of equipment that Jessie couldn't identify. The half-moon table with two booths squatted in the back, and to the right was more cabinetry and a door that Jessie assumed led to whatever served as the bathroom.

As old as it all was, Patsy had clearly spent some money on upgrades. Where there was usually a picture window on the back wall, there was instead a flat-screen TV that currently showed the back view from the Winnebago. Picture-in-picture squares on the screen displayed each side view and the front as well. The cab of the vehicle was equally tricked out: another smaller screen showing the same as the one in the back, and switches and lights that were unlabeled but clearly not factory installed.

Jace, Alton, and Walt had taken seats at the back table. Otomi was leaning against the table itself, her arms crossed and looking forward intently. Toby sat on a pile of blankets stashed behind the driver's side, and Jessie, somewhat reluctantly, took the passenger's seat.

Patsy put her War Rig in gear and let out three quick toots, waving out the window. Jessie looked at the screen that showed the rear view. She could see Birkenstocks and Tevas glaring daggers from the store's front window.

"Why'd you tell them your name was Wanda?" Jessie asked.

"Because my name ain't nobody's business," Patsy said. "And when I first met their uncle years back, I was Wanda."

"Is your name even Patsy?" Jessie asked.

"Aw, kitten," Patsy smiled. "Would I lie to you?"

Toby looked gobsmacked. "Clearly," he said. "Absolutely, yes, you would."

"It's like what Bing Crosby told the Andrews Sisters," Patsy said, taking a curve, "*Ask me no questions and I'll tell you no lies.*"

They headed up and out of Ward, back to the Peak to Peak. As they did, time seemed to reverse a bit as they exited the shadowed valley and once again saw the sun. They were going about fifty, which Jessie hoped was "rabbit" enough.

"Is it really that important that we get there before dark?" Jessie asked.

"Naw," Patsy said. "What's really important is that those cops—or whatever they are—don't catch up with us."

Jessie looked at the screen showing the rear view. Two

black-and-white police cruisers were bearing down on them, lights blazing. Even through the war-clad RV, she could hear the cops over their loudspeakers telling them to pull over.

"What do they want from us?" Jessie said.

"Shit," Toby said. "What are we supposed to do?"

"Not get caught," Patsy said, and floored the RV as she took a near two-wheeled turn onto a county road with a sign they moved past so quickly that all Jessie could read was something about a Boy Scout camp.

And that was right about when the police started firing.

# CHAPTER FOUR

JUST SHY OF BRAINARD LAKE RECREATION AREA
USFS/COLORADO

"They're shooting at us?" Walt cried from the back of the RV. "I've never been shot at before!" His voice was a mix of panic and some sort of pride.

"Relax, old man," Otomi said, trying to keep her balance while the RV lurched on the unpaved road. "Hear that pinging? That's their little state-issued bullets deflecting off the back. Our coyote must have some serious bulletproofing mounted on the rear of this old thing."

"On all sides," Patsy shouted. "Same for the glass in the windows. Doc, how are you with a gun? There's a rifle under that bench seat you're sitting on, and if you slide that panel up on the right of the screen, there's an embrasure there."

"I'm not shooting a gun," Alton said flatly.

"No one's shooting anyone!" Jessie yelled.

"Might want to tell them that," Patsy said, and then called

to the back. "Anyone of y'all not have some moral compunction against self-defense?"

"Returning fire at cops is not self-defense," Jace said, staring at the police cars behind them on-screen.

"The only time I've ever shot a gun is playing *Duck Hunt*," Walt admitted, but he'd scooted Alton off the bench seat and lifted it up. Sure enough, there was a rifle there, a polished walnut stock that had clearly seen both heavy use and a lot of loving care.

"Give me that," Otomi said, and grabbed the gun. "Duck under the table and get out of my way," she ordered Jace, who instantly did what he was told, with only his head popping up on the other side. ".308 Winchester," she said, turning the rifle from one side to the other, inspecting it, holding the sight up to her right eye. "Top-quality Griffin & Howe scope. Old school. I like it."

"Admire while you're shooting," Patsy yelled, taking a hard turn and throwing everyone off-balance for a moment. The road was thinning; the split-log fence that they'd been seeing on their left suddenly vanished. There was evidence of a burn, pines blackened, and needles browned. Rocks—boulders, really—began marking the sides of the narrowing dirt road.

"We haven't *done* anything," Jessie said, almost pleading. "Do *not* shoot at those cops."

Otomi paused long enough for Alton to grab the gun—not out of her hands, but enough to prevent her from doing anything.

"Jessie's right," Toby agreed. "We haven't done anything to warrant the cops chasing us."

"Which means something's off," Patsy said, steering onto the shoulder to avoid a couple of kids—a tween girl and a younger boy with a yellow lab trundling happily next to them—walking on the other side of the road. "Goddammit," Patsy muttered.

And then to Jessie, she snarled, "Look, princess, I know we haven't done anything. You know we haven't done anything. But those cops shooting their guns at our tail feathers clearly have a difference of opinion."

"Still . . ." Jessie said.

"Christ on a cracker," Patsy said. "Fuck it. We're getting up near the trailer park anyhow. They'll stop firing, at least for a bit."

And she was right. As soon as the RV crested a small hill, Brainard Lake revealed itself in its deep-blue majesty, small boats dotting the distant waters. Up ahead, there was a small trailer park—more a vacation camp, really, with both single-wides and tumbledown homes jigsawed together where the lake met the shore. There was both a boat launch and a pier, with a bait shop nearby. Outside the rickety structure were two coolers: one marked Ice and the other marked Worms.

Patsy floored her War Rig over a concrete overflow channel built into the road—there was enough water in it to splash up, which made the police cars fishtail a little before regaining control. But they'd lost a beat. By the time they were able to get back up to speed, Patsy had nearly completed the left curve around the trailer park, fishermen and families in webbed plastic lawn chairs looking over curiously.

Beyond the trailer park, the road got even worse. They were heading up into the Indian Peaks Wilderness now, a trailhead to their right the last bit of governmental signage they'd see. They passed several No Trespassing signs of increasing levels of threat. The police were still following them, but the roads were getting tougher to manage. Jessie didn't know if it was their greater weight, special tires, or some sort of modification that Patsy had done to her vehicle, but there was no doubt about the effect: they were outpacing the cops.

Up ahead was a gate, with more No Trespassing signs

emblazoned on either side. There was a cattle guard too, all the way across the gap between the rocky-sloped stream on the left and the cliffside on the right. The fat metal bars of a fence were crafted so only pedestrians could wind their way ahead—and even that was clearly discouraged.

"They really don't want people up here, do they?" Jessie said only seconds before Patsy barreled full speed through the gate, which was sturdy enough to knock the RV onto two wheels before slamming hard back down to the dirt road beyond it.

Everyone was watching the back monitor and could see that the police cars had pulled up to the ruined gate and stopped. Whether it was because it had fallen across the road and was blocking the squad cars, Jessie didn't know.

"They stopped," she said simply. The cops were out of their vehicles, their shapes receding as the RV scooted toward an incline. One of the cops was shouting into a radio. The others were just watching.

"Why would they stop there?" Walt asked from the back. "They could have gotten around that gate."

"It really doesn't make a lot of sense," Alton agreed.

"I'm not complaining," Jace said, finally getting up off the floor and taking a seat.

"You and me both," Walt said, and the two high-fived like they'd accomplished something.

"Seriously," Jessie asked Patsy, "what the hell was that? Why were those cops shooting at us?"

"If they was really cops at all," Patsy mused. "Anyway, it doesn't matter. They're gone now, and thank God and Greyhound they are."

"You're not answering anything," Toby said.

"Not really trying to," Patsy admitted with a tone that suggested the conversation, such as it was, had ended.

The RV plodded along a rutted dirt road that clearly didn't see much use anymore, if it ever had. There was barbed wire along the road, almost military grade, but only in spots. Patsy slowed around a bend, and pulled off the road nose first into the scraggly grass, and started to back up into a three-point turn. She gunned the RV up a road that didn't look like a road—Jessie figured it had been perhaps deliberately hidden, because it became more road-like once they breached the tree line.

Not that the ride was smooth. As the vehicle advanced, the canopy of trees on either side of the road encroached enough that branches snapped clean off as the RV bull-rushed through with significant force, if not speed.

"I'm feeling pretty sick," Toby said, and he did look a little green.

"Almost there, Tubby," Patsy said. They passed a few remnants of what looked to be old homesteads—cabins in the mountains that might have predated the Forest Service. None of them looked like they'd been inhabited for years, maybe decades. One, gated off by a timber frame that looked like it was the entrance to an old ranch, had an unreadable sign hanging from a pair of thin chains. To one side were what looked to be some old snowshoes and a busted Victrola. There had been life up here at one time, Jessie considered. She wondered what happened to it all.

*Nothing left but ghosts*, was all she could think.

---

At the end of what served as a road was what looked like an old dude ranch that had since been converted into a logging camp, now clearly abandoned for some time. The Forest Service had put up signs all over, declaring the lot as reclamation, probably after a fire in what looked like the main house. It sat over to the left, overlooking a small lake, burned down to its stone foundation. With all the overgrowth, it wouldn't have been recognizable if not for the grand stone hearth and chimney that still jutted up into the cerulean sky.

There was what looked to be a machine shed that listed to one side, but still looked safe. Smaller ruined cabins dotted the rest of the clearing, in various states of decomposition. In the center of the pull-around squatted the cab and flatbed of a 1968 International truck, its wheels flattened to the rims.

"We walk from here," Patsy ordered, lighting up another cigarette and opening her door. Everyone else followed suit.

"Shit, it's cold," Jace said.

"Ten thousand feet or more," Patsy shrugged. "Wait until that sun is fully down."

Everyone grabbed jackets and put them on. "What is this place?" Alton said as he donned an immaculately tailored fleeced denim jacket.

"Nothing, now," Patsy said. "Used to be one of the first guest ranches in the state, one of those places where East Coast dandies come out to play cowboy for a while. Eat some beans, ride a horse, drink some coffee with grounds in the cup, that sort of thing. But now? Now it ain't nothing." She turned to the group. "Get all your shit together and wait for me by the side of that shed," she pointed. There was something like a trail leading away from it, though it was tough to tell with the dying light of the sinking sun.

The group did as they were told. Walt went over to Alton and presented the lapel of his own denim jacket—no lining, and baggy on him. "Jean jacket buds!" he smiled, and Alton offered a generous laugh and a thumbs-up.

"Don't encourage him," Jace muttered as he passed them with his bag over one shoulder.

Patsy opened the doors to the machine shed, which let out a painful shriek as they rolled to the right, then pulled her War Rig into the darkness as far forward as she could. She began rolling barrels behind it, stacking some things up to look like it had been there a while. She threw a tarp over it, and then pulled on it a bit to simulate that it may have been here long enough to shift and settle. Between the road dust and the general look of the RV, Jessie had to admit—it fit right in.

"Anything I can do to help?" Jessie asked, Toby standing next to her.

Patsy looked at them as if suddenly reminded they were there. "Sure," she finally decided. "Take this and go cut off some pine branches. Get some with lots of needles coming off. Maybe three or four feet long." Patsy tossed a six-inch knife at her feet.

Jessie nodded and picked up the knife. She and Toby headed over to the trees to pick out some branches thin enough to cut.

"This is crazy," Jessie said conspiratorially. "It's already out of control, and we're not even in the complex yet."

"What did you expect?" Toby replied, giving her a half smile. "You're literally leading a group of strangers into a secret complex. You're breaking and entering and trespassing, at the very least."

"I didn't expect to get shot at," Jessie said. "At least not so soon."

"I'm not sure the timing is your biggest worry here," Toby pointed out. "Cops shooting at us is cops shooting at us. And now they know we're here, whoever *they* are."

Jessie considered this as she started cutting low branches off a small cluster of pines just up the slope. "Yeah," she finally said. "I don't know what I've gotten myself into here. The only one that seems normal is Alton. Everyone else besides us is kind of crazy."

"I don't know," Toby said. "Walt's just a boomer out of his depth. Jace is a dick, but seems harmless. Otomi . . . I don't know. Between her flying in on a chopper and knowing her shit about firearms . . . yikes."

"You're forgetting Patsy," Jessie said, cutting the last of the branches. "She's one beer short of a case."

"Don't start sounding like her," Toby laughed. "I can't take any more folksy shit."

"Fair," Jessie smiled. "Let's get these back down to her, whatever they're for."

What they were for, it turned out, was hiding their tracks. Patsy walked with them dragging behind her all the way back to where they'd turned off the main road, and when she came back, she did the same with the various footprints in the clearing.

Alton and Walt had started a small fire in the sparse area where they'd been told to wait. Everyone was warming their hands.

"Put that shit out," Patsy ordered through her teeth, keeping her voice low. "You want everyone here in East Jesus to know where we are?"

"Who exactly?" challenged Jace. "We haven't done shit yet, and we're already being chased. That's fucked up."

"You do owe us an explanation," Otomi said sullenly, and Walt and Alton nodded.

"I don't owe you shit," Patsy cackled. "You're paying me to get you to where you need to go, and out again. That's my job. Who might be following you, I don't know. In my experience, it's better to assume that someone's always watching. But this ain't my bivouac, kids, and I'm telling you, unless you want more folks shooting at you . . . put out that fire."

They did as they were told, Walt smothering the small flame with dirt. The embers were still glowing underneath the soil. "I'll go to the lake and get some water," he said, grunting a little as he got up from his crouch.

"I saw a bucket around the other side of the shed," Patsy said, taking a long pull on her cigarette, standing back, and looking up at the moon in the sky. She exhaled without a sound, and from where she was sitting, Jessie could swear the smoke ate the whole moon right up.

---

"Got me some ground rules," Patsy said when the embers had been doused, and everyone moved into the shed. "None of us need any surprises from here on, so no one do anything without running it by me first. Unless I tell you to take point, you stay behind me. If I say run, start running. If I say duck, don't ask why, or it might be the last thing you say."

"Yeah, yeah," Jace muttered. "And if you say jump, we ask how high. We get the drill."

"No, you don't," Patsy snapped. "You don't ask how high. You fucking jump. You take the time to ask anything, and you're dead. And if you die, that's just more work for the rest of us."

"Jesus," Jace said. "Whatever."

"Everyone needs to calm down," Alton said with a preternatural calm, his eyes heavy lidded and serious. "No one's going to die. Not if I can help it. I have a med kit and an emergency kit in my pack. I'll be able to do anything short of surgery, if necessary, not that I think it will be."

"That's a good idea," Jessie said. "We should all share what we brought along, so we all know what we have to work with. Could be important in a crisis. Alton has medical supplies. That's good."

"Any weapons?" Patsy asked.

"No," said Alton.

Patsy shook her head. "Pretty stupid for a doctor."

"I'm here to treat injuries if they happen," Alton said. "Not cause them."

"Injuries don't just happen," Patsy retorted. "They get done *to* you, and there's always a *because*. Inattention. Distraction. Someone literally trying to kill you."

"We all agreed," Jessie interjected. "No weapons. I mean, not really. Camp knives and whatnot are fine, I guess, but no guns. This isn't that sort of trip."

"In my experience, they're all that sort of trip," Patsy said, rolling her eyes. "Be sure to write down what y'all want on your tombstones."

"I have rope," Walt interjected. "I have two canteens, a waterproof tarp, camp binoculars, and a compass. Some plastic bags full of fresh toilet paper. Lots of energy bars and chocolate drop trail mix for some quick energy." And then to Patsy, he said, "I do have a Swiss Army knife, and also a camping hatchet in a frog sleeve."

"That's something," Patsy nodded.

"Oh," Walt added. "Also, my cholesterol pills, which I'm supposed to take every night, so someone remind me."

Most of the group had the same sort of supplies—hard rations, water containers, purifier tablets. Otomi only had a change of clothes, her phone, and some granola bars. Toby had even less than that.

Jace was especially encumbered, mostly with surveillance and recording tech. He'd also brought everyone earbuds, each one serving as a two-way communicator with his own more substantial headset, an antenna coming up from his left ear.

"What did you bring?" Alton asked Patsy.

"The necessities of life," she answered, and didn't offer more.

"And everyone has their phone, right?" Jessie said, holding up a small Pelican case that glinted in the moonlight. "With extra SIM cards? We'll switch them out each night, like we agreed. And then one more time when we're all safely out."

"I can edit it all together, so everyone has a copy," Toby said.

"My job, chief," Jace insisted.

"Just offering," Toby shrugged.

"Y'all want to sleep a bit, or get moving?" Patsy asked. "Once you're down in the hole, you won't know if it's day or night anyway."

"What would you suggest?" Jessie asked, wishing that Patsy was spelunking down with them, and not just waiting up at the shaft for their retrieval.

"This is your keelboat, Mike Fink," Patsy said. "I just work here."

"Wasn't that some old ride at Disneyland?" Jace asked.

"It was something else before that," said Walt, visibly annoyed. Jessie wondered if Walt had finally reached the limit of his patience with Jace. "You might want to read a book sometime."

"Walt comes alive!" Toby beamed. Even Otomi had to crack a smile.

"I say we camp," Jessie decided. "This might be the last safe place we get for a while, and we all need the sleep. We can start fresh at daybreak."

Everyone seemed to agree—everyone but Patsy. "Ain't no such thing as a safe place up here," she said. "But it's your call. I will insist that we cold camp in the shed, though, and we'll have to cover our tracks again in the morning before we head out."

They set up a makeshift camp—really just a ring of blankets for most of them except Patsy. Jace had suggested that a few of them could sleep in the RV, but the coyote had said no. It wasn't that sort of RV, whatever that meant. Jessie wondered if it was more that Patsy just liked saying no to Jace, but it wasn't like she slept inside either. The older woman had climbed up the side of the RV in the dusty half-light of the old machine shed and lay flat on her back on top of the War Rig, using her coat as a pillow and a flap of the tarp as a blanket. Based on the snoring, she fell asleep in minutes.

No one else was that lucky—or that practiced in sleeping when the opportunity presented itself. But all of them caught a few fitful hours, listening to the sounds of the surrounding forest—and what sounded at times like the low humming of . . . something. There was also an occasional howling, which everyone considered might be chupacabras, mythical doglike monsters they'd heard about from the *Escaping Denver* podcast, but were more likely wolves. Not that the thought was all that consoling. Were chupacabras worse than wolves? Somehow it seemed so, but they didn't know. And none of them wanted to find out. Despite all this, they all drifted off to sleep.

Jessie woke suddenly in the predawn to the sound of machine gun fire followed by a high whine, some small and distant explosions, and finally, a nose-diving metallic crash that broke the night's silence.

*Maybe we should have listened to Patsy after all*, Jessie thought as everyone shot to their feet and looked around groggy and scared and unprepared for everything coming.

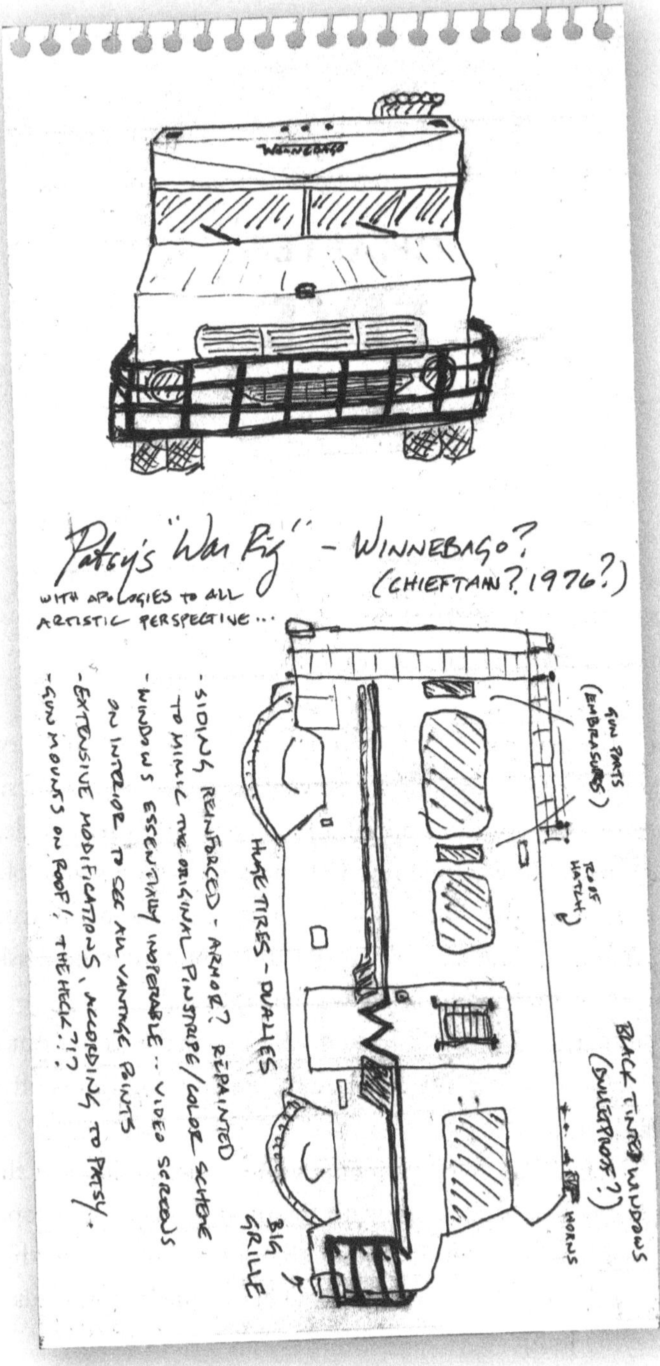


Walt's Field Journal, page 6

# CHAPTER FIVE

ABANDONED DUDE RANCH
INDIAN PEAKS, USFS/COLORADO

When the group piled out through the shed door, they saw Patsy crouched in the middle of what had once been a guesthouse but was now just a pile of splintered wood with a buckled shingle roof. She was holding a Kalashnikov that was still smoking from the barrel. Off to one side of the shed, something on the ground was similarly smoking in the mountain mist. Jessie shivered and assured herself it was just the cold.

"What the hell?" Alton shouted. "You make us put out a fire, but you're out here shooting a fucking machine gun at five in the morning?"

"Drone," Patsy said, rising to her feet, and nodding at the wreckage. "And we're done with the hiding. There are people whose job it is to keep people away from this place, and they know we're here. Get your shit, and get it quick, y'all. This is me saying jump."

"I know there are bears and stuff out here," Walt said to

Otomi as they packed up quickly. "But I don't think we need an AK. Seems like overkill."

"It's not for the bears," Otomi said, slinging her pack over her shoulder. "It's for the 'and stuff,' old man."

"Everyone needs to cut it out with the old man crap," Walt said to Jessie, as she was raking the area where they'd slept.

"She doesn't mean anything by it," Jessie responded, leaning on the upturned rake.

"You know, I've hiked more of this country than any of you put together," Walt said, but he was smiling again. "I know you've all got your skills, and I respect that, but this old man has some surprises left in him. You don't watch as much nature programming as I have without learning a little something about survival."

Jessie didn't know if he was kidding, but she finished up, and followed Walt out of the shed, pulling the door as closed as the old rollers would allow.

"You ready?" Toby asked her. Jace and Alton were up standing near Patsy, who was smoking another cherry hand-roll. Otomi was leaning against a tree, just waiting, and Walt was off relieving himself at the tree line.

"As ever," Jessie said. "So far, this hasn't gone like I thought."

"Nothing ever does, right?" sighed Toby. "Except for the cops shooting at us, it's been sort of what I expected."

"I'm a little surprised at how poorly everyone is getting along," Jessie said. "We were pretty tight online."

"Easy to do on the internet," Toby said. "And if you're really concerned, we can just call this off now. We can go home, and you all can go back to armchair quarterbacking this conspiracy theory or whatever it is. Do your thing from the safety of your living room. That's what the podcast is for, right? You can live vicariously through it without the authorities shooting at you and drones hunting you down and whatever the hell comes next."

Jessie looked hard at Toby. She hadn't noticed his reticence before, but it made sense. None of this had any context for him; he'd never listened to *Escaping Denver*. He wasn't here for that—he was here for *her*. And now, because Carla hadn't shown up, he was in with both feet. "I get it," she finally said. "But I'm pushing on. If you need to pull up stakes and head back to Ward to pick up the Lincoln—even drive back home to Chicago—I'd totally understand." She took a deep breath. "This is my thing. And I'm going to see it through. It's something I have to do. I'm not even sure why. But it feels like unlocking this mystery is a huge step in understanding everything else, you know? I can't explain it."

"No," Toby said softly. "You are explaining it. But have you looked up where Patsy is taking us? There's a path there, even if it doesn't look like one. It's old, overgrown—but there's also busted branches along the way that show something—God knows what, but something big—pushed its way through, and at some point not that long ago. And it left no tracks."

"What are you saying?" Jessie asked.

"That we don't want to find whatever that is," Toby said. "Even if Patsy has an AK and a grenade in her boot."

"She has a grenade in her boot?"

"We don't want to find that out either," Toby joked.

"Seriously, Tobes," Jessie said. "If you need to go, go. I'll catch up with you. Or you can camp out with Patsy and wait with her, if you want. But I have to do this."

"I can't leave you," Toby said simply, and with a heavy sigh. "I won't."

Patsy let out a sharp whistle, circling her finger in the air as she began her climb up the rocky slope. Everyone fell in a rough line behind her. *More of a gaggle, really*, Jessie thought. But at least they were off.

The sun was in their eyes as they all headed east and up.

The group was quiet except for occasional out-of-breath huffing when they'd climb a little too fast. Walt asked how far it was, but Patsy didn't answer. Jace asked how long they'd be walking, but Patsy didn't answer that either. Alton recommended they take a short rest to let everyone slow their heart rate, and by everyone, he meant Walt. Patsy again said nothing. She did stop occasionally, looked around, touched the bark of a nearby tree, and even sniffed at the air. She even crouched down and tasted the dirt once, which made Otomi grimace, but no one said anything. The only curious thing about Patsy's behavior, Jessie noted, was that this was the longest she'd seen the older woman go without lighting up a cigarette.

The route they were taking couldn't even really be called a path. They were essentially bushwhacking, the way marked only by strange detritus that had untold stories of their own. At one point, Jessie spotted a single dirty sneaker stuffed with something Jessie didn't recognize, but silently hoped wasn't the remains of a foot.

Walt pointed out some scat that he said didn't look like the work of any animal he was aware of. Jessie wondered what some of the jagged pieces in the pile of scat might have been, but there was no telling, and that was a discovery that Jessie had no interest in making.

They were cresting yet another furrowed line of rock, the elevation climb being anything but level, when Patsy called out, "Mind the fence."

At first, Jessie didn't see anything, but as they approached a small rise in vegetation, she could see it: wires twisting out of the foliage, blackened like the leaves around it but still somehow fading back into the greens and the browns of the forest floor.

"I guess something else found the fence before we did," Jace observed, crouching down and examining the twisted metal. "Looks like something blasted right through."

"No tracks," Walt said. "Not of an animal that size, or a herd, or a vehicle either."

"No," Jace agreed. "But something was here. Is this fur?" He reached out and plucked a tuft of dark hair from a snaggy piece of fence.

"Don't touch that," Otomi said.

"Circuit's been broken, sweetheart," Jace said. "It was definitely electrified, though, and stronger than your usual ranch stuff. Seriously, what animal is this from?"

"Hairy alligator, anyone?" Walt murmured.

"Do you think the creatures from the facility can actually get out?" Alton asked.

"If they can't," Jace reasoned, "I don't know why we think we can get in so easily."

"A hairy alligator?" Toby questioned. "Sounds like some shitty cocktail only a barfly would order."

"You should remember to tell that joke again when one has you in its jaws," Otomi said.

"I'm actually not sure how much we should believe," Jessie explained to Toby. "It's all so . . . out there, I know. The creatures, the cryptids, the conspiracies. Apparently, the Collective was initially formed to fight back against an alien takeover of the world by some race called Firbens."

"Fear-beans?" Toby scoffed. "Alien invasion? This is even more warped than I thought."

"Again," Otomi warned, "probably not wise to dismiss things you know nothing about."

"Yeah, yeah," Toby said. "*More things in heaven and earth than are dreamt of in my philosophy.* Whatever."

"Let me see that," Alton interrupted, approaching the dead fence with care, just in case. He took the fur and rolled it between his fingers thoughtfully. "It's from an animal, that's for sure. Patsy, you have any insight into this? This ringing any bells for you in terms of scent or anything?"

Patsy side-eyed Alton, but took the fur from his outstretched hand and gave it a quick sniff. "Bear," she finally said.

"Bear would leave tracks," Walt pointed out.

"Sneaky bear, then," Patsy said. "Who the fuck cares? The fence is down—one less thing for us to worry about. We should move, though. They probably know there was a breach, and they'll be out looking to fix it. We shouldn't be here when they arrive."

Jace picked up a stick and thumped the ground ahead of them on the path. "Just making sure," he said to Jessie as she looked at him quizzically. "No pitfalls, no electrocuted corpses of sneaky bears."

"Is it weird that I'm imagining this bear wearing tennis shoes now?" Toby asked Jessie with a grin.

Jessie smiled back, but it was forced. Part of her got what Toby was saying. It was all so . . . yes, it *was* weird. And that was saying something for a trip they'd planned in order to uncover weirdness.

They had descended into an aspen grove in a small valley when they first saw the shaft. It was so well hidden that they were almost on top of it, camouflaged against a rising butte in this natural dip in the landscape. It was concrete, but dyed with a mottled slate gray that faded into the rock behind it, especially as it sat in the middle of towering aspens that trembled in the breeze that wound through them.

"There she is," Patsy said.

It was silent in the valley of aspens except for the wind fluttering the leaves in the trees. It sounded almost like a whisper, Jessie considered, if you turned your head just right. But whispers of what?

"It really does resemble a take on the Velsertunnel," Walt

said as the group approached. The shaft seemed to increase in height as they descended the slope of the valley toward the structure. The vegetation got thicker and taller too, so the group was wading through green up to their chests and shoulders.

"The what?" Toby asked.

"The Velsertunnel," Walt explained. "In the Netherlands, built back in 1957. Lots of the same characteristics on this, though it's just one big shaft instead of several small ones. But see those rectangular intakes near the top there? That's exactly what the Dutch did in Velsen-Noord. Supposed to enhance the airflow."

"This was modeled after that?" Jessie asked. "So, it's post-'57?"

"Or that was based on this," Alton said. "Which would make it the other way around."

"Y'all want to carbon-date this sumbitch," Patsy drawled, "or get on inside?"

No one answered, but everyone moved.

"I'm surprised there's no cameras," Jace said when they were at the base of the shaft. The ground had risen sharply in the final twenty feet or so, and there was a rusted metal ladder leading up the near side.

Patsy was already busy hacking away with a machete from her belt, making a spot to camp while they were gone. "There are," she said. "Just not all over. Why do you think we've been zigzagging to get here? We've been dodging coverage."

"So, you know the blind spots?" Otomi confirmed. "How?"

"It's my job to know, sweetheart," Patsy winked. "And these guys? They're all about recordings. All about surveillance, all about expanding their base of knowledge. I don't know who or what sits at the top of their organization, if you can call it that? But whatever else they're wanting, data is at the top of their list."

"I'd know if there were cameras," Jace boasted. "It's like a sixth sense to me. I can feel the waves of data brushing past my ears."

"No," Patsy said simply. "You wouldn't. You didn't know there was cameras on you in the War Rig, now did you?"

"You were filming us in the RV?" Jessie asked. "Why?"

"Maybe just to have video evidence of who they're looking for," Patsy said. "In case y'all don't come back."

"You should have let us know," Alton said.

"Yes," agreed Otomi, crossing her arms.

Patsy waved them all off. "I'm the one who'll be up here topside waiting to pull you out of that hole, so the more I know, the better off you all just might be."

"At least there's a ladder," Toby offered.

"Think there's another ladder leading down the inside?" Walt asked.

"I doubt this place would be that kind," Otomi said, but she was the first up the ladder.

"Wait," Jace said. "We're just . . . *going*? Don't we need to prep or something?"

"Haste is pretty much the only thing y'all have on your side," Patsy said. "That and the element of surprise. So yes, get on up. I'll finish setting up here, and I'll wait to hear from you."

"Testing," Jace said into his headset.

"Loud and clear, ace," Patsy tapped on her earpiece. "Stop namby-pambying around and go. All of you. The sooner you're down there and see what you need to see, the sooner I can get you out."

"Right," Jessie said, taking a breath. "I'll bring up the rear. You guys go."

"No," Toby said. "I'll bring up the rear. Just in case."

"You sure you're not just wanting to look at her ass, man?" Jace chided Toby as he passed, laughing at his own joke.

"That's not necessary," Walt said, climbing behind Jace.

"Thanks, Patsy," Jessie said. "See you soon."

"Remember only to go as far as the first landing," Patsy directed. "There's plenty for you to see on that level, and anything below that, I doubt we're going to retain any way to communicate whatsoever. The signal just don't go that far, okay?"

Jessie nodded. At this point, she didn't need convincing to make this a relatively short trip. Spelunk down into the shaft far enough that they access the interior, bust a lock or two, rifle through some drawers, record everything on their smartphones, and when Patsy pulls them out, upload all of it to the web where they and countless other internet sleuths could dissect every frame for information. It wouldn't be their last foray into the underground network centered on Denver International Airport, but it would be enough for them to get the discoveries started. Maybe start their own podcast.

But mainly? To get some answers.

She started climbing, and heard Toby fall into line behind her. The thin-railed ladder didn't feel especially safe, particularly when it moved a bit in the spots where the concrete wall had crumbled. But she kept climbing.

The top of the shaft flared out slightly, creating something of a platform around the rim. The entrance was wider than it looked from down below—probably thirty or forty feet. Enough that the hole seemed like the maw of some great leviathan beast, ready to swallow them all. Jessie shook off the thought.

Toby touched her shoulder. "You okay?" he asked quietly.

"Yeah," Jessie replied. Otomi was already setting up the rappelling equipment, checking the stopping knots and the anchors and the relative sturdiness of each of the ropes before starting on each individual harness.

"I got pretty good at this down at the climbing wall at the Y," Walt said as Otomi checked the straps on his vest. He peered over the lip and down into the darkness. "Never did anything from this height, though."

"Height is a construct of perception," Otomi said tonelessly. "Outside, on the ground, you were eleven or twelve thousand feet above sea level, and that didn't bother you at all. This shouldn't either. It's all in your head," she added, finishing up and tapping a slender finger on Walt's forehead.

"Guess so," Walt said.

"I have a massive headache," Toby admitted to Jessie.

"That's the elevation," Alton explained. "It affects people differently."

"I was a little sick to my stomach last night," Walt said. "But I got through it. Drink a little water."

"That won't do much," Alton said, "but it's always good to hydrate."

Toby took a swig from his canteen. "Mmm . . ." he intoned sarcastically. "Warm like bathwater."

Jessie shone her Maglite down the shaft, illuminating a beam down into the dusty murk. Below, some fifty feet down or so, was the platform for which they were heading. It was a simple concrete pad with no stairs or evident manner of access. No railing either—nothing but a door in one wall that they believed was access to a room that sat right under the ground level outside where Patsy remained. If they aimed it right, they could rappel straight down and land on the close edge of the ledge, with no swinging or complicated moves necessary.

"Here we go, guys," Jessie said. "Down just a little ways to that door, and then we see what's what."

"Moment of truth," Alton said. "Hopefully, everyone's practiced their rappelling skills because there's no telling exactly how long that drop is."

"Not helping my anxiety," Walt laughed, his voice shaky.

"Mama Bear, Mama Bear, come in Mama Bear," Jace said, putting his finger up to his earpiece. Jessie wondered for a moment if that was actually a thing, the ear touching, or just an affectation Jace had seen in any number of movies.

"Don't call me that, you little shit," came Patsy's voice over the small speaker Jace had clipped to his vest. "I'm not your mama, or a bear, thank God for both. Watch that first step, y'all."

"So folksy," Otomi deadpanned. "Not tiresome at all."

"Aw, she's funny," Walt said.

"She's more scary than anything," Toby said.

"Well bless your little chickenshit heart," came Patsy's voice again.

"I didn't know you could still hear us," Toby said.

"You'll be free of me soon enough," Patsy retorted. "Get going, and try sending up a signal when you hit that landing. Might be we still have coverage from there, but if not, you've got my Pigeon."

"Roger that," Jace said.

"Pigeon?" Alton asked.

Jace held up something small and bladed, made of black plastic. He shoved it back into one of the many bulging pockets on his vest. "Mini drone," he said. "Can't do a whole lot more than fly straight up and beep, but that'll be enough to grab Patsy's attention."

"Talk to you in a few minutes, Patsy," Jessie said. "I hope."

"Lord willing and the creek don't rise," Patsy said with a static crackle. Jace clicked off the speaker.

---

The descent was perhaps the stupidest thing she'd ever done, or so Jessie considered as she leaped from the relative safety of the lip of the shaft. It was only a short hop, down a couple of measured yards, to plant her feet against the wall and get used to her weight being supported by the rope. To reset, stabilize, and get ready for the next step, and the one after that.

Otomi had gone down first. It was clear she'd done this before. Alton was right behind her, with Walt and Jace going at the same time, side by side. That left Jessie and Toby to bring up the rear again.

"Hey, this isn't bad at all," Walt said. "I can't even look down unless I try super hard. That helps."

"Focus," said Otomi. Her voice from below rang hollow off the shaft walls.

"And don't get cocky," said Alton.

"Seriously, everyone, be . . ." Otomi started, but her voice trailed off.

"Otomi?" Jessie said. They'd all stopped their descent.

"Shhh," Otomi hissed. "I hear something."

They craned their necks in different directions, and after a moment, they could hear it too. A buzzing—no, more a humming. Subtle at first, but quickly getting louder.

From where she dangled against the wall, Jessie could just make out what looked like dozens of tiny red dots in the gloom below the platform. As they approached and grew larger, she could see they were pairs of eyes. "Hold on," Otomi yelled. "A whole lot of somethings are flying up out of the hole!"

"What are they?" Walt shouted back.

But the creatures were on them in an instant. "Cover your eyes!" Alton yelled.

"No, your necks!" Toby screamed. "They'll try to get your neck!"

It was impossible for Jessie to hear if anyone said anything after that. They were besieged by what looked to be greasy-feathered birds the size of cranes, but with wings that flapped so quickly that it was almost impossible to catch sight of them. What was more apparent—and more concerning—were their long proboscises, thin beaks that glinted with a metallic sheen and were tapered to a sharp point.

Whatever their intent, the monstrous birds succeeded in one thing: inciting panic. In the chaos, somehow, Alton lost the tether on his line. "*Shit! Shit shit shit shit shit!*" he cried as he began to plummet deep into the shaft with a sudden unreeling sound. The attacks from the hovering needle-beak beasts continued, and Jace was the next to fall, grabbing Walt in sheer panic and causing them both to hurtle down and hit Otomi. All three of them disappeared into the blackness.

And then Jessie heard one of her ropes snap, and she, too, began free-falling.

# CHAPTER SIX

MAIN AIR SHAFT, WESTERN QUADRANT

It was a darkness that seemed to breathe on its own, Jessie thought as she hung there in midair, suspended by a single stop tie that had—at least for now—held throughout a long drop and a sudden, halting jerk. She heard something coming from above her, and was relieved to hear Toby whispering her name, descending on his gear, lit by a glow stick zip-tied to his belt.

"Jessie," he said. "You there?"

"I'm here," Jessie said. "Where'd those bird things go?"

"I'm not sure," he said. "Up and out, I think? I don't even know if them attacking us was purposeful or not."

"Purposeful enough," Jessie said. "One of them clipped one of my ropes."

"Same here, I think," came Alton's voice from the darkness, a little lower than where Jessie was hanging.

"We're here too," Walt said as he lit up a flare that flooded the shaft in crimson. He, Jace, and Otomi were snarled in a ball. Walt and Jace seemed to still be attached to their ropes, taut and vibrating. Otomi had ripped free of her vest and was literally perched on top of the other two, holding on to a rope.

"Jesus, Otomi," Toby said. "Are you okay?"

"I'm fine," she replied. "But I'll be better when we get over to that landing." She took out a small disc from a pouch on her belt and threw it in the darkness. It landed and lit up with a welcome white light, unveiling a platform much like the one they'd been aiming for, including the door in the far wall. "Hang on," Otomi said, and then leaned back hard, holding fast to both Walt and Jace's ropes.

"What the fuck?" Jace shrieked. "And get your foot out of my face!"

"Don't squirm," Otomi said, leaning forward to gain momentum. "This has to be smooth."

"We're not going to clear that lip . . ." Walt said, just before the trio barely did. They swung a bit, and then back again. Otomi pulled a thin blade from her hip, planted her feet firmly against the far wall on the backswing, and thrust forward with impressive force. The three swung once again over the landing, this time significantly farther over the lip, and she sliced the ropes at the apex of the arc, sending Walt and Jace tumbling on the concrete, rolling to a stop. Otomi landed on her feet and walked out the rest of her momentum in a way that looked almost casual. She stowed the blade back on her hip.

"Fuck no, you didn't just stick that landing," Toby said, admiration shining in his eyes.

"Fuck yes, I did," Otomi responded with just the hint of a smile appearing on her normally stoic face.

"Some of us are still hanging here," Alton said. "Literally at the end of our ropes. Can you all banter a little later?"

Otomi instructed the three still on their ropes to do the same as she had; she cut the ropes for both Alton and Jessie, leaving only Toby's still fastened up at the top of the shaft. Otomi took a piton from her backpack, along with a small hammer, and drove the spike into a concrete seam on the wall closest to where the ropes hung, and hung Toby's rope from it.

"Well, at least we made it back to solid ground," Walt said with a forced cheer.

"I guess we hit *a* landing, right?" Jessie sighed, looking up. Above them stacked platform after identical platform, as far up as the light would allow them to see. From where they stood near the edge, they couldn't even see the top of the shaft anymore. Not really. Jessie thought she could see a wavering light far above, but she wasn't sure if that was daylight or just some trick of the mind. Or just plain hope.

"Well, hell," Walt said. "Hard telling."

"How did you know we should cover our necks?" Alton asked Toby.

"Too many vampire movies, I guess?" Toby shrugged. "And maybe some old-school gaming. Lots of games have taken on the Greek stories of Stymphalian birds, like from the Labours of Hercules. Either way, if they were bloodsuckers, they'd go for the place where the most blood is closest to the skin's surface."

"Carotid artery," Alton said. "Smart."

Toby shrugged again, lazily thumbing an earlobe. It was a tic Jessie recognized. When Toby got uncomfortable, he'd rub at his right ear. Maybe to calm himself? Everyone had their thing, she supposed.

"They looked like giant hummingbirds," Jessie said.

"And we were their little red hanging jars of nectar," Walt said. "I think when I get home, I might take down the one I have on my porch."

Jace futzed with his receiver. "We're definitely too deep for Patsy to hear us," he said. "But I'm hearing something."

"Maybe she's just ignoring you," Otomi said.

"Call her Mama Bear again," suggested Toby. "That'll provoke a response if she can hear it."

"Shut up," Jace said, waving off the commentary. "Seriously, I heard something. It sounded like . . . like a voice. A Russian voice."

"What did it say?" Alton said with some excitement.

"I don't know," Jace admitted. "I only caught a bit of it, and now it's gone."

"Okay, well, what did it sound like?" Alton insisted.

"It sounded like *I don't understand Russian*," Jace scowled.

They all paused as they heard a whirring getting louder over their heads—not the thunderous reverberations of the killer birds, but something smaller—a little drone that approached just close enough to drop something that hit the concrete of the landing. It was a note.

Jessie picked it up. It was hastily scrawled, but clearly from Patsy, communicating in the only manner she had available.

*You went too far, like I figured you would. New plan: get yourselves back up here quick as a whistle. The lower you go, the more dangerous it'll be. Whatever you do, don't go down any more than you already have.*

*One more warning, since you are where you are. There's a creep down there named Elmo. Former associate of mine. He's dangerous. Absolutely crackers. Do not seek him out. If you meet him . . . run.*

*Actually, that's just good advice in general right now. Run like hell. Get back topside. You're in over your heads in more ways than you know.*

*I'll wait for you here until it doesn't make sense to hope anymore. Good luck.*

"Love, Patsy," finished Jace.

"No," Jessie corrected him. "She didn't sign it at all."

"This guy Elmo . . ." Toby grinned. "Short, high-pitched voice? Red fur?"

"Don't tickle him, whatever you do," Jace cackled.

Jessie stuffed the note in her pocket and joined Otomi in checking the door. Jessie turned the handle, half expecting it to be locked, for a new conundrum to present itself. But it wasn't. The handle turned easily. With a confusing mix of surprise, excitement, and dread, Jessie looked over at Otomi. They nodded their readiness to each other. "Everyone shut up and get lights and cameras ready," Jessie said. "I'm about to open the door."

The group immediately quieted. Jace turned on his GoPro, which had a small but powerful light. Glow sticks were snapped, flashlights were turned on, and smartphones were out and ready.

*We're here,* Jessie thought. After hearing about it for so long on the podcast, after talking about it online for years with this group and so many others. After all the conjecture, all the hope, all the trepidation . . . they were finally here. About to get some answers.

"Can we fucking get on with it?" Jace blurted, jarring Jessie's moment. "I'm burning juice here, and this isn't exactly riveting footage I'm getting."

"You, sir," Walt said to Jace, looking him straight in the eye, "have no romance in your soul."

Jace pushed past them all. "I'll show you no romance, Mr. Potato Head," he said, and nudged Jessie to one side as he grabbed the door handle. "Here we go," Jace said. "Open sesame, motherfuckers!"

But the room beyond the door was nothing like they'd expected. It occurred to Jessie that she didn't know what she'd expected—an office space or something, maybe? Something with filing cabinets and desks. Whiteboards with arcane symbology?

Or maybe even a nest of chupacabras? Or Bigfoot wearing a tux and offering her a fancy drink in a severe British accent? Maybe. But not this.

---

The room wasn't so much a room as it was a cavern. A big one. The ceiling, if it had one, was so far up into the darkness that it was essentially invisible. The floor was literally dirt beyond the threshold of the concrete landing, and that soil provided fertile enough ground for a veritable lawn of mushrooms and moss in varying colors of greens and browns and even some purple dotted here and there. Water dripped from somewhere overhead, forming small pools on the ground. Some of them looked natural, but others were clearly purposeful, circular rings of stone built perhaps to contain the focused precipitation. How they drained—or if they did at all—was anyone's guess. There were trees, too, but small, sort of sad ones drooping on little islands in the mire. Weeping willows, Jessie surmised, from their characteristic slump. But why? And what were those in the distance? Giant mushrooms?

The walls looked much like those Noah had mentioned in the podcasts, but it was still a shock to see the rough natural rock that had somehow grown over the concrete.

"Nobody move," Otomi said.

"Fuck that," Jace said, turning around in order to record as much of the enormous chamber as their light would reach. He knelt and dug a bit in the dirt floor. "This is packed soil," he continued, carving clods with a small lock knife from his belt. "It goes down at least eight inches."

"Gotta be more, with these trees," Alton said. "The mounds are probably to give it some extra root space, but you wouldn't get growth like this without a purposeful level of soil."

"So this is a Bio-Dome," Jace marveled, though it was clear that he was narrating his video, and not particularly talking to anyone in the room.

"Maybe," corrected Otomi. "This place wants us to make presumptions like that. Every riddle sits inside another riddle. This seems larger somehow."

"It could be the same," Toby offered. "Why build more than one ginormous indoor woodland plant festival?"

"We don't know," Jessie said. "That's the point. We don't know why they built one, so we don't know if building more than one is questionable or not."

"The one from the podcast was full of trees," Otomi added. "And the dome was one of hundreds. Unless each one is so large that you can't see the outside when you're in it, this isn't that."

"But we're comparing objective witness to subjective reporting," Alton said, looking around in wonder. "So who really knows?"

"The Bio-Domes they mentioned on the podcast had a waterfall too, remember?" Jessie said. "It was through some passages behind the waterfall that they accessed the shaft. Or at least, the shaft they found, which might or might not be our shaft."

"Their shaft had one bar of coverage," Jace said. "We still got nothing down here."

"Okay, so this isn't the Bio-Domes," Jessie said. "Nothing looks right, nothing fits. This doesn't feel like a forest either—it's more of a . . . woodland maybe? A swamp?"

"Why would anyone build a swamp?" Toby sounded skeptical.

"For the hairy alligators?" Walt suggested.

"Okay, well, this room just lost a lot of its charm for me," Jace said. "Let's get out of here before we run out of luck."

"Luck has nothing to do with this place," Otomi said softly. "Everything is designed."

"Footprints," Walt said from just a bit ahead. No one had heeded Otomi's warning. They'd all been wandering, taking it all in, and Walt had forged ahead deeper into the room.

"What kind?" Jessie asked, approaching him carefully.

"All kinds," Walt said. "And nothing that really looks normal, outside of some rabbit tracks. There's something much larger here, but it's an older print. Some standard-sized canine prints, too, but they have pretty serious claws."

"Chupacabra?" Jace wondered out loud, rushing up and pointing his GoPro down at the tracks in the dirt, which was wetter here, and looked to contain a little more clay. "Man, I'd love to get one of those on video. Shut all the naysayers right the hell up. We all got our whistles, right?"

"We don't know those are chupacabra," Jessie said. "We don't really even know these are rabbit tracks."

"I'm pretty sure," Walt countered.

"Then where are the rabbits?" Alton asked. They were all in a group again. "Where are any of these things, for that matter? I don't see anything, and I don't hear anything. Not a bird, not an insect, nothing. How does a place like this thrive without an ecosystem? Without any sun at all?"

"Riddles within riddles," Otomi intoned.

"Okay," Jessie said. She was getting annoyed at Otomi's shift from acrobatic badass to doomsaying philosopher. She'd always been separate from the group in some way. But this . . . this was new. Just the stress of being down here? Or was it more? "This looks like a game trail," Jessie said after taking a beat. "Maybe we follow it?"

"Or is following it what they want us to do?" Toby asked.

"We're not going to get anywhere if we keep second-guessing the intent of literally everything we run into," Alton said, shaking his head, and Jessie was impressed to see that the curl in his impressive hair hadn't missed a bounce. "Sometimes a game trail is just a game trail."

"What other options do we have?" Walt said. "I say we follow it through this room and see what's on the other side. It goes back to why the chicken crossed the road."

"And got run over by a Mack truck," Jace said. "But nah, I agree with Walt. My badminton coach used to quote Abraham Lincoln all the time: *Things may come to those who wait, but only the things left by those who hustle.*"

"That's apocryphal," Alton said.

"Hey, thanks man," Jace said, and raised his hand for a high five. Alton started to explain what that word meant, but decided it wasn't worth it, and accepted the high five with a nonplussed air.

"More importantly: *badminton coach*?" Toby laughed.

"Fuck you, Tubby," Jace said. "I was good."

"I'm just saying," Toby said. "Next time you tell that story, I'd just refer to them as your coach, y'know?"

"Cut it out," Jessie reprimanded. "It seems to me that we have two main options here: one, perimeter the room and take its full measure. That's going to take a while. Or we cut across the diameter and get to the next room, or at least the next part of this one. Thoughts?"

Jace voted with Walt, saying he was jumping to get to the next thing. Alton said he had no preference, but would follow the group, and Toby indicated that he was fine with whatever Jessie wanted. Otomi shrugged off the matter entirely, consumed with looking around the room, apparently scouring what was visible for any sort of movement. As Jessie was just about to turn away, Otomi's head cocked to one side, and she grimaced.

"Was . . ." she started. "Did you guys see that light there before?"

Sure enough, ahead of them in the general direction of the game trail, was a very small bit of light in the distance. It looked ambient, like it was coming off something that wasn't its source, but in the darkness of the room, it might as well have been a beacon.

"That wasn't there just a minute ago," Walt said.

"Is it moving?" Jace said. He was whispering now, looking straight at the light.

"Don't think so," Walt replied.

"Okay," Jessie said. "We push on, then. Quietly. And everyone, keep your heads down."

"Not a chance," Jace said, adjusting his GoPro and checking its feed on his phone. They crept forward through the mud and the moss that, by all rights, shouldn't have been there at all.

---

It was a hut. That was the only way they could describe it. A hut apparently built, on the exterior at least, from materials found in the room itself: bare branches used as corner posts, around which were tied hundreds upon hundreds of willow switches. A door that was more like a thick curtain of those same thin, reedy tree limbs and a roof crafted from the broad leaves of giant philodendrons or something that looked much like them. The light was coming from the pseudo-door, filtering through the plant material just enough to be seen. Above the door was a small rough-looking sign, really just a large piece of bark with a single word burned into it: Bwana.

"Bwana?" Jace read, recording the sign.

"It's Swahili," Alton said. "Means anything from 'boss' to 'master,' depending on the context."

"So this is the boss's hut," Jessie said.

"Okay," Jace deadpanned. "Boss of what, though?"

"Amateur wood burning, from the look of it," Toby said. "Should we knock or something?"

"What, on the curtain?" Jace said, laughing at his own joke. "We've made enough noise to announce ourselves." He pushed aside the thick brush that served as a door, and a dim light spilled out.

It was a single room, furnished more or less like a bedroom. The walls had been finished with what looked to be 1970s wood paneling; there was an overstuffed mustard-yellow chair with a small table next to it and a digital clock radio perched on top. The red-numbered display was faint, but it no longer showed the time, if it ever had. It just read EE:EE.

Against one wall was a bed, neatly made with an old, thin-looking bedcover, tightly drawn at the corners. It had a polished maple headboard and a matching footboard—the former was unadorned, but the latter had a rather grandiose R carved into it in bas-relief. The low bedside table had a small lamp on it, and a closed drawer within. There was a desk, too, with a simple wooden chair, and sitting on the desk was what looked to be a vintage camcorder.

"Groovy," said Jace. "Makes me want to watch *The Brady Bunch* or some shit." Apparently unable to control himself, he suddenly rushed over and jumped heavily into the easy chair, and a visible cloud of dust spouted up from the seat cushion with a flat squeaking. "That was the chair, by the way."

"If you say so, man," Toby joked.

"Hey, I used to have one of these back in school," Walt said, picking up and admiring the camcorder. "It's an old Panasonic Omnimovie. It was the new toy for the A/V club back in . . . man, must have been '85? It was awesome because it used full-size VHS tapes, and not those little mini VHS-C ones."

"Is it still working?" Jessie asked.

“Seems dead,” Walt said, clicking around with the controls and holding the viewfinder up to his eye. “These old models used tube tech, not to mention internal belt drivers and whatnot. So much to go wrong on these old things over time. Still, might just be a power thing. But there’s no cord.”

Toby sat on the bed. “Hey, this is a pretty nice mattress. Feathers, I think.”

“Can everyone please get up and stop checking things out like we’re thinking of renting the place?” Jessie pleaded. “We’re going to stumble into something we don’t expect, and that could be dangerous.”

“C’mon, Jess,” Jace said. “Lighten up. It’s a chair and a bed and a decrepit video camera in what looks a lot like what I imagine Walt’s basement to look like.”

Walt looked around and seemed to consider the idea, and then nodded. “I’d have a TV there in front of that chair, though.”

Alton looked up from the floor near the wall opposite the chair. “Looks like someone did,” he said. “Or something similar. There’s scratches in the wood floor here. Something heavy was here, and then got moved.”

“Here’s why the light went on,” Otomi said, holding up an old dial-front plug-in timer. “It’s set to come on and go off daily, but the times seem random.”

“They’re not meant to come on at EE o’clock?” Jace laughed at his own joke again. “I wonder if they got any reception down here?” He turned the radio on, but it was, as Jessie expected, just static. Jace left it on, monitoring it with his ear close to the speaker.

“Aw,” Toby said, “there’s a note in the nightstand drawer here. *Dearest Roger. Come back. All is forgiven.* And it’s just signed *Melissa*. That’s . . . sweet, I guess?”

“So this is Roger’s place,” Jessie put her hands on her hips. “Now the question is: who’s Roger?”

"And who's Melissa?" Otomi added.

"And what did she need to forgive?" Toby asked.

"We might find out, if we can get this camera working," Walt offered. "There's still a VHS tape in here." He ejected the tape as if to demonstrate, and clicked it closed again. "This camera had playback through the viewfinder, so if we can find the power cord, there's a chance we could see it."

"Shit," Jace said, putting his ear closer to the radio. "Everyone shut up."

"Why?" Alton said. "Did you hear something?"

"Yeah," Jace said. "I've heard it twice now, but it's still gibberish to me. Something like *Vony u kimnati starogo*? Tough to make out, and then there was some noise, and then . . ."

"Back to static," Walt finished.

"Sounds Russian. Or Ukrainian. Something about an old man's room?" Alton guessed. "It was a woman's voice? Are you sure?"

"Maybe that was Melissa?" Jessie offered.

"Wait, this room?" Otomi pounced.

Toby rose from the bed and stepped closer to Walt. "Do you think Roger was an old man?"

"His tech suggests he was," Jace said, standing up and brushing off the dust.

"Hey," Walt protested, but there quickly came the sound of something—maybe a door slamming open somewhere out in the Bio-Domes?—that curtailed all further conversation. Walt put the camcorder down, ejected the VHS, and stowed it in his pack. Alton held the brush door to one side so everyone could quietly creep out.

"Where are we going?" Alton mouthed in a barely audible whisper to Jessie as she exited with him close behind.

"Away from that noise, now that we're out of the hut," Jessie whispered back. "It sounded like it came from where we entered, didn't it?"

"Tough to tell in here," he said.

"Too many echoes," Otomi agreed.

Jessie crouched down and started hustling in the opposite direction from the door back to the shaft. She motioned with two fingers for everyone to follow her, not knowing if anyone but Toby would. But they did.

The game trail didn't extend directly behind the Bwana Hut, but Jessie figured that bushwhacking was a little better than staying on any established path. The vegetation hid them to some degree, and the ground here was wet, muddy, and quiet.

"Is anyone even following us?" Jace said.

"Stopping might be a bad way to find out," Otomi said.

"This sucks," Jace complained. "I'd rather be . . ."

But no one would ever find out what or where Jace would have rather been, because three things happened in such rapid succession that everyone—even Jace himself—could only watch.

First, Jace's ankle caught and pulled on a vine hidden in the foliage.

Then, Jace stood up from his crouch, surprised. He looked down at his feet.

And that's when a spiked log snapped up from behind him, its wickedly pointed tips slamming into Jace's back with such force that they bloomed from his front in a sudden shower of blood and viscera. It made a wet, slapping sound when it hit. A pitiful sound, really, nothing heroic or memorable about it. Still, it was the last sound Jace would ever hear, and Jessie would later hope that somehow, someway, he'd been gone before he could hear it. It wasn't much of a goodbye.

# CHAPTER SEVEN

WETLANDS OVERFLOW

"What the fucking shit?!" Toby shrieked. He'd been right behind Jace when the trap went off. Jessie heard the whoosh, but Toby had been close enough to feel the turbulence in the air as the log had shot forward.

"Nobody move," Otomi said again, this time with some urgency—or maybe anger, or both?—in her voice. This time, nobody did. They were too busy taking in what had happened to Jace. He was pinned to the log like a collected butterfly. The log had been carved with no small amount of skill—split in half to provide a wide, flat surface, leaving enough wood attached such that spikes of varying lengths could be whittled to a deadly point. In the middle, where Jace had unfortunately found himself, the spikes were a foot and a half long, maybe more, and the force of the blow had driven several clean through his body, piercing or pulverizing whatever got in their way. One had driven right through his skull, emerging from his forehead like a vulgar parody of a unicorn's horn. Four spikes were spaced neatly in his chest and stomach, two to either side of his groin, one in each thigh and calf. His left arm was bent at the elbow, bearing some of his weight, and his right arm dangled free, the only limb to escape the trap's effects.

Alton took a few tentative steps toward where Jace and the trap stood. "Damn, kid," he whispered, examining the body, which still dripped blood. Alton reached out to check for a pulse, just in case, but Jace's wide-open eyes, still showing evident shock, told enough of the story. "He's gone," Alton confirmed, closing the younger man's eyes with a pass of his hand.

"Seriously . . ." Toby was panting a little, his hands on his knees. His voice was lower now, more collected. "What in the fucking shit?"

"Oh god," Jessie said, looking away. "Who would make something like that? And why?"

"And how?" Walt pointed out. "We didn't see any tools in that hut, and none of the trees in this room are big enough to have a trunk that thick. That's not willow wood, either. Pretty sure that's oak."

"It's not like we've seen this whole area," Alton said. "There could be a grove of old growth somewhere we haven't seen. Even if that's not the case, we already know this isn't the Bio-Dome from the podcast, and that room did have very tall trees, right? So maybe this came from there?"

"Which means that room probably isn't far?" Jessie reasoned. "I mean, whoever did this wouldn't lug a tree trunk that size very far, right?"

"Am I the only one still working on accepting that our friend here is a Halloween decoration?" Toby said.

"He wasn't our friend," Alton countered. "He was one of us, but none of us really know each other. And we all knew the risks coming down here."

"You're cold, man," Toby said.

"We should take him down," Walt said.

"And do what?" Alton asked, ignoring Toby and gingerly removing the GoPro from Jace's bloodied head. "It's not like we can bury him."

"We have to do something," Jessie said. "My god. I can't believe . . ."

"Poor kid," Walt picked up where Jessie had trailed off. "If it means anything to anyone, I don't think he felt a thing. Happened too fast."

"That's one of those things that people say just hoping it's true," Alton murmured, cutting the straps on Jace's backpack to remove it from between the spikes and Jace's corpse. "So they can live in some peace thinking it'll be true for them too."

"Quite the bedside manner you have there, Doc," Toby said. "Especially since you're saying all that while looting the body."

"Not looting," Alton said in measured tones as he examined the bloodied pack. "Recovering. Most of this is completely ruined. I don't even know what half this stuff is, but I know it's not supposed to look like this."

"We don't have time for this," Otomi said. "We were running, remember? That doesn't stop just because one of us falls."

"She's right," Jessie said.

"She's talking like the kid just skinned his knee," Toby said. "We're talking about one of us fucking dying here. Impaled like horror-movie style."

"The trap seems somewhat . . . rudimentary?" Alton added and dropped the bloody and broken GoPro. He fished a couple of energy bars and a battery pack out of the backpack and then dumped it at the feet of Jace's suspended body. "I got his phone too," he said. "For the data."

"Should we . . . grab his headset too?" Jessie asked, pausing as she realized that the earpiece was hanging from one of the uppermost spikes—along with the ear to which it had been attached.

"No, I'm good," Alton said.

"Leave it," Otomi ordered. "Leave all of it."

"I'm sorry, Jacinto," Walt said, putting a hand on Jace's shoulder, one of the few places on his body that wasn't bloody. "I'll remember you to your grandmother when the rest of us get out of here."

Toby swore but fell into line behind his retreating companions and then muttered, "Maybe leave out the part where we left his dead body hanging there like a goddamn scarecrow."

---

It was slow going, now that the simple act of walking could literally be lethal. Otomi had taken point, casting a stick she'd picked up out in front of her, thumping in an arc, looking for anything that could be another trap, trip wire, anything. None of them had any jokes left in them; what joy they'd had died with Jace.

The darkness hid the edges of the room well. They were almost on top of the far wall—once again, mostly reclaimed by what looked to be natural stone—before they saw that they'd reached the other side. It was a pair of oversized doors this time, both institutional and metal with no center strut, wide enough to drive a car through.

Otomi was already listening at one of the doors, her hand cupped to catch the sound. She looked back at everyone and shook her head, pointed to the door handle, and raised an eyebrow to ask if she should turn it. Jessie nodded.

The doors opened into a plain-looking hallway running to the right and left, lit with fluorescent lights humming in the ceiling above. It wasn't unexpected; according to the accounts they'd all heard from the podcast, hallways were what most of this facility was made up of. Otomi stuck her head through and around the corner. "Clear," she said.

They entered the hallway, leaving muddy prints as they did. "Perfect," Alton said. "We'll be as easy to follow as that game trail."

"Scoot your feet," Walt instructed. "Don't step, slide. It'll wear the mud off faster, and they won't get as much information from the footprints, if they're paying attention to them at all."

"They seemed to know we were in that hut," Toby pointed out, "without following our tracks."

"We have to consider all the risks though," Jessie said.

"Shh," Otomi hissed.

She pointed down the hallway to the right, and they could all hear the sound of footsteps. And as they stood there, listening, they heard voices too. Loud enough to tell they weren't bothering to stay quiet. These people—whoever they were—weren't bothering with anything approaching stealth.

"We move," said Otomi, sotto voce. She turned left down the hallway, and everyone followed, no longer scooting their feet, no longer worrying about mud on their shoes or leaving a trail. Just getting away. Pure flight.

They ran as fast as they could, Toby bringing up the rear. Jessie could hear him huffing behind them, and she fought away pangs of guilt for putting him in danger.

Then the gunfire started. First one AK volley, and then another; the second was a little more precise, as Jessie could hear the ricochet of a couple of bullets hitting something—fortunately not flesh, by the sound. She heard one shot whiz past her ear like an angry bee.

Jessie was out in front of the group with Otomi. Jessie realized that all the running she'd made herself do—that she'd trained herself to enjoy, or at least believe she enjoyed—had been worth it. It was paying off, if only in that she was able to run for her life from guys who may or may not be Ukrainians with guns, and were apparently all too willing to use them.

"Left, left!" Jessie called, taking a corner to get out of the line of fire. She kept her voice low so it wouldn't carry back to the soldiers, or so she hoped.

"Whose idea was it again to not bring guns?" Toby wheezed as he took the left with the rest of them. "What's that old line about not bringing knives—or anything else for that matter—to a gunfight?"

"This isn't a gunfight," Jessie snapped. *And shut up, Toby,* she said to herself. *You're not helping.*

"No, it'll be a massacre," Toby said, his words as halting as his labored breath. "Like Valentine's Day in 1929 Chicago, and I haven't even . . . had the pleasure . . . of being a made man."

"You should really stop talking," Alton warned. "Save your wind for running."

"He talks too much when he's nervous," Jessie said.

"And I get nervous"—Toby panted—"when I'm running for my fucking life."

"We've got to do something," Jessie said to Otomi, glancing behind her. "If they get much closer, they might just start hitting what they're shooting at." Their pursuers were gaining ground, their voices getting louder, and it didn't look like there was much the group could do. They'd passed a few doors, but stopping to try them was risky. If they were locked, they'd most likely get caught. And even if they were unlocked, there was a good chance they'd then be trapped.

Up ahead, they saw another turn to the left. "That way," Otomi said. "And keep running, all of you. I'm going to slow them down."

"You can't sacrifice yourself—" Jessie started, but Otomi cut her off.

"Are you kidding?" Otomi scowled. "I'm not. I have a contingency. Just run."

They sprinted as they took the corner, and heard yelling from the men chasing them. Even Jessie's legs were starting to feel it—she could only imagine how close to the bottom of the gas tank Walt and Toby might be. But they all kept running.

Behind them, Otomi spun around and flattened herself against the wall after taking the turn, and crouched five feet from the corner they'd just rounded.

*She is sacrificing herself,* Jessie thought, and at the same time, she realized that the hallway in front of them was about to end with a single, simple door. Their only option, it seemed.

Jessie pulled up and stopped, motioning everyone else to do the same. Toby and Walt seemed only too happy to do so, while Alton didn't look like he was even breaking a sweat. But he, too, stopped, hands on his hips, and looked back.

"What's she doing?" Alton whispered. "What's she getting out of her pack?"

The three men who were chasing them appeared from around the corner, also taking the turn wide and trying to maintain balance as they shifted direction at full speed, their guns still up and ready to fire. Otomi raised her hands—she had a gun. And then she pulled the trigger: three shots, close range, square in the center of the forehead of two pursuers, who fell to the floor like sacks of meat. She caught the shoulder of the third, who fell in a panic all his own, witnessing the precision with which his companions had been killed. He tried to bring the AK to bear on Otomi, but it was too late. She sprang to her feet, gun still pointed and ready, and put a bullet between his eyes, the fear in them still showing even as the life drained quickly from the body to which they belonged.

"I'm sort of tired of saying this," Toby said from down the hall. "But what the fucking fuckity fuck?"

"We agreed to no guns," Alton shouted at Otomi, who was walking up to the rest of the group while reloading her clip.

"Are you complaining?" Otomi asked simply. She'd brought along one of the Kalashnikovs, its long strap dragging on the floor behind her.

"I'm not," Walt volunteered.

"Nobody is," Jessie said. "Just no more surprises, okay? From any of us? No more secrets." She looked at them all, one by one. Otomi shrugged. Alton just looked worried and suspicious of everyone, and so did Toby.

"I think we're all agreed," Walt said. "We're all on the same side here. We just want to get what we came for, and get out safe."

"Wait. Don't you already have what you came for?" Toby asked. "You wanted to verify . . . what? The weirdness you'd heard about in this podcast, right? So you've done that. We've seen teenage mutant ninja hummingbirds, fallen like a hundred feet or more, found some guy's mystery hut, and one of us caught a platform of spikes right in the fucking face. Oh, and Russians are shooting at us, but it's okay, because we just MURDERED THEM."

"Ukrainians," Otomi corrected.

"SAME THING!" Toby was yelling now.

"Not since 1991," Walt said. "And even before that. It was actually settled by Scandinavian traders—"

"I DON'T CARE!" Toby shrieked.

"Toby!" Jessie barked. "Get it together."

"And be quieter," Otomi said. "These weren't the only three hunting us."

"We should go back and get those two other guns," Walt suggested. "Maybe search the bodies for information?"

Otomi threw him the assault rifle. "Take it," she said. "I don't need it."

"I don't want a gun," Alton insisted.

"Neither do I," agreed Jessie.

"Didn't do them much good," Toby said.

"I think we just need to go," Alton pointed out. "Staying in one place hasn't served us well so far. It just gives them a chance to locate us, however they're doing that."

"That is weird," Walt said, putting the AK strap around his neck so he could wear the gun like a sling. "I haven't seen any cameras, but maybe it's like what Patsy said . . . maybe there are cameras we can't see? Seems like we would, though, given the tech down here so far."

"Look, we clearly need to talk," Jessie said. "And maybe regroup and think about strategy. But here in the hallway isn't the place to do it."

"We could go back," Toby said, purposefully subdued, but his teeth gritted. "There were doors in the hallway we couldn't take the time to check."

"When you're being chased, going back is the worst thing you can do," Otomi said.

"We're not being chased anymore," Toby snapped. "You made sure of that."

"Yes, I did," Otomi replied. "And in here? We're always being chased. Count on it."

"Okay," Alton said. "So, through this door?"

"Through that door," Jessie confirmed.

"There's no way that's unlocked," Toby said.

But when they tried the handle, the door glided open easily. Beyond it was a room no larger than a toilet stall, just concrete block walls with a single black ladder leading up.

"I guess we go up," Jessie murmured to no one in particular.

---

The ladder only ascended one floor and ended in a trapdoor that also opened easily.

"Awful convenient," Alton said, and Jessie had to agree, even if she didn't voice it. She pushed it open, wondering not for the first time why she was the one in front.

"What do you see?" Otomi whispered from just below her.

"Absolutely nothing," Jessie whispered back. "Someone hand me a glow stick or something."

"Here," Otomi said, pressing something into Jessie's left hand. "Push it in the middle, then toss it to where you want the light to go."

Jessie saw that it was another disc, the size of the half-dollars her dad used to bring her now and then. She hadn't thought of that in a long time—either her father, or those fifty-cent pieces. Up on the top shelf of her closet in the apartment, she and Toby split was a music box she'd gotten as a kid. It was a dim memory, getting the music box; she thought it was from some older relative, but Jessie didn't recognize who, and the dress Jessie wore in the recollection was impossibly out of date. But her mother had always dressed her like she was a little doll from the 1940s or 1950s. Frills, white pinafores, bows in her hair. Like some fake TV kid who had wardrobe and makeup to keep her perfect.

Anyway, the music box was where she kept those half-dollars from her dad, at least the ones she didn't spend on a whim on some comic book or magazine from the grocery store. And she'd lost some along the way too.

Just like she'd lost her father somewhere along the way.

Jessie clicked the disc, wondering exactly who Otomi was to have stuff like this. She'd never seen one of these before, and she would have imagined they'd be all over late-night infomercials or available in a twelve-pack on QVC if they were anywhere on the market. She tossed the disc into the shadows of the room, and it lit up like a bonfire.

"It's . . . it's someone's office, I think," Jessie said, climbing out of the thin ladder shaft. As her eyes adjusted to the light, and the group piled up through the trapdoor, Jessie took inventory of the room. It was divided into two parts: one was a standard office, with a small half wall crafted from fabric and batting over a metal frame. Against that was the side of an industrial desk, metal and Formica, with a calendar blotter on top that read 1986. There was a high-backed leatherette chair behind the desk, and some shelves behind that, with some binders, a plastic philodendron, and a single framed photo. Otherwise, it was fairly sparse, though there was a door set in the far wall.

The other half of the room resembled a sitting area. One wall contained a bank of old tube TVs, with a low console cabinet beneath. Two chocolate-brown couches ran perpendicular to the bank of screens, and a long coffee table filled the space between them. At the other end were two plush orange swivel barrel chairs.

Walt moved directly to the wall of televisions, checking the edges for where there might be a catch or a latch or anything to swing the panel out and access the sets themselves.

"What are you looking for?" Toby asked.

"I'm curious if there's any VCRs back here," Walt said, peering into the darkness of the nook holding the TVs in neatly spaced rows and columns. "I want to see what's on that tape we found."

"Find any?" Alton asked as he crouched down to examine the console under the screens.

"No," said a clearly disappointed Walt.

"This might pick you up," Alton said, swinging open the leftmost cabinet. "It's a mini fridge. And it's still running, so there's power in here."

"Anyone see a light switch?" Jessie asked, and started looking around herself. She soon found one on the wall next to the door on the office side. The fluorescent panels in the ceiling flickered to life as if loath to do so after sitting idle for so long.

As the lights came on, Walt seemed to notice the orange chairs for the first time. "Swanky!" he beamed, and sat heavily into one of them, immediately rotating back and forth to test out the swivel. "Smooth as butter on biscuits."

"Please don't channel Patsy," Toby moaned, taking a seat on the far couch. Jessie sat next to him, and Otomi sat on the opposite couch by herself.

"Have a seat and tell me I'm wrong," Walt said. "And that's not Patsy I'm quoting. That's my grandmother."

Alton spun around smiling, holding in one hand a six-pack and a small flat carton. "Snacks, anyone?" He sat in the other orange chair and put the two items down on the coffee table with something approaching triumph. It was a small, unopened package of Hydrox cookies and a cold six-pack of New Coke.

"You've got to be kidding me," Toby marveled. "New Coke?"

"Hey, I remember loving this stuff," Walt said, pulling one out of the plastic rings.

"I'll pass on the forty-year-old soda and cookies," Otomi sniffed.

"I'm a medical professional," Alton said, opening the cookies and popping a whole one into his mouth. "And I say these are perfectly fine." He happily munched away and grabbed two more from the pack.

"I'm in," Walt said. "Throw me one?"

Toby took a handful of cookies and tossed the bag over to Walt, who clumsily caught it with his free hand. Toby crunched happily away, and then seemed to realize that Jessie was looking at him with a raised eyebrow. "What . . . ?" he mumbled through the crumbs.

In the end, they all drank the soda and finished off the cookies. Even Otomi. There was an unspoken agreement, apparently, that they all needed a break. Once the cookies were gone, Walt sat forward in his chair and raised his can of New Coke. "To Jace," he said.

"To Jace," Jessie said, and everyone raised their cans in a toast. And then the quiet fell again, everyone apparently lost in thoughts all their own.

It was Toby who broke the silence. Toby, who wasn't supposed to be here at all, Jessie reminded herself. "I'm just gonna say it," he announced, slapping his knees and leaning forward. "We have to double back and get the hell out of here. Like *now*."

And just like that, the pleasant moment disappeared for good.

# CHAPTER EIGHT

MONITORING ROOM SIX

It wasn't meant to be a come-to-Jesus meeting, but that's what it turned into.

There were definitive sides forming, and it troubled Jessie that she and Toby were more or less opposing team captains. Toby was advocating for a full-on retreat, but Jessie was adamant that they had to press forward. Alton seemed to agree with her, while Walt was on Toby's side more and more. Otomi didn't seem to have a side at all, though Jessie suspected—or maybe that was hope?—that if pressed, she'd agree with her and want to move forward.

"I'm just saying this isn't worth it," Toby said. "You've all had your little adventure, everyone got shot at multiple times, and you've seen some shit to add to whatever crazy myth you've all been obsessed with. You're done. Hell, *I'm* done. This is already more than I bargained for, and I'm only here to help Jessie."

"Then help," Jessie said. "Help me push through."

"I am helping," Toby responded plaintively. "Helping you to survive."

"Survival isn't always the point," Alton said quietly, but with a firmness that surprised even Jessie.

"It's always the goddamn point," Toby blurted out. "If you don't survive, nothing else matters. A pyrrhic victory is a loss. You get that, right?"

"You've never worked for something larger than yourself," Otomi said. Her voice was flat as ever, but she also seemed tired, more than the circumstances would warrant, if that was even possible, Jessie thought.

"Fuck you," Toby countered. "I don't know what secret spy agency you're supposed to be from, or what weirdness the doc here is hiding under that fabulously toned bod and romance-novel-cover hair. But I'm just a guy looking out for his friend, and I'm doing what any good friend would. Saving her bacon, whether she wants me to or not."

"My bacon is fine," Jessie said. She was getting annoyed, but tried to maintain composure. "And I appreciate your help, Tobes, but I don't have a choice here. We're in this far, and I have to keep going. If you want to bail, like I told you before, just bail. This isn't your deal. Stay here, sleep on the couch until we get back, if we can get back. But I'm going on. I have to."

"Okay, Jess," Toby said, throwing up his hands. "Tell me why. This isn't just curiosity, not for you. Tell me why and help me understand."

Jessie looked at the group, wondering if she could trust them. Alton seemed the least worthy of her confidence—he was still a mystery, still too quiet even on the important stuff. Otomi . . . well, she was definitely hiding something, but if her aims were her own—or more likely, those of some outside organization she was unable and unwilling to name—they were parallel to Jessie's. Walt, she was pretty sure, was really only here for the discovery of it all. For the adventure. But maybe that was his cover?

*Stop thinking like that*, Jessie berated herself. She knew these people—well enough at least.

"Okay, cards on the table," she finally said. "I'm here because of my father."

"I thought your dad took off on you and your mom?" Toby raised an eyebrow.

"He did," she admitted. "But later, years later, I was getting the mower out of our shed, and the wheel hit this plywood wall that had always been nailed to the studs in the back. Sort of a shitty attempt at drywall or something? I don't know, it had just always been there." Jessie took a breath and steeled herself for the rest. The stuff she couldn't explain. "Anyway, the wheel hitting the corner of this wood board made the whole thing topple over. It looked like the nails had been working their way out for a while by then. I don't know. At the time, it felt like a sign. Even more so when I saw what was on the wall behind it."

Jessie looked around to take stock of how her story was going over. Alton looked intrigued, if a little suspicious, as though this were a joke waiting for a punchline. Walt and Toby just looked concerned, both entirely focused on her. Otomi didn't look like she was paying attention, but Jessie knew her well enough by now to understand that this was how the woman concentrated—by staring at an indistinct point in the distance, so that what she was listening to would sink in. Jessie wasn't sure if this was a practiced technique or some neurodivergence on Otomi's part.

"It was a set of symbols," Jessie continued. "Silver ink. I don't know if that's important, but that's what it was, why I even noticed it. It looked almost like they were glowing, but I think they were just reflecting the light from the shed door."

"You think?" Toby laughed a little, but there was no joy behind it. "You're actually considering the possibility that they were glowing? Like magic runes from *The Ghost Tower of Inverness*? I hate to say it, but maybe you played too much D&D."

"I'm not kidding, Toby," Jessie insisted. "And I'm saying it was the light, not that they were magical. But they were . . . mysterious, I guess. I took a Polaroid of it. Nine symbols, in a circle, around a center point that just looked like a sort of grandiose M."

"Or a symbol for the mountains," Alton said.

Jessie nodded. "That thought occurred to me too, which is one of the reasons why that mystery has led me . . . well, here. I looked everywhere for some definition or source for those symbols, but nothing. No known languages match up. No invented languages, like from Tolkien or *Star Trek* or something. I used the photo to draw them in a book I kept with all the questions I had—the same one I started taking notes in later—when I found the podcast."

"This is at your mom's house?" Toby said.

"It was," Jessie answered. "When I went back in the shed a few days later, it was gone. Someone had replaced the entire section of brick. They tried to match the color, but it's impossible to match years of wear, especially in the mortar joints. The silvery script was gone. All I had left was that one photo."

"And you connect this with your dad because . . ." Toby pressed.

"Because that shed was his place," Jessie said. "He had a workbench out there, but I never saw him fixing or building anything. He did bioresearch for U of I, and I don't remember him as handy at all. There weren't really even tools out there. I mean, there were some—there was this pegboard over the workbench with painted outlines of where the hammer went, where the wrenches sat, the saw hanging vertically next to a long metal level. But I never saw him use any of it. He had a little laptop—one of the old ones, with the built-in monochrome green display? Heavy as shit? He'd be on that out there sometimes. I saw him using it once and asked what he was doing, and he shut the thing down like he was hiding porn or something."

"Not possible on those old models," Walt said. "Believe me, my friends and I tried."

"Lovely," Otomi muttered, still staring off in a singular direction. *But yes,* Jessie thought. *She's listening.*

"You said it was one of two things that brought you to this point," Alton said. "What was the other?"

"It was the last thing my dad said to me before he left us," Jessie went on, taking another breath, this one catching in her throat a little. She hadn't talked about this—or given it voice at all—for years. Not even to Toby, who seemed to understand her anyway. It was one of the things she appreciated about him—how much he seemed to understand about her without even having to be told. "I remember it distinctly. He came into my bedroom in the back of the house. He was leaving for another university lecture trip the next day, the one he'd never come home from. He always said goodbye to me, always promised to bring me something when he got back. This time, he sat next to me on the bed—I was playing with my Polly Pocket Sparkle Style House, I remember, because he moved it to sit where it was. We talked for a little while, the usual dad stuff. Be good, you know I love you, that sort of thing. He gave me this stuffed animal—even then, I thought it was weird that he was giving me something before he left, and not when he got home—but it was this purple horse. *Caballo Morado* I called him, because I was learning Spanish. It was just one of those silly gift shop things, but I loved it anyway."

Jessie smiled to herself just a bit when she remembered it was the only reminder she had of her dad's voice—it was one of those early-2000s things that used what was then the latest in small recording and playback devices, something that her dad recorded for her and would play back when you pinched its left hind hoof. She remembered it with crystal clarity. *We can ride anywhere!* in her father's softest tone. It helped her when she was younger and made Jessie miss him both much more and slightly less at the same time.

"I wondered why you kept that old thing," said Toby. "Makes total sense why you'd keep it, now."

Jessie nodded. "It was the last thing he gave me," she said. "But it was what he said last that made me remember it. He took my chin in his hands, looked me straight in the eyes, and said *You remember that you're you. You're not anyone else. You're better.* He made me repeat it back to him. And then he left, and I went back to playing with my dolls. Caballo Morado made an appearance at the Sparkle Style House, and my dad left and never came back."

"That's sweet," Toby said. "But it was just a dad saying goodbye, right? The usual *You're special* stuff parents say, especially when they're about to break your heart."

"I don't know," Jessie said. "It just always stuck with me, like it was important in a way I didn't understand yet. I don't know what relation those symbols have to that memory, if any. They could have just been coincidental, happening around the same time, so I've conflated them. But then I found the podcast, and I thought this place might have answers. I mean, we know there are mysteries explained here. Why not mine?"

There was another quiet in the room as everyone let that last question hang in the air. Jessie was suddenly aware of the dead silence in the room, in this whole complex when it wasn't being interrupted by gunfire. *It's almost peaceful,* she thought. *And also—almost like a grave.*

"Because you want to ascribe some meaning to your dad leaving you," Toby said gently. "And I get it. I do. My dad left without even that much. He went to work one Saturday morning while I was playing *Super Mario Bros.*—or said he was going to work, anyway—and just never came home. I knew he was fine, because I'd get some weird Christmas or birthday present from him in the mail once every few years. It was always something that only served to prove he had no idea who I was. I got a finger painting set for my twelfth birthday. Got two Ninja Turtles for my sixteenth, and two years later, I got a congratulations on your high school graduation card with ten bucks in it."

"I remember that," Jessie said. "You bought us beer."

"Yeah," Toby said. "That's how some dads are. They're just shitty mysteries with no good solutions."

"Some moms too," Jessie smiled grimly.

"Some moms too," Toby agreed. "But that's got nothing to do with what we're deciding here. It really doesn't, Jess, and you need to recognize that, because while you're snipe hunting down here, we're all in serious danger. These are real fucking bullets. She just killed three actual people who were admittedly trying to kill us. Jace is fucking dead. I don't want to say that this isn't fun anymore, because I know none of you guys are here for fun. But it really isn't. It's deadly and serious, and I'm done with it."

"I gotta say," Walt interjected. "I see what Toby is saying. Honestly, losing that kid back there was it for me, and I think I'm just getting around to seeing it. I knew this would be dangerous. I didn't know one of us would get killed. This isn't what any of us thought it would be. Hell, I'm just here because my kids turned me on to this podcast and it was something cool we could talk about. Then I sort of fell into it, and my kids ate it up. They're all older now—they lived with their mom until college, and now they're out on their own. I was the weekend dad, you know? Always looking for a way to make my time with them memorable." He took a sip from his New Coke. "It never worked, not really. Only so many water parks, you know? Only so many movies, takeout, arcades with pizza. And then I found this, and I could talk with them again. Like, really talk with them. They wanted to talk to me, too. That's a thing, you know? Your kids are in their early twenties and still want to talk to their old man? That's a thing.

"So I did this for them," Walt continued after taking a beat. "To impress them, just like I tried to dive off the high board at the pool when they were kids even though my knees were shaking. I belly flopped then, too. And here I am again, belly flopping. I don't want to go back. But I also want to see my kids again. They were the point. They were the whole point."

"You're saying that as though 'back' is safe," Otomi interjected with some surprising compassion. "It's not. We just proved that it's not. We go back, we're potentially running into range of more men with guns."

"But the same could be said about moving forward," Alton said. "At least back, we know what we're expecting. It's the devil we know."

"Agreed," Toby said. "Anyway, since we're all telling stories, what about you, *American Ninja Warrior*? What's got you here with all your James Bond shit?"

"I don't have James Bond shit," Otomi said.

"You came in a helicopter," Toby countered.

"Which means I'm a pilot," Otomi shrugged. "Jace came on an expensive motorcycle."

"Which meant he was a dick," Toby said, and before Walt could protest, he held up a hand and added, "God bless his soul. So, why are you here, Otomi?"

She didn't look up. "Pass."

"Pass?" Toby said, laughing. "You can't pass."

"I just did," Otomi replied with purposeful disinterest, and leaned back on the couch and crossed her arms.

"Trading stories isn't why we're here," Alton pointed out. "And honestly, it's nothing we have time for."

"Fine," Toby said. "Not to be all *Robert's Rules of Order*, but that's three to two for retreat. Motion carries."

"It's not that simple," Otomi countered. She looked directly up at Toby, her emotionless face suddenly accusatory. "You know that."

"I don't know anything!" Toby said. "Other than that I'm missing too many shifts at Osco, and I'm not sure how I'm making rent in a couple of weeks if we don't get back home soon."

"You hide behind this cowardice," Otomi said. "But all you have behind that is more cowardice."

Toby looked nonplussed. "That . . . that doesn't mean anything."

"Guys," Walt said, "we've made a decision as a group. Let's just accept it, get a move on, and get back to where we came in. I'm not sure how we'll all get up that one rope we have left, but I assume it'll be some variation of one at a time and also very carefully. And hopefully, we'll be able to get up far enough to contact Patsy."

"Shit," Jessie said. "Her drone. The Pigeon or whatever. Jace had it in his pack."

"It's probably in pieces then," Alton said. "I didn't root through it all to identify everything, but given the condition of what was in there, I doubt it would turn on, let alone fly."

"We can check to be sure when we go back through that area," Jessie said. "I can't believe I forgot that, of all things. Our lifeline out of here."

"We had other, more immediate concerns," Walt reasoned, and even Otomi nodded in agreement.

An audible click came from nearby. A mechanical engagement of something unseen, something with a terrible finality to it, Jessie thought.

"What was that?" Alton said.

"Came from the floor over there," Otomi answered. "The trapdoor. It's closed. Was it closed before?"

"I . . ." Jessie started, but realized she didn't know. "I don't remember."

Toby ran over to it and pulled hard, so hard he fell to one knee. "Locked," he finally muttered. "And no key, keyhole, nothing."

"Someone is watching," Otomi said. "Someone is listening. Someone who doesn't like the results of our vote."

"Bullshit," Toby responded, but stopped as the trapdoor he was standing on lurched up, the whole floor moving with the weight of a blow from beneath. "What the fuck . . ."

The floor shuddered again, and the floor around the trapdoor began to splinter—only slightly, but enough to suggest that the whole thing would give way if the pounding from below continued.

"Time to go," Otomi said. "Forward."

"No choice now," Alton agreed, and everyone grabbed their stuff and ran to the door on the other side of the room.

"What's doing that?" Toby said as he backed away from the trapdoor. Another powerful blow resounded through the office floor, with the unmistakable sound of wood splitting.

"We don't want to find out," Jessie said, grabbing Toby's collar and wrangling him forward while Otomi flung open the door in the far wall.

"Of course it's unlocked," Toby said, letting Jessie lead him through the door. "They want us in there."

"Shut up," she said, and with a tone that she hoped brooked no dissent. Toby complied.

The other side of the door wasn't so much a room as it was a catwalk over rushing water. Some fifteen feet below the metal floor of the bridge leading about a football field away, ending in another door, was churning water coming from channels in the far wall. The walls were brown-glazed brick, vaulted above in an even curve, and at the surface of the water below were several huge ceramic intake pipes with mouths as wide as a small car.

They ran, and despite the terrifying sound of the impacts behind them, Jessie noticed the details in this new room. It had the vibe of an old European sewer, like the one Orson Welles and Joseph Cotten ran through in the underground of postwar Vienna in her favorite movie *The Third Man.* Orson Welles and Joseph Cotten and the nature of good and evil set to incessant bouzouki music. It's said that Welles extemporized the most famous line from the film: *In Italy for thirty years under the Borgias, they had warfare, terror, murder, and bloodshed, but they produced Michelangelo, Leonardo da Vinci, and the Renaissance. In Switzerland, they had brotherly love, they had five hundred years of democracy and peace, and what did that produce? The cuckoo clock. So long, Holly.*

Toby had introduced her to it. *One of the benefits of being besties with a film major,* Jessie thought, but the smile she felt didn't reach her lips. The present moment loomed back into her consciousness. But Toby had clearly been flashing on the same thing—he caught up to Jessie and winked. "Bouzouki, amiright?" She didn't have long to ponder that, or anything, really, because a voluminous screech from somewhere below suddenly filled the vaulted space. It was something between a bird and a jet engine—so loud that Jessie could feel the sound waves like physical blows. She wasn't the only one. Everyone stopped running and tried to maintain their balance as they put their hands to their ears to help block the audible attack.

Everyone but Walt, who brought up his new gun, fumbling it a little in his haste, looking around for whatever was coming. Otomi saw him and pushed him forward. "Don't be stupid," she yelled, already pulling her gun from where she'd stowed it in her waistband.

Whether Walt would have followed that order became an utterly moot point. Rising above the lip of the metal catwalk was an impossible creature—something chimeric and impossible, a thing from nightmares. But it was also beautiful in its way, rising up on vibrant crimson wings, with a body as large as a cow, but covered with iridescent scales of green, red, and black. It had a whiplike tail that looked prehensile in the way it moved, and an elongated neck—but its head was almost obscene. Somewhere between a man's and a tiger's face, with antlers like a rutting deer, and bloodred orbs for eyes. When it roared, its jaw seemed to dislocate, opening far more widely than seemed possible.

"RUN!" Otomi yelled, and planted her feet there in the middle of the catwalk above the churning water. The thing's screech was dying down, and it reared its head. Otomi started firing, and everyone else took off running.

Jessie looked back over her shoulder, hoping that the pistol would be enough, or that Otomi could place a shot in the thing's eye. Enough to at least drive it back, convinced that this prey was too dangerous to pursue. Otomi was giving it every bullet she had while she dodged its attacks. The thing bit at her, lunging its head forward with teeth the size of butcher knives, but Otomi moved too quickly, too balletic, for the monster to catch her. She fired again, and again, choosing her shots as precisely as she'd clearly been trained, and trained well, to perform.

Until there was a click. An empty clip. It was that moment of pause, Jessie would later consider, that was the end of Otomi, the end of her mystery, the end of the questions as to who she was, where she came from, and what exactly she was doing there. Because just a moment later, as Otomi threw the spent Glock to one side and pulled a thin blade from her belt with impossible speed, the beast's head turned slightly, and it bit down, its teeth finding purchase in Otomi's midsection.

She tried one last move—to shove her Glock into the thing's right red saucer eye, but if Otomi had some hope to have been swallowed whole enough to carve her way out, it was made impossible as the thing's jaws clenched through her. With a quick series of death shakes, Otomi's top half fell to the catwalk right next to her disembodied legs. The blade clattered harmlessly away, and the thing started screeching all over again.

*Fuck* was the only word that Jessie's brain was able to conjure, but what came out of her mouth instead was a scream.

# CHAPTER NINE

WESTERN SPILLWAY

Alton nearly fell from the edge of the catwalk when he threw open the door, but was able to catch himself before tumbling forward, even as Walt and Toby both shoved into his back.

Jessie wasn't sure what he was waiting for—didn't realize the path had abruptly ended at the threshold—but she stole a look back. The monster was eating what was left of Otomi, grabbing her lower half in its mouth and flipping it up to catch and consume it whole. Jessie watched with dull, numbing horror as she watched Otomi's feet flailing about as the thing swallowed her, gulp by gulp.

"It's just a pole, heading down into darkness," Alton yelled back. "If we go down, we won't be able to get back up!"

"Do it!" Jessie said, keeping an eye on the abomination. It had finished Otomi—the only trace left of her was a gruesome puddle on the floor where she'd made her last stand—and was eyeing the rest of them. "We don't have much choice here!"

Alton didn't question her; he slid down the pole on the other side of the door. Walt and Toby followed, and Jessie was right behind them, slamming the door behind her more out of frustration and fury than anything. That beast couldn't get through the door if it wanted to, but still . . . Otomi. She deserved better.

It wasn't until they landed on the small peninsula below that Jessie was able to take stock of where they were. It was, she had to admit, dazzling. The horror of the last couple of minutes seemed to drain away from her as she took in this new space—so immensely huge that they couldn't see where it ended in any direction other than the wall against which they stood. Based on the gentle arc of the walls to either side, it was probably cylindrical—but it was also impossible to tell.

But the most stunning part of the space came from the distant lights above—still fluorescent, Jessie noted, but hanging from a ceiling that was so far above them that it was essentially invisible—and the acres upon acres of geodesic domes. It looked to Jessie like a vast subterranean neighborhood of sorts, only instead of cookie-cutter houses, it was row upon row of glass constructs separated by water-filled canals instead of streets and alleys.

"The Bio-Domes room," Walt said. "The real one."

They could hear the unmistakable sound of a waterfall somewhere in the distance. And birds. Like the podcast had claimed, even down here, there were birds, or at least their songs. They could have been piped in, Jessie thought, like at Disney World. But she dismissed that thought immediately. Why would there need to be fake ambiance when this place had proven so well that it could manifest the real thing? "It's beautiful," she finally said.

Light spilled down onto the domes, a towering field of wilderness contained in terrariums all their own. A fair amount of vegetation had sprouted free from the glass and steel confines, busting through like an ancient creature emerging from its egg. Some even reached up as high as the suspended lights.

"We're not safe here," Alton said. "Remember what was in the water, according to the podcast? Hair and fins. Something that dragged in the Chupacabra Wrangler."

"Warlord," Walt corrected, still marveling at his surroundings.

"What?" Alton said.

"They called him a Warlord," Walt shrugged. "Just saying."

"Save us the semantics, Walt," Alton said. "Two of us are dead."

"Way dead," Toby interjected. "Like super-duper dead."

"We get it, Toby," Jessie said. "And Alton is right. We don't have time to linger or appreciate anything. But on the bright side, we're in a space we know. We can hear the falls in the distance, which means . . ."

"The way back to the shaft," Walt said. "Or *a* shaft, anyway."

"We need to get to a safe place first," Alton said. "Take stock of what we know before we wander off into this maze. Because one of the things we do know is that there are chupacabras here. The ones that slaughtered the soldiers."

"And Mongolian Death Worms," Walt added. "Don't forget those little dudes. One bite and . . . well, you at least lose a hand."

"More likely you're dead," Toby said. "Unless you want to perform a quick amputation."

"The doc here could do it," Walt pointed out.

"Not an experience either of us would relish," Alton replied.

"Okay, okay," Jessie said. Her mind was still reeling with how Otomi had been killed—slaughtered, really—but she steeled herself and forced some focus. She was feeling that creeping sensation of imbalance again, and this was no time for a seizure.

"Over here," Alton called out, surveying the water. "It looks like the closer you stay to the base of the dome, the ground is just under the water level. And there are paths that cut across the domes, too. You can see where they are by the way the water reverses a bit when it hits one of the submerged berms."

"Good," Jessie said. "Can we just go into the nearest one?"

"I vote for the nearest one that's been breached," Alton said. "It stands to reason that if there was anything dangerous living in them they would at least have had a chance to get out."

"Or to get in," Walt said.

"Fair point," Alton admitted. "Okay, closest one."

"At least it looks manageable," offered Walt. "Woodlands, maybe?"

"Let's just get in, Ranger Rick," Toby said. "You can teach us all about ecosystems once we're relatively safer."

The four of them found the door just on the other side of the dome. It, too, was unlocked, and they went in and closed the door behind them. Jessie didn't know if this was a good or bad omen. It just was. Like Jace pinned to half a log. Like Otomi in the belly of a mythical beast that Jessie realized she recognized. Like Carla, who—it was now utterly clear—had been taken out before she'd even set one foot on the journey.

---

The dome smelled like the pine of the Illinois woods Jessie recalled from childhood. They were dim memories, more like snapshots in someone else's album, but she still cherished them—her father taking her to Lake of the Woods downstate, to the old Dickson Mounds that featured underground Native American burial sites with colored spotlights and a recorded voice-over until it occurred to everyone that they wouldn't want their own ancestors' skeletons on display like a macabre fun house, and it was shut down and resealed out of an extremely tardy show of respect. And then there were the Cahokia Mounds, another site shrouded in mystery, a huge community of Native peoples until a massive drought forced them to move. Near there, just north and east of present-day St. Louis across the Mississippi River, was Alton, Illinois. And that was where she'd seen that thing that had eaten Otomi.

"It was the Piasa," Jessie said, perched on a fallen log in a small clearing surrounded by trees near the dome's entrance. It looked and felt like they were in the woods, if you could ignore the dome wall, the door, and the strangely ominous black phone attached to the wall next to it. Alton was squatting nearby, examining the soil, and Walt and Toby had sat on the sparse grass using the same log as a backrest. "The thing that killed Otomi. I think that was the Piasa."

"What the hell is a Pie-a-saw?" Toby asked.

"It means *man-eating bird* in the language of the Illini tribe," Jessie said.

"Like the Illinois basketball team?" Walt looked confused.

"It was a tribe first," Toby explained. "Fighting Illini? Their mascot was Chief Illiniwek for a long time."

"I know that," Walt said. "I've forgotten more about college basketball than you'll ever know. I just didn't know the origin of the name."

"Try me on college basketball, old man," Toby said with a friendly challenge.

Jessie was having none of it. "No. Focus," she reprimanded them. "Otomi is dead and you're swapping trash talk."

"I got a video," Alton said, holding up his phone. "It's far away, and the light was bad, and I didn't have a chance to fix any settings, and I was filming over my shoulder backward. But . . . yeah. Take a look."

Jessie took his phone and played the video while the other three crowded in to look too. They watched as the creature bounced in and out of frame as the grainy low-light video ran. Flying. Shrieking. Diving for Otomi. And then the video cut out.

"This explains why every cryptid video is so crappy," Walt said. "Because the camera guy is running for their life. Still, that's a beaut, Doc. You're going to be famous for that one."

Alton didn't seem to care about that, and took back his phone. "You think this was that bird thing, Jessie? The Piasa?"

"Jesus . . . I don't know. But yeah. Maybe. I mean, it fits," Jessie said. "This place is known for evidence of cryptids, right? And the Piasa is definitely one of those. The explorer Jacques Marquette described seeing a painting of it on the limestone cliffs overlooking the river on the Illinois side. All the details match, at least from later sightings."

"It's just a legend," Toby waved off the idea as if it were nonsense. "A story to tell kids on a field trip. The original mural was wiped out due to mining back in the 1800s. That thing that's there now? That's a recreation of it based on the historical descriptions."

"A lot of people claim to have seen it, Toby," Jessie said. "More to the point, that legend just ate the shit out of our friend."

"She wasn't our friend," Toby pointed out.

"What is *with* you?" Jessie scowled.

Toby took a deliberate breath. "Fuck, I don't know," he said, picking up a stick and drawing idly in the dirt. "I'm sorry. I didn't want her to die. Or Jace either."

"I know," Jessie said, and put a hand on his shoulder. "I know."

"So, what now?" Walt asked.

"I don't know about the rest of you," Jessie said. "But I'm just coming down off the adrenaline from running for our lives—again. And I'm so tired."

They all looked around, realizing for the first time that it was actually getting dark—as if they were really outside. "Is it . . . ?" Walt started.

"Dusk," Alton confirmed.

"Well, that cinches it for me," Toby announced. "It's night night time. I'm not cool running around in the dark out here anyhow."

"Yeah, not a good idea. Toby's right—maybe we should stop here," Alton said. "Rest a little. We can trade off keeping watch. Everyone stands guard for an hour, and everyone gets to sleep for three. Cool?"

Jessie nodded. They all did, and began to settle in, using packs as pillows and taking deep breaths of the pine-filled air. There seemed to be an unspoken agreement that Alton would take first watch.

"Who am I waking up to take over for me?" Alton asked as everyone else was getting comfortable—or as comfortable as they could be.

"Me," Jessie said. "If I can get an hour, I'll be good. Anything more than that will just be gravy."

Toby agreed to take watch after that, and Walt promised he would take his turn last. They all nestled in while Alton stood and began pacing. *Trying to stay awake*, Jessie thought.

"You know, it's weird," Alton said, approaching the black wall phone to the left of the door. "For all the phones ringing in the podcast, we haven't heard one ring once."

"That's what you find weird about a phone on a wall in the middle of the woods?" Toby snickered.

"Well, the *fake* woods," Walt countered.

Alton ignored them, picked up the receiver, and held it to his ear. Jessie presumed he heard nothing on the other end because he put it back in its cradle with an air of dissatisfaction. The last thing Jessie remembered before she slipped into dreamless sleep was that a phone call from someone down here was the last thing they needed.

—

And so, of course, the phone rang right in the middle of Toby's watch.

Alton and Jessie's shifts had gone by without incident. They'd both managed to stay awake and alert the whole time, and Jessie was able to fall back to sleep nearly immediately once her watch was done.

"Shit," Toby said, coming out of the barely-woke stupor he'd allowed himself to slip into. He ran to answer the phone without thinking. The rest of the group sat up, suddenly wide-awake at the ringing.

"Hello?" Toby answered. A pause. "No, who is this?" he countered. "I'm not telling you where we are until you tell me who this is." Another pause. "Yes, I know anyone could be listening, which is why I'm not telling you where we are." He looked over at Jessie, worry sprouting in his expression. "If you already know we're in the Domes, why ask me?"

"Hang up," Alton said.

"Yes," Jessie agreed. "Cut it off. They could be tracing it."

"They must know we're here already," Walt argued. "I mean, they're calling the right phone."

"Toby," Jessie said simply, and her roommate quickly hung up the receiver without another word. He stood there for a long moment, just staring at it. Wondering, Jessie assumed, if it would ring again. It didn't.

"What did the voice sound like?" Alton asked, hoisting himself up off the ground and sitting up against the log, stretching.

"It was a woman," Toby said. "She was whispering, but I'm pretty sure she had an accent. Tough to make out, though."

"Did she sound . . . villainous?" Walt asked.

Toby couldn't help but laugh. "I didn't hear any mustache twirling, if that's what you're asking."

"I'm serious," Walt said. "Noah and Sara got phone calls when they were in the Domes in the podcast. Did it sound like her?"

"Actually, that's a good question," Jessie admitted.

"How would I know that?" Toby asked. "I'm not one of you podcast people."

"Just our luck," Walt moaned. "The only one of us that wouldn't have recognized that voice."

"Oh, whatever," Toby said, annoyed. "Like I said, she was whispering, so I doubt any of you would have been able to tell either. If it means anything, she didn't seem like she knew much more than we do. And she was worried about someone listening in."

"Okay," Alton reasoned. "So potentially she's not one of the Collective. Who is she, then?"

"An escapee?" Walt offered. "I mean, who else could she be?"

"But she knew where we were," Jessie said, arching an eyebrow. "That suggests she has a working knowledge of the systems down here. She didn't just call this phone at random, right? She knew we were here."

"But she didn't seem to know where here was," Toby admitted. "I'm not sure she knew we were in the Domes. I may have messed up there. It's possible I accidentally confirmed it."

"But she must have said it first," Alton pointed out. "You said something like, 'If you already know we're in the Domes . . .'?"

"Right," Toby seemed to visibly relax. "She did. But she also seemed excited to hear me say it. Like it was a guess that she got right, maybe? That was the sense I got, anyway."

Jessie sighed. She was still tired, but was now wide-awake. "Anyone think they can still sleep?"

"I probably could," Walt said, "but I don't think I should. I don't think any of us should. I think we have to book it on out of here before whoever was on that phone finds us here. Or sends a team of guys to do it."

"Agreed," Alton nodded.

"Still dark out there," Toby said. "But yeah."

"Okay, good," Jessie said, and clapped her hands together. "Who's up for finding a waterfall?"

---

It was tough to keep any bearings in the valleys of the Bio-Domes once you were inside them.

It wasn't laid out on a grid like they'd assumed. Instead, it seemed to be concentric circles, which made the crisscross of the paths feel random, and caused them to move diagonally when it felt like they were going straight ahead. They were reminded a few times in the hours they zigzagged through the geodesic maze that they weren't alone here: Walt said he heard dogs panting at one point. Alton saw hair and scales flip in the dim light illuminating the deeper water, but he had no idea what that was, and didn't want to find out. And the gliding beasts above—whatever was casting shadows under the distant lights above—made Jessie's heart leap every time one passed. And not in a good way.

"Do flying monkeys imply a Wicked Witch of any specific cardinal direction?" Toby mused. "And are they wearing little bellhop uniforms from Hell?"

"Wouldn't that be a Hell-hop?" Walt joked.

"Oh man," Toby laughed appreciatively. "It should be."

"Only the east and west witches were wicked," Jessie said. "North and south were the good witches. According to the Baum books anyway."

"Did they all have monkeys?" Alton asked.

"It's not a nature documentary," Toby said, still laughing.

"No," Jessie answered. "But they did help Dorothy later in the books. They were controlled by anyone who wore the magic cap."

"I'd like to find that cap," Walt murmured. "At least they're not dive-bombing us or trying to carry us away."

"All those creatures are just as trapped down here as the rest of us, I imagine," Jessie murmured. "A big, beautiful cage is still just a cage."

"One thing's for sure," Walt said cheerfully. "There's no place like Dome."

Toby cackled at that one. "Walt, you're on fire," he said. "You're killing me here."

But the moment didn't last. They could all suddenly hear the snarls of what sounded like a small pack of chupacabras stalking them from behind.

They ran. Again.

It occurred to Jessie that maybe this was one of those animals that you shouldn't run from, that standing your ground and posing a threat was the better shot at survival, but fight or flight took over, and they all ran like hell, hoping they were still going in the direction of the waterfall. The chupacabras were following but didn't seem to be gaining. Were they herding them? Or were they only moderately interested in them as prey? And either way—why?

Alton had the same question. "Why aren't they catching up?" he yelled, still running. He looked unbothered by the effort, Jessie noted. Like he was only running to keep up with the group, not as fast as he could.

"I don't know," panted Jessie, who was running her fastest, and realizing that Walt and Toby were already lagging behind. The old joke popped into Jessie's mind, unbidden: You don't have to run faster than the bear—you just have to run faster than your friends.

After passing a few more domes—a desert of sorts next to an Arctic tundra next to what looked to be a Christmas-movie-worthy taiga full of frosted pines—Jessie became certain that they were being directed purposefully. But they were running in that direction already—maybe it was just a coincidence? She didn't know, but she was pretty sure she wasn't going to like the answer.

As they passed another dome, the waterfall came into sight. It was a majestic vision of water flowing down over a rocky lip, the mist sparkling in the brilliant fluorescence surrounding it, pouring into what looked to be a small lagoon connected to dozens of channels that led out and away, threading themselves between dome after dome after dome in a near 180-degree arc. The sheer beauty before them was marred by only one thing: a couple of soldiers, presumably from the Collective, standing watch over something going on behind the cascading water. What it was, Jessie couldn't see—but she didn't have to wonder long, since it was clear that the sentried soldiers had noticed the group coming into view. The yells that sounded, the pointing, and the bullets that followed were proof enough of that.

"To the left!" Alton shouted, looking back at Walt and Toby, and physically pushing Jessie in that direction. "Follow the water line and turn again! We have to lose them in the domes."

If Jessie was surprised by Alton suddenly taking charge of the situation—if any of them were—they didn't have time to question it. They followed his plan, turning to perimeter the lagoon, running in a crouch to make a smaller target for the gunmen. There were more soldiers after them now than the original two they'd seen, but there was no time to count. They had to stay out of range of the guns and, at the same time, keep a distance from the chupacabras she assumed were still racing after them. Jessie wondered if turning in this new direction would make the creatures pick up speed? Or would they get distracted by the soldiers running toward them, and attack them instead?

It was at that moment that she realized the chupacabras were no longer behind them. At some point before they came within sight of the soldiers at the waterfall, they'd given up pursuit, for some reason. A bullet buzzed past her ear as if to remind her that sure, perhaps there were no more monster dogs on their tail, but soldiers with automatic rifles? Yep, plenty of those.

Jessie stole one look back before they reentered the canal system of the domes—it was too chaotic, too dark, and too confusing to make out a damn thing, and she swore silently. What she did see was Alton wince as something hit him in his lower back. Had he caught a bullet? *Shit.* But he was still running behind her, and didn't seem fazed by it. Maybe just a muscle tweak from running? Jessie hoped so.

"Keep going!" Alton urged, and somehow Toby and Walt found a reserve tank somewhere within to keep pace with Jessie. Panic, Jessie assumed. Adrenaline. But that wouldn't last long.

Dawn was breaking—or what passed for dawn down here—as Jessie spied a dome up ahead that looked like a potential hiding spot. It was a little scrub plain at the entrance with a small brook and a stone ruin just beyond it, fronting a mass of overgrown foliage and woods that continued on from there. It looked like a quaint little ruined moat house directly from the English countryside, something that would have looked perfectly at home next to a stone fence and sheep grazing in a pasture. Almost like a souvenir snow globe you'd purchase in a tourist town with a name like Upton Snodsbury or Pucklechurch.

Maybe it was the look of it, this cultivated oversized terrarium, or maybe it was just that Jessie knew that Toby and Walt were going to run out of steam at any moment, but she decided now was a good time to hide—and this was a great place to do it.

She poured on enough speed to easily pass Toby and Walt, ran directly for the door to the dome, and flung it open. "Get in, get in," she said, keeping her voice low but her tone insistent.

Toby and Walt did so. Alton held the door for Jessie to go in, and followed, closing it quietly behind him. They all scurried into the dark doorway of the little ruined structure, two crouched on each side of the threshold, and waited.

But they didn't wait long. The soldiers had clearly split up and fanned out to search for them. A lone soldier—tall and lean, was dressed like all the others in the same gray fatigues. He had a beard, thick glasses, and for some reason, a beret. His AK was at the ready, his finger on the trigger, and he was wading quietly through the canal water.

They took turns peering over the broken stone wall and watched him come, working to stay quiet. But Toby, apparently, couldn't. "Walt," he seethed through clenched teeth. "Stop breathing on me. What did you eat earlier, anyway? You need a mint or something."

"I'm not breathing on you," Walt said.

"Yes," Toby said, "you are. And I need you to . . ."

Walt turned on his flashlight, cupping one side to let as little light spill through the doorway as he could. But he did illuminate something: two glowing yellow eyes the size of buffet plates, the glistening green skin of something amphibious, and a mouth—a gaping cavern of a mouth.

The maw opened wider, and then came the scream that split the artificial dawn.

Fig. 7b

The Piasa or Piasa Bird (Fig. 7b) is a bird-like creature 7-10 feet tall. Originally thought to be a creature of Native American Mythology after being depicted on multiple murals painted above the Mississippi River, the Piasa is actually another creature from beyond The Threshold. Having both mammalian and avian attributes, The Piasa stands apart from its Earth-based "cousins". The term "cousin" is used loosely here as there is currently no evidence of The

# CHAPTER TEN

BIO-DOME 466

What at first sounded like a scream was more of a guttural yawp that built up from that first, shrill sound until a bass note rose to engulf it. In a panic, both Walt and Toby stumbled out into the light of the dome and fell roughly to the muddy dirt just shy of the stream.

The thing revealed itself to be a mottled and immense frog-like behemoth, at least five feet at the shoulder, as it leaped forward on powerful legs. In one hop, it moved from inside the ruin to past the stream, sailing harmlessly over the heads of Walt and Toby, who were both covering their heads like it was a safety drill in elementary school. They looked up sideways at the grand white belly of the thing, the only part of the beast that wasn't some shade of green, and saw it land right in front of the soldier, who let out only a single burst of bullets and a stifled scream before being consumed by the giant amphibian. They could hear a hiss from inside the frog—were those digestive acids, already working to dissolve flesh?—and then muffled screams and panicked shifting that quickly stopped in an impressive—and disturbing—dearth of time. The only thing left of the soldier were his boots and part of his legs, still sticking out of the mouth of the giant frog up to the mid-calf, and with another gargantuan gulp, even those disappeared.

Toby and Walt rose as quickly as they could and backed away from the monstrous creature, keeping their eyes locked on it. The frog lazily turned to look at them—the eyes were emotionless, but still somehow seemed . . . well, *bored*, Jessie thought.

"Okay," Walt said. "I had to run a class dissecting frogs one year . . ."

"I thought you taught social studies?" Toby interrupted, continuing to back up carefully.

"Bio teacher was on maternity," Walt explained. He'd stopped where he was on the bank of the stream, and was watching the frog intently. "Anyway, unless someone can think of a way to pith this particular specimen, I think we all need to go while he's busy chewing."

"He's right," Alton said as the body of the soldier slithered farther down into the monster's considerable gullet. "He's calm now—but he might not be once he's made room for second helpings."

They circled the glistening beast carefully, heading for the door. The frog pivoted to follow them, still consuming the corpse, but made no other movement.

"Anyone know what the beret was?" Toby asked as they moved.

"Squad leader, maybe?" Alton suggested, creeping sideways.

"Maybe it was just jaunty," Walt said. "You know, a little bit of style among all the camouflage?"

"Shut. The. Fuck. Up," Jessie said quietly, but with a purposeful edge to her voice. "I don't want anyone ending up like Otomi."

"Devoured by a frog would be an interesting way for a former part-time biology teacher to go," Walt agreed.

There was no more talking as the group backed out slowly. Jessie looked over Walt's shoulder to make sure no other soldiers were approaching. She didn't see any, and before long, they were outside the dome again, the door shutting with a comforting click.

"Anyone know what nightmare of legend that disgusting thing might be?" Toby asked, hands on his knees, catching his breath.

"No idea on that one," Jessie admitted.

"Tiddalik," Alton said simply.

Too simply for Toby. "Tidda-what?"

"Tiddalik," Alton repeated. "It's an Aboriginal creation story, sort of a reverse flood myth. Tiddalik was a giant frog who drank up all the earth's water because of a terrible thirst. Myth says that it took an eel dancing to make Tiddalik laugh, which released all the water back into the world in one big gush."

"So, all the water in the world is this frog's backwash?" Toby shook his head. "That's disgusting."

"Do we know if ginormo-Kermit here could bust through?" Toby asked, but Walt just shook his head at Toby and started taking video through the glass. Jessie had to hand it to the man—he was the only one with the presence of mind to make a record of any of this weirdness once it had actually started. And he still had that video cassette too. If they did make it out of this alive—a big if, at this point—with anything approaching evidence of what they'd seen down here, it would mostly be thanks to Walt.

"Let's not stay here long enough to find out," Alton said to Toby, whispering again. "Head that way." He pointed in the direction they'd been going before they stopped. "Stay on as straight a path as you can. We should be safe as long as we keep moving forward."

"As long as no one heard that burst of gunfire," Toby said.

"Exactly," Jessie said. "So let's get moving."

---

They moved as directed, and with trepidation, having been reminded once again and all too well of the terrors that might have lingered around any corner, in any shadow, under the surface of any water, or flying above them in the atmospheric gloom. But they moved, and kept moving even as Jessie's legs began to register that familiar pain, the exhaustion settling in and her right knee starting to twitch like it always did. It almost felt like an old injury, Jessie thought, but she'd never injured it. Not once. Another mystery related to her body. One with no answer, and one she dealt with anyway.

It took them hours of careful progression, and they stopped breathlessly as they heard something—a soldier, or worse—nearby, perhaps watching them, perhaps just going on about its monstrous cryptid business. But finally, the series of dome after dome seemed to have an end point.

"What is that, a clearing?" Alton whispered as they all stopped to take in a change in the landscape ahead.

"Or something," Jessie said. "I can see something in the darkness just beyond it, but it doesn't look like a wall or anything. It looks like . . . a pillar maybe?"

"It's too big to be a pillar," Alton countered. "It's almost as big around as one of these domes."

Jessie shrugged but didn't argue. Instead, they pressed on, and as they did, it became evident that she'd been right. It was a pillar, of sorts. It was crafted from some sort of black slatelike stone, perhaps to more effectively go unnoticed in the relative darkness of the immense cavern. But this was clearly no structural support, as it stopped right at the level where the fluorescent lights hung. And at the top, it flared out into a bulb of sorts, ringed with what looked to be windows. Or at least glass. From below, they appeared blackened and opaque.

"It looks like . . ." Walt said, ". . . like a control tower or something. At an airport?"

"I doubt there's a lot of air traffic here in need of control," Toby snarked.

"Tell the flying monkeys that," Walt said, still peering up. He reached into his backpack, and pulled out a small set of binoculars and held them to his eyes. "There's a ladder on the pillar. No safety cage, though, and it goes a good ways up there. Anyone want to climb an incredibly tall structure with only a ladder and no means of surviving a fall?"

"Why not?" Jessie answered and began moving forward. "It's no worse than the alternative."

They began crossing open dirt ground dotted with what used to be trees: stumps, fallen logs, some of them clearly run over and mangled by some sort of heavy machinery. It was good to be back on solid ground—the canals didn't extend out here. They were only halfway across the cleared zone when they heard a voice behind them yell something like *vezha*.

"They're yelling 'tower,'" Alton translated.

Behind them, six soldiers had emerged from the canals between the domes, and were converging on a central point at a forward angle toward the group. When they met in the middle, they formed a quick line and slowed their march, sighting their rifles.

"Run for the ladder!" Alton shouted. There was gunfire again, but at a distance too far for them to hit. Jessie didn't hear any telltale high-pitched whines rushing past them, a sure sign that the gunmen hadn't yet drawn a bead. But they would.

It shocked Jessie to realize that she now knew what it sounded like—and felt like too—to be shot at. She was a grad student, for God's sake. She had a little rental near Winnemac Park. Just a couple of weeks earlier she'd been helping a tween named Kira on an L platform take care of her seizing mother. A week before that, Jessie had bailed on going downstate to see her own mother, who sounded just as relieved when Jessie told her she had too much going on to make the trip. Those were her problems then. Now, she was trying to gauge the effective range of a Kalashnikov simply by virtue of the sound of its ammunition. *Time is an accordion*, or so Jessie recalled her dad saying. *It ebbs and it flows, it stretches and it contracts, and there's nothing we can do but follow the music and dance when we can.* Or words to that effect. She wished she remembered more of him. Wished he'd never gone away—or knew at least why he had.

Jessie knew on some level that she blamed her mother. There was little else other than some casual cruelty and occasional neglect to explain why Jessie disliked her mother as much as she did, but there it was. The awareness of it had always been there, just beneath the surface.

Jessie's legs ached. Her knee twitched again, but she pushed the feeling away and gritted her teeth. *Ain't no hill for a stepper*, Jessie reminded herself, and kept going.

And then came another burst of gunfire, and another, and then a slapping thud too close behind her. Alton, who was bringing up the rear almost certainly on purpose, fell out of step with his own run as he took a blow to the back, fell to one knee, and struggled back to his feet again. That, Jessie thought, was definitely a bullet. But Alton was still running. *Adrenaline again*, Jessie assumed. *Amazing shit.* Jessie just hoped he'd be able to make it to safety with the rest of them, and that he'd be able to stay conscious long enough for him to guide one of them through the steps of treating the wound so he wouldn't join Jace and Otomi on the casualty list.

That was when another bullet hit Alton, this time in his left shoulder, and it took him fully to the ground. Jessie spun around for just a split second before Alton screamed at her to keep running. He was already almost back up on his feet. Jessie didn't know how he was doing it, but she was glad he was.

Still, Alton was out of breath and struggling. Two more bursts of gunshots came. He was still running, but it was more of a stagger now, and Jessie realized he wasn't going to make it to the ladder, now less than a football field away. "Walt!" Alton yelled. "Throw me . . ." he gasped, "the gun."

"Holy god," Walt muttered, realizing for the first time that the doc had been shot. He unstrung the strap from his neck and quickly turned to toss it to Alton before pivoting back to running. Given any time to reflect, Jessie would have thought the move showed some impressive grace.

More bullets hit Alton as he caught the AK in midair, the shots jerking him around like a marionette. Toby and Walt continued to flat-out run to the best of their ability, but Jessie turned around and ran back to see if there was anything she could do for Alton. There wasn't, she knew, even as she slowed down. It might have been that Jessie didn't want Alton to die alone, even though he was splayed out in a no-man's-land between a field of environmental domes and some laddered pillar hundreds of feet below ground in a place that shouldn't exist. She watched as Alton brought the automatic rifle up to sight, aimed it at the rapidly approaching soldiers, and emptied the clip.

The soldiers reacted, flattening to the ground. One rolled sideways to find purchase behind a tree far too thin to protect him, while the other two caught Alton's bullets. One of them fell to the ground already dead, or so it looked. The other was holding his hip, which had probably been shattered by the beefy 7.62 round. The barrel smoked as Alton looked to survey what he'd accomplished. Jessie assumed this would be the dramatic movie moment where he'd finally fall to his knees, his last gasp for life spent and a death rattle already on his lips.

But instead, Alton threw the emptied gun down, turned on his heel, and began running to the pillar with an apparent renewed energy. "What are you doing?" he yelled when he noticed Jessie still standing there watching. "Go, go!"

She ran. Walt was the first one up the ladder, already climbing. Toby was at the base, waiting for Jessie, motioning her forward, sweat staining the front of his shirt in a darkened V. "Climb!" Jessie shouted at him, and though Toby paused for a moment, he complied.

Jessie was right behind him on the ladder, and Alton was right behind her. Somehow. More soldiers had appeared behind them, and were rushing the ladder while another tended to his fallen friend who'd been shot in the hip.

The climb felt painfully slow, and the top unreachably far off. But up they went, rung by rung, hand by hand.

The soldiers started firing, and a few bullets pinged off the structure, but Jessie could hear at least one make that same sick thudding sound as it hit Alton. He was climbing more slowly now, leaning out from the ladder so far that Jessie was afraid he was in the process of losing his grip and falling, but that's when she realized: *He's trying to block the line of fire. Doing everything he can to make sure we don't get shot. Killing himself to save us.*

Regardless, they kept climbing. One of the soldiers below stopped firing and started up the ladder too, while his companions reloaded below. Jessie yelled a warning down, but Alton had already seen it and stopped. He hung on to the ladder with one arm and gingerly took his pack off one shoulder with care. Jessie didn't know what he was doing—maybe getting ready to throw his backpack at the ascending soldier? That didn't seem like it would have much effect, but . . .

And then she saw it in his hand. Something small and a dull shade of black. At first, Jessie thought it might be a grenade, but dismissed that quickly. That didn't make any sense. Where would Alton have gotten one of those? Alton, who until five minutes ago refused to shoot a gun? But then—Jessie watched as Alton pulled the pin with his teeth.

She realized it *was* a grenade. And then Jessie noticed: he wasn't throwing it. He was holding it. And he was starting to climb back down the ladder.

"What the fuck are you doing?" Jessie screamed.

Alton looked up and called out "KEEP GOING!" And then he seemed to purposefully let go of his grip on the ladder completely.

He didn't even make it close to the ground before the grenade went off. *Maybe that was the point*, Jessie thought, since it succeeded in destroying the lower part of the ladder itself, preventing any soldiers from climbing up. Not that the soldiers were going to be an issue anymore. The one that had been on the ladder was obliterated, too, and the two who were readying to resume fire had taken shrapnel and were lying still in the dirt below. Only the one that had stayed behind to help his injured friend was still on his feet, and he was stumbling back into the dome canals, doing a fireman's carry of his nonambulatory friend.

Jessie looked away, then up. Toby was reaching down out of an open hatch at the top of the ladder, which was still thrumming with the force of the explosion. Through tears, Jessie climbed and took her friend's hand.

# CHAPTER ELEVEN

DOME CENTRAL CONTROL TOWER

"We're never getting out of here, y'know," Toby murmured.

He and Jessie were both looking out of the trapdoor, down to the Dome cavern floor hundreds of feet below. Walt was busying himself looking over the multicolor control panel, all switches and buttons and levers and lights.

"You're just a font of positivity, Tobes," Jessie said. "Ever since Jace was killed, you've sort of taken his place as the group asshat. Is that purposeful on your part, or just a weird and terrible decision?"

"Oh, I'm sorry," Toby replied in mock offense. "I'm allergic to unnecessary mortal danger. It pisses me off just the slightest bit. People shoot at me and monsters try to eat me and I get a little testy. Please forgive my lack of congeniality inside the *death trap*."

"All right," Jessie said. "I get it."

"Doc might have saved us," Toby continued. "But he took out our only route of escape at the same time."

"I said I get it," Jessie snapped. So they were down to three.

They'd lost their tech guy, their . . . what, spy? And now their medic. This was not good. This was very much not good. "We don't know that's the only way out. Look around. We're clearly not supposed to be up here. Let's see what trouble we could get into that they wanted so badly to keep us from."

But Toby was still gazing down at the ground. It was tough to see anything since there was still so much smoke and dust in the air from the conflagration. "Jesus, Jess, how many bullets did Alton take before he sacrificed himself?"

"I don't know," she admitted. "More than I want to count. I have no clue how he was still standing, let alone climbing a ladder."

"I guess he went out in a blaze of glory," Toby said. "Gotta give him that."

"I always hated that saying," Jessie replied grimly, getting up and wiping tears from her eyes. "When you make a sacrifice like that, it's not you that gets the glorious blaze. It's that the goddamn blaze of glory gets you."

Toby closed the hatch and locked it just for good measure. "And so the tomb doors close," he said, grinning at Jessie.

"Why are you being like this?" Jessie asked, glaring.

"Gallows humor, bestie," he said. "I'm laughing in the face of death, whistling past the graveyard, putting on a brave face, contemptuous to the peril surrounding us."

"Which is super annoying," Walt called out from over by the control panel. "And that's saying something from a guy that taught middle school and abided by the dumbass bravado of pubescent boys every day. Cut it out and come over here and take a look at this."

They did. "Looks like something out of an old movie about NASA. Something that was outdated by the time we had Atari cartridges," Toby said.

"What are you seeing here that I'm not, Walt?" Jessie asked. "It looks like a jumble of unlabeled controls to me."

"It's a switchboard, I think," Walt mused. "At least these controls over here. It's all still working. Some of this, I think, has to do with airflow, environment, and things like that. This section here is lighting. And this . . ." he said, gesturing toward a square bank of thirty-two levers, eight across and four deep, each with a button on its left, and a line of a dozen LED lights on the right. Above the block of levers, a thick black dial was inset. "This knob corresponds to both the lights next to the active lever, and this display."

It was just a simple CRT monitor, Jessie thought, mounted on top of the console. There was a bank of similar-looking screens—though these looked more like the ones in the room with the couches—that were either disconnected or dead. The active display on the console was the old drab green monochrome that was standard decades earlier. The screen was dim, either by virtue of its settings or by the ravages of time on ancient pixels, and Jessie thought it resembled a bowling scorecard: rows of boxes with numbers and a smaller box inset in the upper right corner. But Walt was correct: when he turned the dial, the highlighted box changed, one to the next, and then down a row when it reached the right edge of the screen.

"What is it?" Jessie asked.

"I don't know," Walt said. "But a lot of this tech is similar to what we were using in the school where I worked. I mean, not these levers. But the environmental stuff over there? That's a lot like what we had for the new fire sprinklers we had put in the ceilings back in the day. That thing next to it is just a fancy venting control. Think of it as a giant attic fan or something. We had those in all the science labs in case some kid made a stink bomb. And then the lighting—well, that was standard stuff for the all-purpose room where the kids in drama would put on their plays, or we'd have assemblies or band concerts."

"I never imagined how much this place would resemble seventh grade," Toby observed, and for once, Jessie wasn't sure if he was kidding.

"Look," Walt said, getting even more excited. "This sprinkler system—I think this might make it rain."

"That's . . . what sprinklers do," Jessie pointed out.

"Not like this," Walt said. "This whole cavern, or whatever it is, is a mock-up of a natural environment, right? So, it stands to reason that these plants, whatever they are, would need nutrients. There's a light and dark cycle too—we've seen that."

"Wait, I can make it rain just by pushing this button?" Toby asked.

"I mean," Walt said, "it's just a theory, but . . ."

Toby pushed the button. At first, nothing seemed to happen, but after a few seconds, the outside of the tower was awash in a light drizzle. "Wow," Toby murmured.

"Right?" Walt agreed. "If you turn that dial there . . ."

Toby did, and the shower outside grew more intense. "That is so cool," he said.

Outside and below the windows of the tower, they heard a frustrated yelp and a loud "Fuck!"

"One of those soldiers must have survived," Jessie said, and started for the hatch.

"But there's no ladder," Toby said, turning the rain down again to a gentle level. "Not for the first . . . what, fifty feet? It got blown away."

"I don't know what to tell you, Toby," said Jessie, kneeling down and unlatching the hatch.

"Be careful," Walt warned.

Jessie nodded. She took a breath and opened it. Sure enough, there was a grappling hook attached to one of the lower rungs before the break in the ladder, with a rope leading down to the ground. On the ground far below was the body of someone groaning back up to his feet. He looked up.

"Alton!" Jessie said. "You survived!" And then she paused. "Wait, *how* did you survive? You took half a dozen bullets to the back, and then you blew yourself up with a grenade you weren't supposed to have."

"What are you doing down there, Doc?" Walt called down.

"Well, I was climbing up until it started to rain," Alton shouted with evident impatience. "Can we talk about this when I'm up there?" His shirt was completely gone, Jessie noted, and one full pant leg was cut at the thigh.

"Don't take this the wrong way," Jessie yelled, "but how do we know it's you? I mean, it's kinda weird that you're not dead."

Alton's look of annoyance was almost enough to convince Jessie that this was indeed the real Alton. "I don't know," he finally conceded. "Ask me something only I would know."

Jessie considered her options for a moment, and then said, "Okay . . . what's the name of our friend waiting for us above ground?"

"Patsy Klein," he said, "if you can believe that."

"Good enough for me," Toby said when Jessie looked at the other two for confirmation. Walt nodded.

"Okay," Jessie said. "C'mon up."

"Can you turn off the rain, please?" Alton said, grabbing the rope again. "Gets a little slick out here."

"Oh!" Toby said, and ran over to the control panel. The rain outside slowed to a dripping stop.

"Thank you," Alton said, and pulled himself up the rope hand over hand with an effortlessness that was surprising to

Jessie, considering how many times he'd been shot. He was almost to the remaining section of ladder already. Jessie had so many questions. Important questions. But for now, she was fine just watching him ascend.

—

Alton had pulled up the rope behind him once he was back on the remains of the ladder so no one could follow, which Jessie considered to be good thinking. She was tired all over, but especially in her head, which felt fuzzy. Not seizure fuzzy, but dull from lack of sleep. Maybe they could sleep here for a bit, she thought. But first—she needed to understand Alton's miraculous survival.

"Let me look at you," Jessie said.

She focused specifically on his back, where she swore he'd caught at least a few bullets in the chase. All she could see were deep purple welts. Nasty, and probably painful, but no broken skin. "How . . . ?" she finally asked.

"I'm fine," he said, and Jessie could tell he was hoping that would be all the explanation required.

"Seriously," Jessie said. "It's not like you had a flak jacket on or something. I mean, did you?"

"No," Alton conceded.

"So then, what the hell?" Jessie demanded. "How are you . . . bulletproof?"

Alton opened his mouth, about to say something, then closed it again. Finally, he said, "Okay. I have something to admit to you guys."

"Great," Jessie said.

"We're all ears," Toby agreed.

"Maybe I can find a user's manual in that filing cabinet,"

Walt said under his breath. He was in his own little '80s tech world, Jessie thought. Might as well let him have it for a while. Who knew what he might come up with?

Alton pulled a stool over and took a seat. He looked bedraggled, and hunched over so much that Jessie could see the purple of the welt on his shoulder. That shoulder was—well, *wrong* too. It popped like bubble wrap when he moved it, which he was clearly trying not to do. "My reasons for being here aren't as altruistic as I'd suggested," he started.

"Don't bother trying to soften the truth while you're admitting to a lie, man," Toby advised.

"It wasn't a lie," Alton replied. "It was a version of the truth."

"What are you, Obi-Wan?" Toby shook his head. "What you've said is true, from a certain point of view?"

"Well, it is," Alton protested.

"Just say it," Jessie pleaded, and shot a warning look at Toby to cut out the ongoing commentary. From experience, she knew that once Toby got started, there was no stopping him for a while. And she was running out of patience. With both of them. "Just fucking say it."

"Okay," Alton said. "I'm sort of invulnerable."

"Isn't that like being sort of pregnant?" Walt called over as he rifled through the files in the drawers without even looking up.

"No, actually," Alton laughed grimly. "My skin is puncture resistant, but only to a certain point. I'm immune to bullets, knives, whatever. But the impact of the blow still goes through, as you can see. I don't know if it's as painful as actually getting shot or stabbed, but I can assure you that it's still super fucking painful. My bones can break too." He lifted his left arm and winced. The shoulder crackled and popped under the skin, and Alton grimaced.

"Just like the podcast. Noah with his healing, or Sara with

her bursts of strength," Jessie concluded. "You're not just after answers. You're after revenge for what they did to you."

"Makes sense, right?" Alton said with a raised eyebrow.

"Wait . . ." Toby interrupted. "If you were experimented on . . . how'd you escape?"

"I didn't," Alton said. "I just . . . found myself in the world again. It's why I'm here. Not so much for revenge, but for . . . an explanation. I'm sorry. It's hard to talk about rationally, especially since I don't even know enough to ask the right questions. It's just something I have to do."

"True for all of us, for different reasons," Jessie said. "Is that all? Is there more you can tell us that might help?"

Alton shook his head. "I'm sorry," he repeated.

"We need to get this guy a shirt," Toby said. "And maybe some ibuprofen. You going to be able to move all right, Superman?"

"Believe me," Alton groaned, stretching as much as he could. "I'm no Superman."

"What about the grenade?" Jessie asked. "Where'd you get that, especially since you weren't crazy about shooting a gun?"

"Which you did mighty well for an avowed pacifist," Toby added. "Just saying, that was some Rambo shit out there."

"I never said I couldn't shoot," Alton said. "Just that I preferred not to." He turned to Jessie. "The grenade came from Patsy. She took me aside and said I might need it, that one of us should probably have it, so she was giving it to the one of us who probably wouldn't pick up a gun. She had a couple of them in each of her boots, from what I saw."

"Ha!" Toby winked at Jessie. "Told you."

"Okay, okay," Jessie said. "Thanks for taking all that damage, Alton," she said, and she meant it. "We'd be shot up six ways from Sunday if you hadn't done what you did. And I'm super glad you're still with us."

"Me too," Alton smiled, but it was a tired smile, and one that disappeared as quickly as it came.

---

"This is weird," Walt said from over by the filing cabinet. Alton was resting his welted back on the cool metal of the control room floor, and Toby and Jessie were leaning back against the wall next to him. Jessie had just been about to suggest a quick nap before they did anything with the control panel—Alton was already there, and Toby was nodding off too. Jessie wanted an excuse to do the same, without guilt, but Walt had found his second wind. Or maybe his third.

"What's weird?" Jessie asked out of a sense of obligation.

"It's a corporate memo from the NFL," Walt said, lifting his glasses to read the faded type. "From 1984."

"The NFL?" Toby asked. "Like the National Football League?"

"Yes," Walt said. "Something about additional agreed-upon technology having been installed in the new Skycam system."

Jessie was suddenly a lot more interested. "What new technology?"

"It doesn't say," Walt replied. "This doesn't even specify who it was written to, only who it's coming from."

"According to internet chatter," Alton murmured from the floor, "pro sports has been scripted for decades. Maybe that has something to do with it."

"That's crap," Toby said. "Some 4chan shit."

"Maybe," Jessie admitted. "But you have to admit, it's weird that the NFL would be communicating with the Collective . . . not to mention talking about tech they installed on their behalf."

"Trust me," Alton said. "Tom Brady isn't what he seems."

"Are you kidding me?" Toby asked, incredulous.

Alton laughed then, and pretty soon they were all laughing.

*This was ridiculous,* Jessie thought. *We're in an air traffic control tower hundreds of feet underground, hiding from a world-encompassing cabal and mutant beasts, reading memos from the Reagan administration about a secret plan to manipulate sports. It's all too weird. Why would they need to control the outcomes of professional sports, anyway?*

Money was the usual answer, and maybe that was part of it. But the real tinfoil-hat reply would be distraction, she knew. Smoke and mirrors for the masses. Don't look at what's happening here—look at this exciting ball and what these men in shiny helmets do with it. Identify with this regional team, and spend one day out of seven every fall paying attention to nothing but that. It was the old ploy—an inattentive populous was far easier to convince of anything. *Anything.*

"I thought I was coming here for answers," Jessie said. "But the only answers I'm finding are to questions I didn't even think to ask."

"What sort of questions did you come here with?" Walt asked.

"I don't know," Jessie replied. "Something about my dad? Something more about . . . well, the nature of the world maybe? I feel like I've been mystified by everything for so long. My mother, when she was around, used to tell me how I was named for Baby Jessica, and that's sort of been the story of my life."

"Baby Jessica?" Alton asked drowsily.

"Jessica McClure," Jessie explained. "She was just a kid, some random toddler, who fell down a well a long time ago. A really thin well. More like a pipe. She became famous because TV crews were there for the whole process of getting her out, which they finally did. Big news. All over. Jessica became the number one name for girls for a while, and some people say that's why."

"Your mom named you after Baby Jessica?" Toby asked. "How have I never heard this before?"

"It's nothing noteworthy," Jessie said. "At least not until now. I'm a girl lost in a hole named for a girl lost in a hole."

"Jessica McClure survived," Walt pointed out. "So that bodes well."

Jessie smiled at Walt. He'd given up on the filing cabinets, and had slumped to the floor next to it, taking a load off. "Let's hope so," Jessie responded.

With that, Alton let out a shallow snore of a breath, having fallen asleep. Without another word, they all silently agreed that it was a fine idea and that they should do the same.

Jessie curled up on the top of the trapdoor, the only way in or out of the room, and slept. She dreamed of people gathered around a well like mourners at a gravesite. Her mother was there, dressed in a long black frock she would never have worn in real life. She was staring right at Jessie. Scowling at her. It was a look that Jessie recalled far too well.

—

When Jessie came to, Walt was at the control panel. If a person could look worried from the back, simply by virtue of the way he was standing and looking from side to side, Walt certainly did so in that moment. He'd gotten the monitors working, and they were flickering in black and white.

"Walt, what's wrong?" Jessie said, getting to her feet quickly. Alton was still sacked out, and Toby was actually drooling a bit, he was so gone. They both stirred a little, but didn't wake.

"Not sure," Walt answered, scanning the monitors. The

darkened glass of the tower itself allowed a 360-degree view, but was so large that no single person could take it all in at the same time without the video screens. "There's something going on down there—probably more than one thing, actually. There's some chupacabras prowling around, but I don't know if that's new or just something I'm seeing now. But those soldiers . . ." He pointed to one of the monitors, which showed a squad of men with guns. "They're definitely searching for something."

"But they must know we're here," Jessie argued. "I mean, I'm assuming they can monitor what's going on . . . ? Or the group Alton took out below must have called something in?"

"Or both," Walt added.

"Or both," Jessie agreed. "Right. So why would that team be looking around like they didn't know where we are?"

"Maybe they think we left?" Walt guessed.

"Or maybe they're not looking for us," Alton said, yawning and joining the other two at the control panel.

"That would be refreshing," Jessie said. "Okay, so who are they hunting?"

"Or what." Walt surmised. "There's another squad . . ." He pointed at another monitor. "There."

"Is that the same one?" Alton pointed to a third monitor. "Just from a different angle?"

"No," Walt shook his head. "That's one more. And a fourth over there."

"Well, this is getting a little ridiculous," Jessie said. "If they all converge on the tower, we're done for."

"Let's see if we can even the odds a little," Walt said. "See that dome in monitor four? The first squad is about to reach it. They're giving it a pretty wide berth. I think . . . something is in there."

"Just looks like mulch to me," Alton said, and then looked closer. "Wait, no . . . is it moving?"

Sure enough, the layer of whatever it was—tough to make out on the monochrome monitor above—was undulating of its own accord, almost visibly eager to break out of the confines of the dome. "Whatever that carpet of muck and sticks might be," Jessie observed, "it isn't strong enough to bust through that glass."

"Let's see if we can give it a little help," Walt said, and pushed a couple of buttons in a sequence that meant nothing to Jessie. But they did the trick—the door to the dome began to open.

The soldiers apparently knew what was in that dome, and were scared shitless, because they panicked right away and opened fire. And it was no wonder—what looked like mulch spilled out of the dome door; it separated out and became more distinct. It wasn't one giant organism after all—it had been a pile of tightly packed individual small beasts. As Jessie watched, she realized they were . . . rabbits? With horns?

"Well, I'll be damned," Walt said. "Jackalopes."

"What-a-lopes?" Alton asked.

"Jackalopes," Jessie repeated. "Southwest legend."

"Midwest too," Walt said. "But I always thought they were just some taxidermy con from back in the day."

"So, they're just bunnies with antlers?" Alton mused.

"Yeah, I guess," Jessie said. "I mean, why the soldiers look so . . ." She stopped as they witnessed a jackalope leap at a soldier through a spray of gunfire, and dug its antlers directly into the soldier's eyes. Both man and rabbit tumbled to the ground. "Oh shit," Jessie swore. "That is a mean motherfucking bunny."

"Is that one . . . eating that guy?" Alton murmured in shock. He pointed to one that had torn open a soldier's throat and looked very much to be nibbling voraciously at the torn-open neck.

The three watched as the jackalopes took out the entire squad of soldiers within the span of a single minute. And then, they all began to feed. "Holy Jesus on a cracker," Walt said. "I used to have rabbits in my classroom for the kids. I always did think they looked at me funny."

"What in the fucking fuck?" Toby exclaimed, wiping the sleep out of his eyes and joining the party. "Are those rabbits?"

"Yeah," Walt said. "Sorta."

"Anyone else getting serious *Watership Down* flashbacks?" Toby commented, his sleepy eyes now open wide.

"Okay, so that's one squad down, in disturbing fashion," Jessie thought out loud. "But we still have three others to deal with. Can we . . . direct the jackalopes somehow?"

"I don't see how," Walt said. "But they're not the only creatures trapped in these domes wanting to get out. Remember in the podcast when the Bigfoot took out the bad guy? I think we can play that same gambit."

"And fill the cavern with uncontrollable rage beasts with a hunger for human flesh," Alton pointed out.

"Not sure what choice we have," Jessie countered. "We're sort of trapped up here anyway, and until we deal with those soldiers, we're just sitting ducks."

"Here's one," Walt said, who'd been continuing to work the monitors and control board. "Remember those hummingbirds from the shaft? Here's a few more."

Releasing the birds, however, wasn't as effective as a ravenous blanket of attack rabbits. The first to emerge from its dome—a meadow with rather enormous flowers—was shot down instantly by the combined fire of the soldiers in the vicinity. Then two, then four or five. But soon, the soldiers were forced to reload, and that's when the charm of birds—*Could you still call a group of hummingbirds a charm when they were twenty times oversized, and had metallic needle beaks?* Jessie wondered—made their attack. Jugulars and carotids were punctured and drained. The birds flushed from iridescent green to an equally glossy red as they drank deeply from the soldiers, only disconnecting and flying away when there was nothing left but uniformed husks sprawled on the thin shore of the canals.

"It's just like *Wizard of Wor* at the old Gold Mine arcade at the mall," Walt said, and opened another door near a third group of soldiers. This time, the squad rushed in, thinking they'd cornered something, only to find themselves confronted by some sort of tree. It reached down with snakelike arms, plucked them up, and began eating them from a mouth in the trunk where the main branches split. A few of the soldiers were able to commence fire, but the bullets had no apparent effect. One by one, the men and women serving the Collective were eaten, disappearing whole into the thing's leafy gullet. "Only this time . . ." Walt said, apparently to himself. ". . . *I'm* the wizard."

Jessie patted Walt on the back to bring him back from what seemed to be a slightly . . . maniacal edge. "Stay with us, Walt."

"Sure," Walt said, smiling. "Sure, of course."

"How about we let Walt be Walt until all the squads are gone?" Toby said. "He's two for two, but we're only halfway there."

"Man's got a point," Alton agreed.

"Toby, go hit the rain again, and turn it all the way up," Walt pointed down the panel. "I think I've figured out a way to . . ." But he didn't finish, at least not out loud.

Toby did as he was told, and an antediluvian deluge began outside . . . except in the sector where the third party of soldiers was standing.

"So, we're keeping that group dry?" Toby looked confused. "Why would we . . ."

But his question was immediately answered as creatures converged from all sides of the hapless soldiers, the beasts trying to escape the sudden and torrential rain. "We figured there were things all around us, just watching," Walt said, crossing his arms over his chest and watching the monitors. A hairy alligator took one soldier down by the legs, and dragged him back into the water—there was some thrashing, but the water calmed quickly. Another soldier was taken by two flying humanoids of some sort, who carried him high up into the darkness beyond the fluorescents, and then dropped him from that height. The soldier plummeted to the ground, landed on his head, and didn't move again. The rest of the soldiers found themselves face-to-face with what looked to be draconic kangaroos, five-foot T-Rexes with leathery wings that looked too small to let them fly. They attacked with punches and kicks, and once their prey was prone, bared their teeth and sank them into whatever flesh was handy. Only one soldier survived that first attack, and that one only because the thing attacking him had bit off his right leg under the knee. He was gushing blood but trying to hop away when another of the kangaroo beasts rose in front of him. The soldier stopped, eyes glued on the thing in front of him, and another came around on his left and bit deeply into the soldier's neck.

"Rain off," Walt said, waving his hand down at Toby.

Toby did as he was instructed, and the rain dripped to a stop. All was quiet again.

"One squad left," Alton said. They'd taken refuge from the storm under a broad elephant ear fern and, now that the rain had stopped, were emerging, looking around cautiously.

"Not sure I have another rabbit to pull out of my hat," Walt said, a little crestfallen. "I don't see . . ."

A pack of wet, glistening chupacabras suddenly burst from the canals nearby. The soldiers, soaked and exhausted and unprepared, put up little fight. One chupacabra fell in the initial gunfire, but soon there were no soldiers left—half of them were already in the bellies of the feeding lizard dogs.

"That was either incredibly lucky," Jessie said, "or whoever they were searching for down there had control of those chupes."

As if on cue, a heavily muscled figure crept out into the clearing. It was a woman with one of the soldier's ball caps on. She had two guns across her back on bandoliers, a tank top, and some camo pants ripped off at the knees.

"Wait, is that . . ." Walt began, but Jessie cut him off with her equally mystified answer.

"It is," Jessie said. "I'll be damned. That's *Carla*."

(continued from page 1)

find it absolutely mandatory that Commissioner Rozelle be kept out of this loop, despite his clearance level both within the NFL and as it concerns the aforementioned "Collective." Rozelle's aides have in the past supported plausible deniability as standard practice such that the Commissioner is able to remain stalwart and incontrovertible when on-camera and representing the NFL, its ownership team, and American corporate interests.

To that end, it has been agreed that all Skycam equipment be routed through pre-defined facilities (confirmation of specific regional addresses provided on pages following) before implementation on-field. The "Collective" will at that time be able to install the additional agreed-upon technology within a closed circuit of need-to-know parties and individuals.

The NFL has been assured that Skycam modifications will not add significant weight to an already carefully-measured system; the four cables that suspend the camera by rings will not in any way affect performance, nor will it cause any sort of line-drooping that might interfere with the natural action on the field. The speeds of Skycam (23 mph laterally and 27 mph vertically) will likewise remain unaffected.

Already this technology has been employed to complete success in two exhibition games (NBC and CBS, specifically). It will next be tested at the World Cup soccer qualifier between the U.S. and the Netherlands at St. Louis, Missouri's Busch Stadium (Oct. 5). Assuming this deployment occurs without complications, the NFL agreement will go into full effect, and will be fully implemented in all stadiums by the end of the 1984 season.

As previously stipulated, the Collective confirms not to divulge in any way when and how that technology comes into use. Given the invisible nature of its effects, there should be only the occasional "unbelievable" moment in gameplay—which have historically happened during unenhanced sports performances anyway. We consider this a "double blind" arrangement that will achieve the ends desired by all parties, and still allow the match-ups to appear organic. As far as the perception of the NFL and its millions of viewers are concerned, they will be.

The National Football League joins the "Collective" in not only the denial of this agreement, but also the denial of the existence of the Collective itself, as a matter of public record. Furthermore, the the sole copy of this agreement will be held by the Collective, which as previously stated the NFL does not confirm the existence of, in a secured location known only to them, who again do not exist.

Signatories, witnesses, and notaries supplied on 2nd page following. For more information, see

# CHAPTER TWELVE

BASE, DOME CENTRAL CONTROL TOWER

They prepared to climb down using the ladder as far as it would go, and then lowering Alton's rope and grapple—salvaged from a fallen soldier, he'd said—to carefully get back down to the ground. The rope mishap from the shaft was all too fresh in their minds, and they didn't want to risk running into the Stymphalian birds, or whatever they were, that Walt had let loose. For perhaps the first time since they'd entered the massive cavern of domes, Jessie was grateful for its huge scale.

"How will she know it's us?" Walt asked, but Jessie surmised that the question wasn't how *would* Carla know it was them, but rather how she *already knew.* Because she clearly did. She waved and grinned up at the control tower like this was all part of the plan.

"Those were Jersey Devils, by the way," Walt said as they made their way down. "The dog-faced kangaroo things. They have lots of names and none of them have stuck like Jersey Devil . . . Wozzle Bug, Hoodle-Doodle Bird, stuff like that.

Personally, I like Jabberwock, but some say that's a whole other creature."

"Or a thing made up for a nonsense poem by Lewis Carroll," Alton suggested.

"I'm not sure how you can be down here, living through what we are," Walt said, "without having a little more faith in things existing that we once thought to be fiction."

"Fair," Alton admitted. "But sometimes a poem is just a poem."

"I don't know," Jessie said, watching Toby descend the rope. "The more I'm down here, the more I think there's no story in this world that doesn't have one foot in reality."

"So, there's no fiction?" Alton asked. "That's just swinging the pendulum too far the other way. Some things have to still just be stories told around a campfire."

"You want to hear a story around a campfire?" Walt murmured, almost to himself. "Let's talk about the myth of a free America. Democracy itself. Everything that I've been teaching for my whole life. If the Collective really has been in charge—and whoever the Collective is working with or for or against? Then the real myth is the history we've all been taught. That I've taught myself. We've all been fools, and I've been one of the fools leading the parade."

"It's not as bad as all that," Alton suggested, but in a way that seemed to admit that Walt might be right.

"It is to a social studies teacher," Walt responded.

"Let's just get down to the ground," Jessie said. "Safely. And then we can talk about the state of the world, and what's true and what's not."

"We can get down to the ground," Walt sighed. "But getting to the bottom of things? I'm not sure that's even possible anymore."

Jessie worried Walt was right about that too. But for that

to really mean anything . . . ? They had to get out of here first. And that was still in question—at least for all of them but Jace and Otomi, who had no more questions to pose.

---

"Hola, guys!"

Carla ran over and embraced Jessie like they were back-to-school friends reuniting at the end of a long summer break. She was taller than Jessie had imagined her to be, taller than Jessie by a fair amount, and that was saying something.

"Oh my god, Carla," Jessie exclaimed once she was unburied from Carla's tight embrace. "How are you here?"

"Here where, chiquita?" Carla asked. "Here in the underground? Or here as in *I'm not dead, as you probably assumed when I never met up with you guys, or even called*?"

"Yes," Jessie said. "All of those things."

Carla hugged Walt, and then Alton too, who winced a little as she squeezed him. "Where's Jacinto? And Otomi?"

"Well . . ." Jessie started, but paused long enough for Toby to jump in.

"Dead," Toby interjected. "Like . . . big nasty dead, too, the both of them."

"I kind of figured, when I didn't see them with you before," Carla said, and glared a little at Toby. She turned back to Jessie. "Who's Mr. Brightside over here?"

"Oh, right," Jessie replied, glad to talk about something else. "You haven't met Toby. Toby, Carla. Carla, Toby. He's my roommate, and was my ride out here. When you went MIA, he decided to tag along."

"Not one of my better decisions in life," Toby said, putting out his hand. "And that's saying quite a bit."

Carla shook, but still looked wary. "You're the dude from the couch," she said. "Couch guy movie man."

"I suppose," Toby replied.

"What did you mean earlier?" Alton asked. "When you said you didn't see them with us before? When did you see us? And how?"

"So many questions," she said. "I got a bunch for you guys too. We need to pool our information. But somewhere where we won't be interrupted by teenage mutant ninja whatevers, you know?"

"Behind the waterfall?" Toby suggested.

"Fuck no," Carla scowled. "Why would you want us to go there?"

"Because that's where the shaft is," Jessie answered.

Carla looked at her and then back to Toby warily. "So is almost the whole Collective army, or might as well be, plus a menagerie of trained hunting monsters they keep half fed so they're ravenous when let loose. Also, a maze of a cave system, remember? We don't want to go near there."

"So, what are you suggesting, then?" Toby asked, annoyed. "Just wandering around and trying to find another way to the shaft?"

"There are dozens of ways out," Carla said. "So yeah, wandering around, but not aimlessly. They know you're trying to get back to where you came from, and they've been right so far. That's making them overconfident. Now's the perfect time to switch it up and get the jump on them by going in a different direction. By the time they realize you're not following the path they expected, we should have a good lead."

"You talk like someone who knows their way around," Alton pointed out.

"So does this guy," Carla pointed to Toby. "But only one of us actually knows what they're talking about."

"Fine," Toby threw up his hands. "I admit it. I don't know this place, and I don't know the way to go. But I do know that you being here all of a sudden seems really fucking fishy to me—and I hate fish." He looked around. Walt grimaced a bit. "Sorry," Toby finally said. "That sounded way cooler in my head. But you know what I mean."

"I know exactly what you mean," Carla nodded. "And you're right, I have lots to explain, and I'll lay it all out. As soon as we're safe."

"Okay," Jessie said, nodding. "Safety first. And then it sounds like we do have a lot to talk about."

Carla took a deep breath, but smiled at Jessie. "You ain't kidding, sister."

---

Carla was able to lead them out of the Domes with relative ease. *Maybe too much ease*, Jessie considered. As much as she'd always liked Carla, her not showing up for the rendezvous in Chicago and then suddenly showing up here, and knowing a bunch of stuff to boot—it was all super suspicious.

Carla led the group back out to the curved exterior wall of the cave where the rock had seemingly grown over the concrete as though it were simply moss or vine. She ran her hands along the wall until she found a seam, invisible to the eye because of the combination of dim light and the growing stone, and searched all around, pressing on random spots. Nothing happened until the third piece of wall she'd stopped at, and then, finally, they all heard a click, and some rock fell away like thin shale as a doorway popped open slightly. It was dark beyond, but Carla clicked something attached to one of her bandoliers, and a reddish light shone out from her chest, casting a glow back on her face. Carla motioned with her head for everyone to go in, her index finger to her lips.

They were back in a hallway, with doors on the left and the right, spaced about twenty feet apart as far up the hall as they could see.

"These go on for miles," Carla whispered. "I'm not even kidding. Like miles and miles—at least the longer hallways that connect major multileveled hubs."

"How do you know that?" Jessie whispered back.

"Because I started in a whole other area," Carla said. "And I've seen a map of the entire place, or what I think was the entire place anyway. It's . . . bigger than we thought. Bigger than it has any right to be."

They heard a noise off down the hallway—it was unclear to Jessie if it was footsteps, but whatever it was, she decided they needed to not be standing in an open and well-lit hallway if and when whoever it was turned their way.

Carla motioned for Jessie to check the door up the hall on the right while she went over to the one on the left. Carla's was locked, but Jessie's opened easily. A light in the room flickered on, and Carla rushed them inside, taking care to shut the door as silently as possible behind her.

"This is a good room," Carla said. "Maintenance. These are almost never open." She dragged a bank of lockers over, as quietly as she could, just a foot or so past where the door opened into the room. They were clearly heavy, but Carla moved them with relative ease.

Jessie looked around. It looked more or less like a changing room at a gym, with a stock of cleaning supplies in a shelved alcove. There were three banks of lockers on the other walls, and benches in front of each one. Some of the open lockers held uniforms, both soldier and what looked to be custodial.

Alton made a beeline for the clothing, hunting for something close to his size.

Carla got a look at Alton's naked back as he passed her. "Holy Mary, Mother, what the fuck happened to you?" she asked.

"Gunshots," Jessie said.

"He's apparently bulletproof," Toby added.

Carla raised an eyebrow. "Okay, that's another thing I need explained to me then," she said, and sat down on a bench. Jessie sat too, straddling the bench, and laid out what had happened to them from the meetup in Ward to Patsy Klein to the shaft. The wetlands Bwana Hut, the trap that took Jace, the escape from the soldiers, Otomi being a badass, and then finally getting torn apart and eaten by something that looked suspiciously like the Mississippi Piasa. And then into the Domes.

"That's where I saw you," Carla said. "I'd found myself in this monitoring room that showed a bunch of the domes. They were numbered, and there were these couches—"

"We were there!" Jessie exclaimed. "With the big orange swivel chairs?"

"No," Carla shook her head. "The chairs in my room were wicker things with these throw pillows, and there was a black lacquer conference table with chairs all around it . . . in like some sort of dark denim stitching? There were a whole bunch of screens on the wall, though, and under that was a whole planter of ferns. I thought they were fake at first, because, you know, hundreds of feet underground. But no, they were real. The soil they were in was even a little damp."

"Weird," Jessie commented.

"Right?" Carla said, and took out a pack of cigarettes. "I did find these, along with a book of matches. I'm thinking whoever cleans up in there and feeds the ferns must have left them. I haven't smoked since I finished high school, but I figured why the hell not?" She lit one up and pointed the pack of Winstons at Jessie. "Want one?"

"No thanks," Jessie replied. "So, you saw us in the domes. Was that you who called us?"

"Yeah," Carla said. "I figured out that the dome numbers under each monitor were extension numbers for the phone system. I called the number of the dome you were all in, and there you were. Or someone was. I thought it might be Jace, but I wasn't sure. I couldn't see the screen from where the phone was, but . . . anyway, I didn't want to waste time having this conversation we're having now over the phone, and I didn't know who else might be listening. So, I hung up and raced to where I thought you were. By the time I got there, though . . ."

"We were already gone," Jessie finished.

Carla nodded.

"I can't believe that was you," Jessie said. "And if this place is as huge as you say—and I believe it, based on what we've seen, it's amazing that you found us."

"One might call it unbelievable." Toby had sauntered over to the two of them, having run out of lockers to plunder.

"Fuck off," Carla said, but it was more casual than serious. "You're just pissed because you didn't find any sweet loot in those lockers."

"That is true," Toby admitted. "But it's also super weird that you'd show up here, in the way that you did. Hard to trust anything down here, especially wild coincidence."

"Cut it out," Jessie told Toby. "Let her explain before you start passing judgment." She turned back to Carla conspiratorially. "Okay, spill. Tell us everything, but the short version. I don't think we can stay in any one place for long."

"These rooms don't have cameras, I don't think," Carla said. "So this is probably safer than most. But you're right—staying in one place is just waiting for death to catch up to you."

"Believe me," Jessie confirmed. "We've discovered that over and over." She looked around the room. Carla was right about there being no visible cameras, but that didn't mean anything. They were recording everything they could, sure—but Jessie was certain that they weren't the only ones.

—

Carla's story was disappointingly unspectacular for one that began with an attack from behind and a kidnapping, Jessie thought. To be fair, Carla wasn't trying to entertain, and the holes in the story were just places where Carla was either unconscious or in the dark, either literally or figuratively.

She confirmed that she had been attacked at the end of their last Zoom meeting, and she fought back hard. "That motherfucker was tough," she said. "I would have had him, if he hadn't sliced me right off the bat with a blade coated in something. I could see it glistening on the edge. It took a few minutes to kick in—and in that time, I kicked his ass around my apartment pretty good—but I was too loopy after a minute or so to even stand. And then it all went black."

From there, Carla said she didn't know what happened, but she woke up in a surgical theater. "And I was the star of the goddamn show," Carla added somberly. She'd been bound, but loosely—more to keep someone unconscious from thrashing, she'd guessed, than to prevent escape. "There was no one around," she said. "Silent as a tomb." She made the sign of the cross over her chest and kissed her thumb.

She'd been able to wriggle out of the straps binding her

without too much effort, and immediately took inventory of herself—trying to figure out if they'd done something to her in that surgical suite, or if they were just prepping her for something that hadn't happened yet. After checking herself carefully, she decided she was still whole—no wounds, no sutures, nothing.

"Getting out of that room wasn't the hard part," Carla said. "But once I was out the double doors, I was in a hallway going left and right as far as I could see. I tell you—this experience is gonna stay with me in a lot of ways, but one of them is definitely that I fucking hate hallways now."

Carla explained that she went left. No reason. Opened doors at random, also for no particular reason. "I wasn't mapping or anything," she admitted. "I wasn't even sure where I was at that point, to be honest, or how much time had passed since I'd been taken."

"How long have you been down here since you woke up, do you think?" Alton asked.

"A little over a week," Carla said. "At least I think so. Time is super weird down here, and not just because you can't see the sun. The clocks all seem to be set to different times—or else I've been losing track. Just like in the podcast, they left me with a phone—not even mine, because that either got left behind or busted in the fight—but this phone didn't have anything on it. No apps, nothing. I've been recording what I can, but it didn't occur to me to start until the second day. Or like I said, what I thought was the second day."

She'd wandered around, recording now and then and investigating what she could understand, which she admitted wasn't much. That all changed on the sixth day, Carla said, when she first ran into a group from the Collective. She'd been coming out of an office that was connected to some sort of warehouse, which in turn had been connected by a wide tunnel laid with tracks for a handcart to another room, this one also large but empty. There was something in the middle—Carla called it a "landing pad," but she admitted she didn't know what it really was, other than maybe a place where crates were dropped off for storage. And she'd only gotten to that room, she said, by sliding down an air shaft.

"Anyway," Carla continued, "The Collective dudes. Yeah, I was coming out of that office just as they were coming in, I think. They were as surprised to see me as I was them. It was a scientist-looking guy and a soldier. The only reason I'm sitting here talking to you is that I was a second or two faster than the guy with the gun—he brought up his AK, but I pushed the barrel to one side and punched him in the throat. When he went down choking, I put him in a headlock and snapped his neck. Bill Nye the Science Guy—he actually kinda looked like him—was backed up against the wall, trying to call someone on his old-ass flip phone. But he stopped when he saw me stand up. I told him he had two choices: help me figure out some shit, or end up like the soldier. He took option one."

"Wait, so you had a prisoner?" Alton said. "What was he able to tell you?"

"Bill told me a lot of things," Carla answered carefully. "Including that you guys were here."

"And that was what, yesterday?" Jessie pressed.

"I think," Carla said.

"Is anyone else finding it hard to believe that she wandered around blindly for six days without meeting anyone or anything?" Toby asked. "We were only here a few hours before we started losing people."

"I'm just telling you what happened, man," Carla said with a scowl. "Anyway, Bill didn't want to go anywhere. Said they'd know where he was, and they'd eventually figure out he'd been taken captive, and they'd send a squad out who wouldn't be choosy about who they shot. Bill said their motto was *Crunch all you want, we'll make more*—whatever that's supposed to mean."

"Doritos," Walt said. "Doritos commercials from the '80s."

"That actually tracks," Carla mused. "Bill talked about the '80s and '90s like it was just last year or something. Weird dude."

"So, what happened to Bill?" Jessie asked in a way that suggested she already knew the answer.

"Oh, he's dead," Carla said. "But I didn't kill him. Like I said, he didn't want to go anywhere, but I made him. Wasn't easy, and he was getting more and more resistant. But I was the one with the gun, and so we kept hunting. He's the one who thought you'd eventually make it to the Domes. We finally found a room with some chupacabras in a cage, and a soldier sleeping on a cot nearby. The chupes were loud as hell, man. I don't know how that soldier was still sleeping. He was easy to take out."

"You killed him?" Alton said, somewhat aghast.

"No," Carla balked, a bit offended. "I knocked him out with the butt of his own rifle, and then tied his ass up good. I'm not gonna murder someone in their sleep. We're supposed to be the good guys."

"And yet Bill is sleeping with the fishes," Toby pointed out.

"Like I said, I didn't kill him," Carla retorted. "I took the soldier's AK and the dog whistle he had. I also changed into some fatigues, at least the pants. What can I say? They were clean, and it had been a week."

"Fair," Walt said. "I'm already wishing this dressing room had a shower."

"Was it the chupacabras?" Jessie asked. "That got Bill, I mean?"

"Nah," Carla said. "Those puppies were just the sweetest,

especially when I let them out of their cages and let them chow down on as much of the food they had stored in there as possible. One even came up and licked my hand. Did you know they have different colored tongues? I thought they were all black, but some are bluish, and some are almost purple. Anyway, after that, I had my own little army. Bill wasn't happy. He was wondering why no one had come to find us. I have to admit, I was beginning to wonder the same thing. At one point, we found ourselves in a sort of zoo. I'd left the chupes in another office down the way. They were sleepy after eating so much."

"A zoo?" Jessie questioned.

"Okay, not a zoo," Carla corrected herself. "But animals in cages, anyway. A lab, maybe? But there was no equipment, just the cages. And I'm using the term 'animal' very loosely here. Some looked normal, but others? Creepy, yo. They looked messed with. Larger than they should have been, or some sort of cross between themselves and something else. I was over looking at a mouse with a wicked barb for a tail, like a scorpion's . . . Bill started getting all freaked out. Said we shouldn't be in here, that this area had been surrendered and marked as offline. He started backing away, and that's when his farm got bought."

"What got him?" Walt asked.

"Big ol' worm dropped from the ceiling right onto his shoulder," Carla said. "Bit down hard on his neck. The skin around the bite was already turning black before poor ol' Bill hit the floor, but it took him a few minutes to die. Bad way to go."

"Mongolian Death Worm," Alton offered.

"That was my guess," Carla agreed. "It came for me too, but I was able to shoot it to shit before it got close. After that, the animals in the cages went a little crazy. Hooting and buzzing and barking and howling. It spooked me, and I didn't know what other creepy-crawlies were in the shadows, so I booked it back the way we'd come, rounded up the pups, and kept hauling ass. Eventually I found that room I mentioned before, with the wicker chairs and all the TV screens. I messed with some of the controls in there a bit, enough to know I didn't know fuck all about them, but then there you were, wandering around on one of the screens. The rest, you know."

"So, you were able to direct the chupacabras to attack the soldiers?" Jessie asked. "Why aren't they still following you?"

"Honestly," Carla said, "outside of being a pretty effective attack pack, those pups are a pain in the ass to have around. They remind me of the greyhounds my abuelita used to bet on at the track. She adopted a retired racer once—she was a sweet girl, but was the laziest thing I'd ever seen. She could bolt something fierce, for sure, but if she wasn't sprinting? She was lying down asleep. These chupes were more or less the same, so making decent time with them in tow wasn't a good plan. Besides, I still have the whistle, so if we run into more, we're good. I think."

"You think?" Toby shook his head.

Carla shrugged. "I'm not sure of anything down here. You shouldn't be either."

"I'm not," Toby replied tersely, looking Carla straight in the eye.

"You can shoot me the *ojo malo* if you want, man," Carla said. "But I'm giving it right back to you, three times over."

"All right, all right," Jessie said. "We don't need to turn on each other here."

"Not that simple, unfortunately," Carla said. "There's one more thing Bill let spill. About you guys. He said you guys have a mole in your group."

"What?" Alton said, startled. "Who?"

"No idea," Carla said. "He wouldn't elaborate, and then he

died horribly before I could circle back to press him on it. It wasn't something he meant to say, I don't think."

"Let's stay calm," Jessie said, realizing that the group was already on edge, and something like this could really tear them apart. "All we know is that some random scientist said we had a mole in the group. That's not exactly proof there is one, you know?"

"Why would he say it otherwise?" Walt asked.

"I don't know," Jessie admitted. "To sow dissent? To save his own ass? Could be anything. I'm just saying we don't know."

"That's true," Carla nodded. "I mean, he sounded sincere, but anything's possible."

Jessie took a deep breath. "Okay. Everyone good now? Everyone okay with each other? We're going to have to work together, and we're already spending too much time here. We've got to get moving. Keep moving. We have to be able to know that everyone is watching each other's backs."

"And not stabbing anyone in theirs," Toby said. "But yeah, I'm in." Everyone in the group nodded affirmatively, and Toby turned to Carla. "I'm sorry if we got off on the wrong foot. I know I'm a jerk sometimes."

"No worries, I get it," Carla said, nodding to Jessie. "But if you cross my girl here, I will kick your ass."

"Same here," Toby said.

Alton jumped up and went back to digging through the uniforms, having decided his first choice—a no-name janitorial jumpsuit—apparently wasn't good enough. "I think the soldier fatigues might actually help us blend in a little more," he explained, rifling through camouflage with name patches embroidered on the left breast pocket: Guthrie, Ballew, Davis, Shoemaker. "But I'd rather find one without a name. They're getting slaughtered down here same as some of us. Hell, we've killed a few ourselves. It doesn't do any good to think of them as real people."

"They *are* real people," Toby argued.

"Do we know that?" Walt asked. "I'm serious. We know there's cloning tech at work. Who's to say the whole army isn't made up of clones?"

"They'd know, wouldn't they?" Toby said. "I mean, they'd know they're clones, right?"

"I don't know the rules," Walt said.

"I'd prefer it if they were all clones. Better than killing human beings," Alton said, buttoning up his fatigues. He'd chosen the one that said Shoemaker since it was the largest and almost fit.

"Wouldn't clones also be human beings, though?" Toby pressed.

"Like Walt said, we don't know the rules, Toby," Alton said with a dismissive air, and then changed the subject. "Maybe we should all put on uniforms. It could help us to bluff our way out of things instead of shooting people in the head."

"Not a bad idea," Walt admitted.

"Unless the uniforms are bugged somehow," Jessie pointed out. "I mean, even Bill the Science Guy was talking about being tracked. It's something I would do, if I was in charge."

"Well, shit," Alton said, and started unbuttoning his fatigues. "Fine. But I need a shirt. I can't just go around half naked."

"There's some civvies in this one," Walt called over, and pulled out a white ring-necked tee with Papa Smurf on the front, smiling above the words HAVE A SMURFY DAY.

"Ugh, seriously?" Alton grumbled. "Whatever. Toss it over here." Once he had it in hand, Alton squeezed himself into the slightly too-small shirt.

Carla offered her second gun to the group, and Walt quickly

accepted. "You fellas head out into the hallway and see if we're still clear," she ordered. "I have to talk to Jessie about some time-of-the-month girl stuff."

"Say no more," Walt said, and dutifully went out the door.

"Oookay," Toby said with suspicion, but followed Walt.

"Is this supposed to make me uncomfortable?" Alton said, but he was falling in line for the hallway anyway. "I'm a doctor."

"A doctor in a Smurf shirt," Walt laughed.

Once the others were in the hall, Carla pulled Jessie to one side. "I just need to tell you one more thing," she whispered. "There was something else Bill told me while we were together. After he did, he panicked and said he'd be killed outright if they heard he'd spilled that particular cup of tea. Begged me not to say anything, to forget he'd said it at all. *One of the most highly classified secrets in a world of highly classified secrets*, he said. And it was about you."

"About me?" Jessie whispered back.

"You know the woman who runs this place? The boss lady? Big bitch in heels?" Carla paused, trying to find the best way to explain the rest, and finally settled for just blurting it out. "Apparently, you're her daughter."

# CHAPTER THIRTEEN

MAINTENANCE READY ROOM 613-B

"Her *daughter*?" Jessie said dubiously. "That's impossible. My mother is terrible, but she's not the leader of a secret cabal out to control the world. She can't even control her own book club. They threw her out last year for refusing to stop lecturing everyone on the dangers of chemtrails."

"I'm just telling you what Bill said," Carla shrugged. "I'm not holding anything against you, or even believing it in the first place. But I thought you should know that there are some people down here who believe it. Bill believed it. Maybe we can use that to our advantage, you know?"

"My mother wears nothing but skirts and clogs," Jessie continued. "She's an aging hippie who never believed in her own peace and love rhetoric. She was a social worker, for God's sake. She drives a Subaru and makes granola and criticizes people behind their backs. She begs me to visit her all the time, but hates me being there almost as much as I hate being there. The only thing my mother and the woman running this place have in common is that they're probably both mean as snakes."

"Like I said . . ." Carla took Jessie by the shoulders to look in her eyes. "I don't care. I'm telling you because I thought you'd want to know, chiquita. That's all."

"But why would they lie about that?" Jessie asked. "What's the play there? To make me seem more dangerous? Or less? Or is it just another weird thing down here, and I'm reading too much into it?"

"I got no idea," Carla said. "Who knows? Even if it's somehow true, it's not like it reflects on you. I know you, and I trust you. That's true for all of us in the group, I think."

"But it *can't* be somehow true," Jessie insisted. "I mean, I appreciate the vote of confidence—I really do—but I don't want you thinking there's any way this could be real. My mother is just a normal person—a little broken by the world and not great at living in it—but she's not a supervillain."

"Okay," Carla said.

"I'm serious!" Jessie said in a raised voice.

"Okay!" Carla shouted back. "Now get it together. Like my mama used to say, we got shit to do, sunshine."

Jessie smiled despite herself. "Did that mean you had something to do, or nothing to do?"

Carla grinned back. "Both," she confirmed. "It was like her version of aloha."

Jessie took a deep breath, gathered herself, and fought back a sudden wave of dizziness. "I'm sorry," she said. "That's just a hard thing to hear out of nowhere."

"Yeah," Carla responded. "You better believe I asked Bill for more information, but he was clammed up tight. Wouldn't say another thing about it, and then . . . you know, death by worm. But shake it off, girl. We'll figure it all out as we go, or we'll make it home and it'll be one of those big, weird things that we can unpack once we're safe. Hell, maybe you can laugh with your mom about it, when you ask her if she's been moonlighting as the leader of a world-dominating organization."

"If she was," Jessie said, "I doubt she'd live in a little blue-clapboard house in Champaign, Illinois. At the very least, wouldn't she live in Denver or something?"

"I'm with you," Carla said, and took a beat. "You okay now? You back?"

Jessie nodded. "I'm back."

"So, let's go," Carla ordered.

Toby poked his head back in. "If you guys are done talking about maxi pads or whatever, we're just standing out in the hallway like sitting ducks."

"Are you sure he's your best friend?" Carla asked, and strode out of the room, brushing past Toby.

"I think she's starting to like me," Toby commented as Jessie got up and followed.

"You wish," Jessie said, but she was thinking about her mother, and all the ways that she'd always been impossible to understand.

—

Another hallway. It sometimes seemed like this place was nothing but long halls peppered by empty offices and labs and storerooms and occasional terrifying oases of mystery. Jessie reflected on how many times she'd heard those on the podcast complain about the place being such a maze, but now she was surprised that they hadn't remarked on it more often.

They'd grown tired of office after empty office, of dusty conference rooms and abandoned labs with the scattered detritus of past use. They'd found a Spuds MacKenzie calendar open to February

1988 that showed the bull terrier on four skis and wearing an orange Bud Light sweater. They'd found more New Coke, ironically sitting in an unplugged Pepsi vending machine that charged a quarter for a can—and also offered up Mandarin Orange Slice, Hires Root Beer, Mello Yello, and something called White Rock Chocolate Time, but no one was in the mood for warm, flat soda. They found someone's briefcase, which was exciting as a prospect but disappointing once it was opened to reveal a petrified peanut butter sandwich in a fold-flap baggie. All the rooms seemed small and forlorn. They'd even stopped recording, for the most part. There didn't seem to be a point in showing one more hallway, one more institutional desk, one more gurney, one more empty cage.

On the plus side, Toby pointed out, they hadn't run into any more soldiers. But the fear was real, and they were always on their toes. Paranoia was the rule of the day—it had been confirmed time and time again as necessary and prudent.

"We're really just wandering aimlessly now," Toby said. "Shouldn't we be marking walls or something, so we'll know if we've been in this intersection before?"

"It would help us," Walt pointed out, "but it would also tell whoever else is here where we were, and potentially where we're going. It might leave a trail leading right to us."

"I'd be more worried about that if we'd seen a soul since we left the Domes," Alton said, pulling the skintight Smurf shirt down over his navel for what seemed like the hundredth time. "We've been walking for hours."

"Is it possible we've landed in some part of the complex that they've completely put in mothballs?" Jessie asked. "And if so, is that good or bad?"

"Hard to say," Carla murmured, peering around the next corner and once again seeing that it was empty.

Jessie was frustrated, but she didn't know if it was because of their fruitless meandering, or because she was still processing what Carla had revealed earlier. What did it all mean, she wondered. If she was—somehow—the daughter of the woman in charge of all this, or at least some of this . . . what did that mean about *her*? Could she even trust *herself*? Could she actually be the mole in the group, if there was one, and not even know she was?

"Short hallway up ahead," Carla said softly. They were still trying to stay quiet, just in case. "That usually means a bigger room, right?"

"Could be," Alton agreed.

"Could mean there are people in there," Toby pointed out.

"Bring 'em on," Walt said, and brought his Kalashnikov up to bear. "We're ready for them."

"Calm down, papi," Carla said. "We're not itching for a fight. Just be ready, is all."

Carla scooted ahead quickly, and more silently than Jessie thought possible. Carla was all sorts of impressive, which made it occur to Jessie that maybe she was too impressive, and then she shook that thought from her head. She was starting to get suspicious of everyone. That line of thinking would come to absolutely no good, she decided.

The doors on the right and left were locked but labeled—one said EXECUTIVES and the other TALENT. The double doors ahead of them, however, weren't just unlocked—they were slightly ajar. Carla pushed on the open door, the one on the right, and it creaked as it opened. It was dark inside, and Toby entered and moved quickly to the nearest wall, clicking on the lights when he found the switch.

It was a TV studio, or so it seemed, a big room with lighting and rigging overhead, a few sit-in cameras big enough to drive on the freeway, some monitors, and editing equipment. In the center of the room was a hexagonal rotating platform, with its surface divided by walls into six separate trapezoids, each one decorated differently from the others. One was a living room set that looked very familiar—Walt claimed it was from *All in the Family*, but Toby was convinced it was the Bundys' place from *Married . . . with Children*. Another was a generic-looking news set, with a huge ornamental 9 in bas-relief on the back wall behind what looked to be an anchor desk. A third was an outdoors set—an extremely plastic-looking woodland—and a fourth was just corrugated metal set on a rotating disk that took up most of the back wall, and a single dining room chair with a brown coat slung over it and what looked to be a rubber Max Headroom mask on the seat. The fifth one was empty but had a single torn piece of paper in the thick dust on the floor, and the sixth was made up to look like the press room at the White House, complete with flags, red drapery, and a white podium with an official-looking seal.

"Well, this is weird," Jessie said.

"There was something in the podcast about a stage set of the moon landing somewhere in the complex, right?" Walt asked.

"Well, this isn't that," Alton said.

"No, but it's along the same lines for sure," Toby replied, picking up the Max Headroom rubber mask and whistling in soft amazement. "Wasn't there some sort of pirate takeover of one of the Chicago stations in the late '80s?"

"Two stations. Signal hijack," Walt said. "They say it was just some punk kids with a powerful transmitter and line of sight to their broadcast antennae on the Sears Tower, but some sources say the same intrusion happened to a station in Los Angeles, but that was quashed because it didn't fit the story."

"Is anyone else worried that they clearly have a setup here to mimic some sort of presidential address?" Jessie asked.

"Wizards behind the curtain gotta stay behind the curtain, right?" Carla offered. "This whole place just gives me the creeps."

"Agreed," Alton said. But he stepped carefully through the untouched dust in the mostly empty trapezoidal set to check out the scrap of paper. "This looks like a tear sheet." He turned it over in his hands. "You know, from the old teletypes?"

"Anything on it?" Jessie asked, but didn't approach. The whole thing had a goose-bump sense to it, like they were rubberneckers at a crash site.

Alton read:

*This is in order that you may share in the great awakening, as the planet passes into the New Age of Aquarius. The New Age can be a time of great peace and evolution for your race, but only if your rulers are made aware of the evil forces that can overshadow their judgments. Be still now and listen, for your chance may not come again.*

"I'm so tired of saying it, but what the fucking shit?" Toby said.

"It's familiar," Walt admitted. "I've heard that before."

"Me too," Jessie nodded, but she couldn't place it either.

"*War of the Worlds*?" Alton suggested.

"Absolutely not," Toby said. "I'd know it by heart if it was."

"Let's just get out of here," Carla suggested. "I don't like it at all. Bad juju."

"Wait," Walt interjected, and pulled something out of his pack. "The tape. I bet there's equipment here where we can finally play the videotape."

"Fuck," Toby said. Jessie saw him scratching at his ear like he always did in moments of stress. "Even if there's something on that tape, we already have it. Let's just keep moving and then watch it when we get back. Hell, I've got six VCRs and a Betamax in cherry shape back at our apartment."

"He really does have all that equipment," Jessie confirmed,

deadpan. "It's what we have instead of a guest room."

"Says the person who doesn't want her mom to visit," Toby said, and Jessie felt her neck get hot. Carla shot her a look.

"Look, it's right over here," Walt said, heading for a wall of A/V dotted with monitors. "Videotape is, as media goes, pretty fragile. We play it, we watch it, I get it recorded on digital, and we get back to getting the hell out of here."

"Sounds logical to me," Alton said.

"Same," Jessie nodded.

"Let's do it," Carla agreed.

Toby shook his head and let out a low growl. "Fine," he said.

Jessie didn't know what Toby's reluctance to watch the video might be—she assumed it was something as simple as sheer exhaustion, or maybe he was irritable because they hadn't run into a facility bathroom in a bit. Anything was possible with him, which was a thought that was simultaneously both annoying and comforting to her. He hadn't changed in the near decade she'd known him. He was maybe the only constant in her life. She watched him roll an office chair from behind a desk at the front of the studio and plop into it with his arms crossed like a pouting toddler.

It didn't take long for Walt to figure out the equipment and find what he needed—the old tech made him whistle a happy little tune as he worked. He watched the monitors above to see which one was connected to the system he was fiddling with, and one finally popped into grainy black-and-white fuzz. "There it is," he said. "Everyone ready?"

The rest of the crew nodded. No one knew what to expect.

"Here we go," Walt whispered with some reverence, and the screen blipped from fuzzy static to video lines to clear picture, all reflected in the wonder-filled eyes behind his plastic glasses.

---

"If you're watching this . . ." the man on-screen began, but then stopped himself. "Actually, I have no insight into how exactly you'd be watching this, or in what context. So that probably wasn't the best place for me to start, was it?" He walked halfway toward the camera, thought better of it, turned around, thought better of it again, turned around with a frustrated shake of his head, and returned to where he was standing against what looked like the wood-paneled wall of the Bwana Hut.

"Walt, you related to this guy?" Carla teased. Alton laughed a bit, and Jessie smiled.

Walt shushed her, shaking his head impatiently.

"Sor-ry," Carla murmured, rolling her eyes, but there was still laughter in them.

"Okay," the man on the screen began again. "Maybe I'll edit that out. If I can figure out how to edit video, and if this camera . . ." He steeled himself. "I'm offtrack again. I'm sorry. I'm nervous. I don't know how much time I have. My name is Roger Zelliger, and this is my confession."

Roger was dressed in what used to be a lab coat—the same kind, Carla confirmed, that Bill the Science Guy wore, only Bill's had been in much better shape. Roger's coat was so ragged and filthy that there were only a few spots where the fabric still looked white. The bottom hem was gone, and frayed fabric hang between the waist and knees. It was unclear what pants he was wearing, if any at all, as his legs were armored in thin strips of wood bound together in some sort of twine. He had no shirt on under his coat, and wore a thick autoclave glove on his left hand, which he kept folded against his chest when he stood. He swayed a bit, but whether that was from agitation or dizziness was unclear. He had horn-rimmed glasses, a receding hairline of still-dark follicles, and a brown beard that looked like he cut it with a knife. When he spoke, whiskers from his too-long mustache would get caught in his mouth, and pop out the next time it opened. He looked half crazed, and half despondent. But his voice was strong—clipped, and obviously emotional, but strong.

"Some quick biological information, just so anyone who finds this can verify that I am who I claim to be. Again, I am Roger Zelliger, born in Ypsilanti, Michigan, to Doris and Don Zelliger in 1984. I studied at the University of Arizona—Bear Down, right?—and later married a woman named Cait who I didn't treat well enough. I worked too hard at Aviation Dynamics, and she left with the three children I didn't get to know. Not because she went away, but because I did. Losing her made me give up on everything. I went away. I went away because it was all too hard. That's on me. I signed on with the Collective because it promised another life, far away, but I didn't really know what I was in for. That's their plan, though, you know? The not-knowing. How many of us would have signed up if we knew exactly what we were signing up for? That's the real question you have to ask yourselves, whoever you are hearing this. Some of us undoubtedly would have enlisted with a . . . with a violent glee, the crazy and the mean and the angry among us. And there are certainly those in our numbers. But there are far more of us who are as much victims as the things upon which we experiment, as the people I see in various stages of distress, as the unfortunates I know who live lives of peril and fear in these tunnels, lost to even their captors, lost to the world. I'm not blameless. None of us are. But I'm not a villain, either, and I lived my life, especially at the end, trying to prove that.

"So as confessions go, this one will be slight," Roger continued, "because I don't honestly know what crimes I've committed, or have been committed in my name. I know that the people I work for—the Collective—have done some things, perhaps many things, with which I strongly disagree.

"And to be clear: I'm not alone in this position. Many others—I'd venture to say most others that I've met and spoken with—feel some measure of that same trepidation. Melissa did. Sweet, sweet Melissa, who's on her way now to bring me back in order to make a plan to leave this place, these jobs, this Collective, and try to start new and build a life that forgets any and all of this."

Roger took a long breath and his face suddenly looked sad and resigned. "Either that," he said, almost forcing the words out, "or she's coming to kill me. With a squad of soldiers of some sort, I'd imagine. But I hope it's the former, for many reasons. I've chosen to trust her when she says that she's ready to leave. With me. I gave her directions for the safe path through the Wetlands Overflow, so my fate is in her hands.

"As it should be." He cleared his throat and corrected his posture. "She and I love each other. We've been together for almost a year . . . or were, before I felt I had to leave. I did abandon my post. I can't say I regret doing that, after hearing what I did."

Roger went on to explain how he'd heard the *Escaping Denver* podcast. He'd been assigned to pick up sensitive scientific materials from a topside agent—he was under orders not to physically leave the convoy, and he didn't. But one of the topside soldiers accompanying him had in his possession an old iPod he'd gotten from a violent Suppressive, which was the term some soldiers used for enemies of the Collective. Roger had idly expressed some jealousy that he had it; such things were considered contraband inside the complex.

"That was the turning point, my poetic volta, as it were," Roger said. "The soldier offered it to me as a gesture of goodwill, a small gift from one to another, a simple human gesture of kindness between two people working for a woefully unkind agency. The iPod was a veritable trove of information—new music with which I was able to woo Melissa, a few episodes of

*Wait, Wait . . . Don't Tell Me!* from NPR; and the first full season of something called *Escaping Denver.* I was so enraptured with the other audio treasures on the device that I admit I didn't listen to the podcast until I'd been back almost a month. And then, during my weekly thirty-six-hour downtime, I listened to it all.

"Well, after that, I realized I was in the wrong place. I told Melissa that, and she listened to the podcast too. Once she did, she agreed. It wore on me more than it did on her—she was able to compartmentalize things better than me. I couldn't focus on my work anymore and couldn't abide where I was or what I was helping to do. Oh, I'd always known something was off. Known there was something larger looming over what we were doing that probably wasn't moral . . . but is it different than, say, working for a defense contractor for a decade or more? I mean, it is, and it isn't, you know? Anyway . . . these were the questions that plagued me. That still do.

"My colleagues got annoyed with me for talking about it. Melissa asked me to stop . . . begged really. Said I was putting myself in danger, and I probably was, but I increasingly did not care. I became a little obsessed with this person the podcast called Tunnel Tarzan—it sounded very much like a legend of our own down here, this figure who slips in and out of the shadows, almost a guerilla-like force in the hallways, always one step ahead of us. Or rather, the soldiers hunting him. It was all my talk of Tunnel Tarzan that earned me the nickname Bwana. Like the old movies. It was meant to be cruel, I suppose, but when Melissa used it, she meant it very differently. With love, I believe. Even when it waned in use among my colleagues, she and I still used it. A term of endearment. It's why I put it above my door. As a message to her that it was me, and this was where she could find me if she came looking.

"Because yes, I did leave. One day, I reached my end," Roger said simply. "It was a dog, of all things. You know the old line about movies being able to kill entire platoons of human beings quite casually, and no one cares, but kick a dog, and everyone falls apart? That was me, falling apart. I stole the dog and left. Just walked out. Had I known I'd do it, I would have prepared better, but I didn't. It just happened, like I was outside myself looking in on someone else doing these curious things. The dog was a Labrador retriever, yellow and rather fat. I wondered where he'd come from. We were supposed to be doing experiments on him to discover new attributes of the chupacabra, but—"

"Pause it," Jessie said, and Walt did, after a second's delay. He, like the rest of the group, had been enraptured. "That's the first outside confirmation that we're dealing with chupacabras, isn't it? Someone on the inside calling them that?"

"None of the soldiers called them that in the podcast recordings?" Toby asked.

Jessie looked over at Alton, and then to Carla and Walt. None of them had an answer. "Okay," Jessie finally responded. "Something to check later, I guess. Sorry to interrupt the filming, Walt."

"S'okay," Walt said chummily, still holding his phone camera at the screen with one hand, and fumbling for the Play button with the other.

The video resumed with a flicker. ". . . I couldn't bear it anymore. Rats and rabbits are one thing. And this was by no means the first dog we'd worked on either. But this time . . . I don't know. I named him Baldr, after the Norse god of light and joy and forgiveness. We needed all of that down here. And off we went. I thought—stupidly, I now realize—that I could find my way out. I greatly underestimated the size of this place. They kept us very much and very literally in the dark when they moved us around, inside windowless panel trucks."

Roger paused and shook his head. "These sound like excuses. I assure you, they're not meant to be. I ran, not knowing where I could run to, and when I realized my error, it was too late. My name had been added to the deserter list, and by then I was being hunted. I found the Wetlands Overflow, which seemed as safe a place as any. Untraveled for the most part, which was good. Inhabited by beasts, which was not good. But I learned to adapt. I girded my legs to protect myself from the death worms, the giant centipedes, and the five-lined constellation fish that can survive in the shallow freshwater pools and can paralyze with a single bite. I built a hut from salvaged materials from decommissioned offices and residential bunkrooms. I made a home for myself and for Baldr. We fed on those paralytic fish once I learned how to weave baskets to trap them and cut around their venom sacs to find the edible meat. They were tasty when cooked with the wild mushrooms in that same area. Occasionally, Baldr would bring a rabbit—even a jackalope, once, though who knows where he got that—and we'd cook those and eat them together. It was a life, and I had thoughts of finding that Tunnel Tarzan person and finding out his story, maybe offering him my help or accepting help from him. But it wasn't meant to be. I don't know how long I was down here—Melissa seemed to suggest in her notes it had been months—but she was doing her work to get me back in the good graces of our superiors in the Collective. Finally, she thought she had. She told me so. I hesitated, because I didn't want to go back, didn't want to think about what might happen to Baldr if I did. And, I had to admit, I had some doubt about what Melissa was able to arrange, and how. It seemed unlikely, but I'd already proven quite effectively that my instincts have always been flawed.

"It was the loss of Baldr that finally made me take the chance. He left one morning as he always did, to perimeter the wetlands and hunt, I suppose. Looking back, maybe I shouldn't have let him do that, but he'd always seemed so capable. But that morning, he went out and never came back. I waited for days before finally admitting to myself that something had gotten him. I checked all the traps I'd set, but he hadn't fallen prey to those. I carefully made forays out in several directions, but nothing. I'm no tracker, and there are no paw prints in stagnant water. I finally made my way into the hallways again, found a phone, and called Melissa. Said I would come back to her. She seemed happy, she really did, but I don't know. This place sows mistrust. I'm ruined, I know. We all are. But what choice do we have but to keep going?

"So back I go. But before I do, I leave you with this—my sad, insipid little story. I hope it helps someone, somewhere. I hope I live to see it have some benefit. It is, at least, some mark that I am more than the Collective scientist I became. I'm not sure what else I can say. I feel like there's so much more, but I don't have the words, and I believe very strongly that in one way or another, I'm out of time. Please pass along to Cait Zelliger and our children that I loved them, even if I didn't know how to show it. Ask them to forgive me. Or if not forgive, then to think of me with some softness, and to know that I thought of them with great love and even bigger regret."

He took a deep breath. "I hope Melissa isn't lying to me. I hope they aren't lying to Melissa. I'm a loose end, I know, and loose ends either get sewn back in the fabric or cut off and forgotten. I go now to find out which."

Roger approached the camera and disappeared to the right of the lens, muttering something about not being very skilled at goodbyes, and then said, "You didn't even say the word goodbye, Roger, you cowardly—" Then the video blipped back to a black screen, and then to the haunting buzz of video snow.

which threatens your world, and the beings on our worlds around you. This is i[illegible] that you may share in the great awakening, as the planet passes into th[illegible] New Age of Aquarius. The New Age can be a time of great peace and evolu[illegible]ion for your race, but only if your rulers are made aware of the evil forces [illegible] that can overshadow their judgments. Be still now and list[illegible]en, for your chance may not come again. All your weapons of evil must be

# CHAPTER FOURTEEN

TRANSMISSION STUDIO T-16

"Thanks for that uplifting moment of zen," Toby said, rocking back and forth in his office chair.

Walt didn't say anything in response, but turned his phone's camera lens over to where Toby was reclining.

"What are you doing?" Toby asked.

"Filming an asshole," Walt said, and clicked his phone to stop the recording. "Guy pours his heart out like that, and all you can offer is a smart remark . . . ? I'd like to think you're better than that, son."

"He is," Jessie countered, but shot Toby yet another look of warning. Yes, he could be an ass, but his heart was always in the right place. It was just the stress of this—an adventure he hadn't signed up for—that was torquing him off a little, she thought. And she felt bad about that—she was the reason he was here, after all.

"That was a *lot*," Carla said, drawing a deep breath.

"Also the best and most clear evidence we have of what's

going on down here," Alton added. "Good job bringing that tape with you, Walt. I wouldn't have thought to do it."

"I'm just glad it was worth it," Walt said, basking a little in the compliment.

"Makes you wonder what happened to Roger, though," Toby said, a little more softly.

*There you are,* Jessie thought. *That's the Tobes I know.*

"Think he made it?" Walt asked.

"I don't know," Jessie responded, "but whatever happened to him, I'm betting it wasn't good. His options were to be reabsorbed into a despotic agency of world domination or to walk right into some sort of punitive ambush, maybe run by 'sweet, sweet Melissa,' you know? And the Collective doesn't strike me as a forgive-and-forget sort of organization."

"Not buying that Melissa ironed out the wrinkles with their bosses?" Alton murmured.

"Not buying the idea that Roger's level of wrinkle is something someone comes back from," Jessie said. "But we're all just guessing. Anyway, I don't think he thought he was going to survive either way. This wasn't a confession so much as it was his farewell."

"And sort of an *I'm sorry,*" Toby suggested. "I mean, in his situation, he probably felt like he had no choices left. But that doesn't mean he doesn't regret the damage he might have caused."

"I suppose," Jessie said. "It's a good reminder for us, especially since we're now armed and ready to kill in order to defend ourselves."

"Again," Alton corrected her. "Ready to kill *again.*"

"Sorry, handsome," Carla said, patting Alton on his Smurfy chest and leaving her hand there just a bit too long. "This is war, and not one we volunteered for. People shoot at us. We have the right to shoot back first."

"That literally makes no sense," Alton shook his head.

"You know what I mean," Carla said.

"Before you go on casting aspersions on our characters," Toby interjected, "maybe you'd like to go into a little more detail on your backstory with the Collective, Doctor Perfect Teeth?"

"I'd like to know that too," Carla jumped in. Seeing the look on Alton's face—sort of a tired frown—she added, "Not because I don't trust you. Just because we have some questions."

"It makes sense," Jessie said, shrugging an apology. "That we have a right to know, I mean."

"I've told you everything I know about the Collective," Alton insisted. "I don't know what else to offer, but if you have questions . . . I'll answer them in the best way I can. But you have to accept that my answer—my honest answer—will sometimes be that I don't know."

"Okay, Doc," Walt said. "I have one. How is it that a twentysomething physician like yourself would know anything about old teletypes . . . let alone what their tear sheets might look like?"

"You too, Walt?" Alton grimaced.

"Hey, I'm just asking." Walt put up his hands. "Could be anything, right? Could be you got it from TV, *WKRP in Cincinnati* or *Lou Grant* or something. Could be your dad was in the broadcasting biz—I mean, if you take after him, he had a face made for television, right?"

"You give me too much credit," Alton said. "I can't even tell you why I know about tear sheets. Just something I picked up somewhere, I guess. Do you know the specific source of everything you know?"

"I have a general idea," Walt replied quickly.

"Then you're a remarkable man," Alton said. "Me, I'm

someone who went through a bunch of stuff and ended up going to medical school to take some control of his life."

"That's why you became a doctor?" Jessie asked.

"One of the reasons, I guess," Alton smiled. "A guy's gotta be able to buy eggs, right? And sure, I wanted to help humanity. I wanted to add something to the world instead of taking away." He rubbed at his injured shoulder, which was no longer popping when he moved it. If it was a purposeful reminder that he'd taken bullets for them, Jessie had to admit, he sold it well. "But you're also asking the wrong questions of the wrong person," Alton finally added. "I'm not the mole, if there even is one."

"You calling me a liar?" Carla bristled.

"No," Alton said with a smooth calm. "I'm saying maybe the Collective guy you heard that from might have been."

"Could be," Toby agreed. "Or maybe it was a rumor, something unfounded but had legs anyway? Maybe there's no mole at all. Maybe we're worrying over nothing."

But Jessie shook her head. "Doesn't make sense that a claim like that would come from nowhere," she scowled. "And if it doesn't make sense, it probably isn't true."

"Well, *that's* bullshit," Toby said. "It's like the old Sherlock line: *When you have eliminated all which is impossible, then whatever remains, however improbable, must be the truth.* I mean, look at you. You're all here because you believe in the unlikely. Or at least like Fox Mulder, you want to believe."

"I don't *want* to believe at all," Alton said. "That's the opposite of the scientific method. I want to prove what *is*. I want to discover answers. I don't want to have my suspicions authenticated. This isn't confirmation bias. This is me, as an individual just trying to live my life, attempting to get answers to questions I don't even know to ask yet. I promise you all: I'm a victim of this place, just like the rest of you. All but possibly one, anyway."

"This is getting us nowhere," Toby said, after a long pause.

"We've just got to get out of here, is all," Walt said. "We have some of what we came for. Information. Enough to keep the conversation going. Enough to answer a few things, and pose a lot more questions."

"Is that enough?" Carla asked.

"It might have to be," Walt argued.

"We can't win the day by lowering our expectations," Alton said. "What do we have? More evidence of weirdness. The final video diary entry of a former scientist who could well have been half crazy."

"Tell that to Jace," Toby muttered.

"You didn't even know Jace," Alton snapped. "Stop acting like he was your best friend."

"You're right," Toby said, standing up and getting into Alton's face. Alton was a head taller, but Toby still bellied up. "This is my best friend," he snarled, pointing at Jessie, "and every time I think of what happened to Jace, I think that it just as easily could have happened to her. This isn't about Jace, or Otomi, or any of you. It's about me getting Jessie out of here and delivered home safely. That's it."

"That's enough," Walt interrupted, putting his hand between Toby and Alton to physically separate them, and managed to do it, if only by inches. "We're all on edge. We can't turn on each other. That's what they want us to do."

"Absolutely," Jessie said. "That's why I think we have a new goal now. We need answers before we get out. And we know who might be able to help us."

"The Archivist?" Carla asked excitedly.

"The Archivist," Jessie confirmed.

"Perfect," Alton said.

"Now we just have to find him," Walt admitted.

"Oh goodie," Toby snarled, flopping back into the office chair and rolling backward a few feet. "Another adventure."

---

They knew the Archivist from the podcast, as much as there was to know. He was a mysterious figure even amongst all the other mysteries of this place—oddly neutral, despite working for the Collective as the keeper of artifacts and relics. He'd been of some help, but his nature and his alignment were still inscrutable. But of one thing there was no doubt: he was a font of information. A resource that could be tapped.

"The sphinx guarding the path ahead if only you solve their riddle," Toby translated. "I get it, I get it. Makes as much sense as anything else down here. So where do we find this guy?"

"That's the question," Alton remarked. They used the space in the transmission studio to compare notes, recalling as much from the podcast as they could, combining that with what Carla had discovered in her wandering through the complex, and what Bill had spilled while he was with her.

They managed to piece together a sort of map of possibility to lead them in what they thought might be the right direction, and set off. They walked for hours, sometimes recognizing that they were going in circles, or at least suspecting that they were. In the end, they found what they were looking for through sheer luck.

They'd come across a large hangar room off one of the main hallways; there was a plaque on the wall outside the door upon which someone had inscribed the words *We all go down together.*

"That seems . . . surprisingly sentimental, doesn't it?" Walt asked.

"Might be something the Archivist would do," Alton volunteered. "He doesn't strike me as an emotional individual, but he's certainly demonstrated a level of respect for antiquities."

Inside the darkened hangar were five single-prop bombers, World War II–era planes, their silvery metal still gleaming under a thick layer of dust, forty feet in length with a fifty-plus foot wingspan. They sat in a staggered row up on their two underwing wheel struts, high enough off the floor that access seemed impossible. There were no rolling ladders anywhere that might have allowed them to peer through the dark cockpit glass.

"Flight 19," Walt said, his voice low out of both respect and awe. He walked up under the plane closest to the door and touched the landing gear like it might break if he handled it too roughly.

"Is that the one that disappeared in the Bermuda Triangle?" Toby asked.

Walt nodded. "December 5, 1945. Routine training mission that departed from Naval Air Station Fort Lauderdale. They were supposed to conduct bombing runs at Hens and Chickens Shoals, turn north, then proceed over Grand Bahama before returning home."

"But they didn't," Carla said.

"No," Walt confirmed. "Fourteen men disappeared in five bombers. These five, apparently."

"Think they're still in there?" Toby asked. "Like . . . skeletons in bomber jackets and hats and whatnot?"

"That's a morbid thought," Alton said.

"What's on that plaque out there were the last known words of Lieutenant Charles Taylor," Walt murmured. "The flight leader. *When the first plane drops below ten gallons, we all go down together*, he said. And that was it." He was taking photos from all sides, looking for serial numbers or any other details on the underbelly and the bottom of the wings.

"And now they're here," Jessie marveled. "But where's here?"

"Bay 94," Carla said, and shone her flashlight over to a small cube of an office nestled in the hangar's corner nearest the door. Sure enough, that's what was stenciled in the glass inset in the small office door. Most of the group went over to check it out, but Walt was still recording the details on the aircraft.

Jessie tried the office door, but it was locked. "Everybody stand back," she instructed, and reversed her heavy flashlight to use the base as a club to smack the glass. The flashlight bounced off harmlessly.

"Let me try that," Toby said, taking the flashlight from Jessie—but his blow had just as little effect.

"Get outta the way," Carla smirked, and smashed her own flashlight's butt into the glass. The impact was louder than the first two hits, but did no more damage. "That's some serious fucking bulletproof glass," she acknowledged.

"Can we pick the lock?" Toby asked.

"It's a card reader," Jessie said. They tried the one Carla had taken from the scientist, but that didn't work either.

Alton peered through the one window to the right of the door, having determined that the glass there was of the same sturdy type. "Well," he said, "there's your bomber jacket and hat, Toby. But no skeletons."

Toby shone his light through the glass and got up so close that he was fogging it. But there it was—on a little display mannequin off to one side was not only a leather jacket and a World War II pilot hat, but a full uniform under it. There were other ephemera on a small shelf, including a C ration pack from the 1940s, some navigational charts, a small hula girl that bobbled at her straw-skirted waist, and something marked Evasion Purse.

Alton was recording as much as he could through the glass. "Look at the desk. Is that a map?"

"Oh shit," Carla said with glee. "It is. That's us, right there, marked 94. What is that mapping back to?"

"The Archives?" Jessie guessed. "The main archives, anyway?"

"Why would the Archivist need a map?" Toby asked.

"He wouldn't," Jessie answered. "But maybe the hired help would, if they needed to bring this stuff back at some point?"

"Could be," Alton said.

"It's a path, at least," Jessie said.

With that, the hangar itself lit up with a flashing red light, followed by an alarm, a squealing siren that resounded throughout the huge room, the sound bouncing off the walls and seeming to magnify with each passing second. On the other side of the room, deep in the formerly invisible recesses of the space, a huge docking door started to open, and soldiers came pouring in like ants escaping a hill flooded with boiling water.

"Run!" Alton shouted, grabbing a fire extinguisher off the nearest wall.

No one had to be told twice. They bolted for the door through which they'd originally come, with Walt taking pictures on his phone as he ran backward, almost tripping, and then recovering and putting the phone away. "Move, move!" Jessie ordered, and held the door for them as she watched Alton carry the heavy extinguisher over to the plane closest to the front doors and start to bash it into the underwing strut supports.

Alton struck at it several times, and finally, the landing strut buckled and snapped under the tonnage of the plane itself, and it lurched as he dropped the battered extinguisher canister and made a beeline for the door. The ancient plane toppled over, its body crashing against the doorframe just as Alton leaped through it to safety.

Jessie wondered if she'd just seen a show of massive strength or just effective knowledge of a construct's weakest point. She wasn't sure, but she knew she didn't have time to consider it, based on the yelling they all heard right on the other side of the now-blocked door. The soldiers were clearly trying to move the plane. It shifted slightly—just enough to make them all start running again.

—

"This way!" Toby cried, his voice tinged with sheer terror. "The map showed this way!"

"Escaping these soldiers is probably our top priority right now," Jessie huffed, momentarily wishing she was one of the two in the group with a gun.

They'd gotten out of the hangar, but in the process had destroyed an antique World War II bomber in the process. But they didn't have time to dwell on such things as history, Jessie reminded herself, even as she knew that wasn't a sentiment that the Archivist would share.

And the Archivist was still their goal, at least for right now. They'd stumbled onto a fairly good lead, and Toby seemed to remember the seen-from-a-distance map well enough to guide them. At least that's what she hoped he was doing. The last thing they needed was to run smack into another monster, another squad of soldiers, or a trap set by a well-meaning scientist with deep regrets about his life choices.

They took a right, Toby still in the lead, but Jessie's brain was working just as fast as her feet, if not faster. She was supposed to believe that her mother was the big bad? The final boss of this twisted little game? The woman wasn't nice, but she wasn't evil—at least not world-conquering evil. And what was that supposed to mean about Jessie, then? That she was a bad seed, the offspring of the villain of the narrative? To what end? What did that signify, and what in the hell was she supposed to do about that if it was true?

Jessie didn't know, but wondered how Carla was taking all of this. If Carla was even really Carla—they hadn't had time to really delve into her story. Carla seemed like the same person Jessie had come to know online for the past several months. And she seemed to have a good heart, too—she'd demonstrated that pretty consistently. She'd only found them because of that good heart, because she went looking for them.

They continued to run straight ahead as Jessie's mind turned.

And Alton—they hadn't gotten enough of his story either. There was something he was holding back for sure, but Jessie considered that was true for all of them, and not always purposefully. Innocently, too—just like she and Carla weren't saying anything about Jessie's supposed origin. It was all too complicated.

Walt seemed too much a mensch to even have secrets, though that in itself would be cause for suspicion for some. But again, Jessie trusted him, just like she trusted Toby after years of knowing him, relying on him. If she could believe in Walt like she believed in her best friend for nearly a decade? That said something.

They took a right, and then a quick jog to the left. They were passing doors and hallway intersections—Toby still seemed to know where he was going. Carla kept looking behind them, her gun at the ready, but didn't seem to see anything. Even the shouts and occasional gunfire—out of frustration, maybe, not being able to get past the fallen fuselage of the bomber?—had subsided, fallen out of earshot.

Jessie took a breath and set her mind to keeping up the pace. They ran for what seemed like an impossible amount of time, Toby in the lead more or less for the entire trip. Finally, he slowed down, and looked left down a hallway—at the end was a simple-looking door, cracked open just enough to see a sliver of light coming from whatever was beyond it.

Toby put his hands on his knees and tried to catch his breath. "I think that's it," he puffed. Jessie wasn't surprised he was spent. That was probably more running than Toby had done in the previous decade. But he was up for it when it counted, she thought. "Good job, Tobes," she said, patting him on his sweat-soaked back.

"No kidding," Alton said admiringly. "I'm impressed you were able to memorize that layout as quickly as you did."

"Years of . . . D&D mapping," Toby grinned with halting breaths, ". . . and video game maneuvering. Knew . . . it would pay off . . . someday."

They took a communal beat, with Carla peering back the way they'd come, around the corner. She didn't seem to see anything, and nothing could be heard from down the hall. "Anyone else feel the hairs on the back of their necks standing up?" Carla said. "First, we get away clean, and now the door we're looking for is already open a crack? No one else finds this weird?"

"No weirder than anything else in here," Jessie said. "And that may not even be the room we're looking for."

"That's definitely the room we want," Toby said, finally getting his wind back. "The Archivist. I'm itching to see what he's got in there. It's like I'm about to go into the cornfield."

"Like in *The Twilight Zone*?" Walt looked confused. "Why would you want to do that?"

"No, like in *Field of Dreams*," Toby said.

"What about *Children of the Corn*?" Carla grinned. "Wanna meet He Who Walks Behind the Rows, Toby?"

"Okay, okay," Toby said. "Maybe the cornfield metaphor wasn't specific enough. Noted, you nerds."

"Who's nerdier?" asked Walt. "The nerd, or the nerds who follow him?"

"All right," Jessie said. "What are we waiting for?"

"For them to stop talking," Alton murmured, and walked down the hall. Everyone fell in behind him.

Alton pushed open the door, which made an ominous creak. It was the Archives, but it was immediately clear that something terrible had happened. Papers were flung everywhere. A desk centered in the stacks of shelving faced the door, but had been swept clean, the grand leather chair behind it cast to its side on the floor behind. The shelves themselves looked rifled through, though some objects had managed to survive—on a high shelf to the left was a glass box, still intact, with an egg perched inside showing a gleaming chicken cast in gold and encrusted with rose diamonds, removing a sapphire egg from a gilded nest. Below that, sitting alone on a shelf as though it were a box of cereal at a grocery store, was a brilliant-looking crown made of thick gold, with a full skullcap and floral adornments on each palisade spike—perhaps Llywelyn's lost coronet. And on the other side, similarly still encased in a protective case was an irregularly-shaped skull of some sort, mottled in bone white and the yellow ochre color of time and degradation. Whether the skull was of alien origin or the lost Peking Man, Jessie didn't know. Either way, she was impressed.

There were other things that had survived as well; on the wall to the left of the door through which they'd entered was what looked like the lower left panel from the *Ghent Altarpiece*, showing robed judges on horseback. On the opposite side of the door was a wide case clearly meant to hold weapons. The glass was shattered, and most of the mounts within stood empty, though many, if not all of them, showed signs of something once being held there. All that was left in the wall-length case were two objects: one a gilded rod of some sort, possibly a scepter, or a baton. Whatever it was, the object was enameled and ornamented with filigree, topped with a small statue of some sort of great bird—maybe an eagle—being ridden by a young man. The other was a gleaming katana which Jessie recognized as the missing Honjo Masamune, perhaps one of the greatest swords ever made by one of the world's greatest swordsmiths.

Jessie was stunned for a moment by what she saw, both the mess and the amazing stuff left behind from whatever had happened. She was pleased to see Walt already taking photos and narrating video of what they were seeing. He'd apparently decided that the crown was indeed the missing Welsh artifact, and was getting as close as he could to it, recording from all angles. Jessie was sure there were countless other artifacts deep in the recesses of this astounding repository, and she wished they had the necessary amount of time it would take to catalog it all.

"I know this is nuts, you guys," Jessie warned. "But come back down to earth for a minute. Something bad happened here. The Archivist is clearly gone, at least temporarily, because he'd never allow this sort of chaos in his space, you know?" She looked down at the floor and could see pieces of glass shattered throughout the scattered papers, file folders, and general debris. "I mean, who knows what we're walking on here."

"She's right," Alton said. "I want to examine all this stuff myself, but . . . something's not right." He picked up a scrap of what looked to be parchment. "This is Sanskrit. I think it's a fragment of the original *Panchatantra*."

"Geez, I hope not," Walt said, coming over and taking a few photos. "You read Sanskrit?"

"A bit," Alton conceded, and put the piece of parchment gently on the desk. "But Jessie's right. We have to get out of here."

"Agreed," Carla said. Jessie considered her to be the least in awe of the place. Perhaps she wasn't as much a student of history as some of them? Or maybe she was more practical, and nervous about what might be coming down the hallway after them.

They were just turning to leave when they heard a *psst* coming from the darkness back in the stacks to their right. Then a bald head popped from around a far shelf, and then a hand motioned them back.

"C'mon," Jessie said, and everyone followed her back to where the man was hiding.

He was tall, built like a professional athlete under his ruddy robes, with a shaved head that looked as though it had never held hair. His heavy-lidded eyes didn't seem to blink. "You've been busy," he said in a sonorous voice—one that was calm and out of sync with the chaos of the room—as they approached.

"Are you the Archivist?" Jessie asked, though even as she asked, she felt it was a dumb question. The man gave a single, solemn nod. "What happened here? Can we help somehow?" She wasn't sure what they could do, but it seemed like the thing to say.

"To answer your questions in order," the Archivist replied, "yes, I am the Archivist. The answer to your second question is indeterminate, as it has several possible answers. And to your third, no. But it's customary for me to thank you for the gesture."

"What are you doing here?" Alton asked. His look was dark, perhaps suspicious, Jessie thought. Which in itself was sort of odd—Alton hadn't seemed dubious of the Archivist before meeting him.

The Archivist smiled slightly. "I could ask you the same,

*physician.*" He drew out the word into what approached a sneer. "Fascinating. You're all a pleasant and, in some ways, unexpected surprise. I'm not often able to say such things."

"What happened to this place?" Walt said, repeating Jessie's question. "Were you attacked or something? Was anything taken?"

"Nothing that happens here is accidental," the Archivist responded. "Nothing here escapes my notice." His eyes flicked toward Jessie. "I see you carry with you a Pelican case strapped to your back, Ms. Boyer," the Archivist said in too-even tones. "Might I ask what that's for?"

Jessie paused, but then decided there was no harm in answering. "Our memory cards. We switch them out of our devices, so we can safeguard the information we've found and recorded."

"Wise," the Archivist said. "But why the special container? And why are *you* the one to carry it?"

"I . . ." Jessie paused again. She felt somehow on the defensive, but she couldn't put her finger on exactly why. "I carry it because I bought the case, and I lined it specially with lead so it wouldn't be as susceptible to erasure. We didn't know what to expect down here."

"Foresight," the Archivist noted. "Expected, but still impressive. And you carry it because it's your burden to do so. Also appropriate."

"What does that mean?" Jessie scowled.

"Meaning, to you, is subjective," the Archivist stated. "Colored by imprecise emotion and impertinent detail. If I were to pause and attempt to explain what I mean, it would be a waste of our time, both yours and mine."

"How about you explain to me, then?" Alton challenged him.

"What, I'm not smart enough to get what he's saying?" Jessie snapped.

"That's not what I meant," Alton said, but didn't take his

eyes off the Archivist. "But I don't think this guy's going to be as helpful to us as he was on the podcast."

"You make presumptions about things you have yet to ask," the Archivist noted.

"So, what can you do to help us?" Walt asked.

"What is it that you want?" the Archivist asked.

"We all just want to get out of here with our lives," Jessie replied.

"Inaccurate," the Archivist stated.

"This is pointless," Toby groaned. "We've asked him what happened in this room several times, and he hasn't even explained that."

"What occurred here has no relationship to you or your true motivations in being here," the Archivist said, his voice suggesting impatience. "Satisfying curiosity isn't a need, it's a want. I'm here to provide you neither one, but certainly not the latter."

"What is it that you do for the Collective?" Jessie asked. She wanted to turn the conversation and put the Archivist on the defensive. She wasn't sure that was wise, actually, but her annoyance won over her worry. "I've always wondered, even from what you did in the podcast, and the way you're responding to us now only makes me question it more. What exactly is your role here?"

"You're looking for more than what my name makes clear," the Archivist said. "I have no more story to tell. I record. I watch. I do not interfere."

"Bullshit," Walt muttered.

"You are permitted to think so," the Archivist bowed slightly.

"You interfered on the podcast," Jessie said. "That's why we sought you out."

"My role here . . ." the Archivist paused, and seemed to be choosing his words more carefully. "Is impertinent to your purpose, and beyond your understanding. You don't even comprehend your own role, Ms. Boyer. And yet you demand me to define mine. You see a tiny fragment of reality, call it enough, and demand others ratify it. It's really quite remarkable. I look forward to recording it later."

"You like talking in circles, we get it," Alton said. "But the fact remains that you were helpful to the folks from the podcast. Why can't you do the same for us?"

"Again, the idea of 'helpful' is relative," the Archivist countered dispassionately. "And therefore, essentially meaningless. It's only in the looking back that we can truly judge what was and was not positive, relevant, influential, or as you so colloquially put it, *helpful*."

"This guy is a trip," Carla said.

"And not a good one," Walt amended.

"They're right," Toby said. "Why'd you even call us over here if you weren't going to actually say anything, you walking fortune cookie?"

"Because *they* were late," the Archivist said simply.

And that was when the group realized that they were surrounded. On all sides. By more soldiers—guns pointed and ready—than they could count.

# CHAPTER FIFTEEN

OUBLIETTE COMPLEX GAMMA

CELL B-23

"I think I peed myself a little," Toby said in a muffled voice from the other side of the wall that separated him from Jessie. "How many soldiers was that?"

"Dozens, at least," Jessie said dully. She was lying on a bed, in a cell exactly like those described by the podcast—but not the ones with bunks where the legs unscrewed into makeshift weapons. These were the serious no-fucking-around cells, apparently. Jessie felt her body relax, just a bit. Being able to lay down on a mattress, even one as thin as this one, was something of a benefit. It felt like forever since she'd been comfortable. "They pulled out all the stops for us, apparently."

"I guess you can only be a fly in the ointment for so long," Toby murmured, "before someone throws out all the fucking ointment."

Their voices carried remarkably well in here, Jessie thought, for being little more than concrete boxes. Even from her cot, she could also hear someone through the wall on the other side, but she didn't think it was anyone she knew. It was a man's voice, but it was broken, a shuddering thing that gasped and whispered madly. She couldn't make out a thing he was saying, and she was pretty sure that she didn't want to.

"You're living the real *Escaping Denver* dream here, Jess," Toby sighed. "I hope it was all fucking worth it. I really do."

"We just have to keep our heads together," Jessie said, realizing that she was, in part, just reassuring herself. "If there's one thing we learned from the podcast, it's that these cells are far from impenetrable. There's always a way out."

"Until there isn't," Toby said. "This isn't a video game. There's no preplanned exit point, some way that the game can continue, you know? Sometimes, the game is just over."

"Don't talk like that," Jessie warned.

"I just want you to face reality here," Toby insisted.

"And you know what's going on?" Jessie laughed despite herself. "That's rich. You haven't even listened to the podcast."

"You're right," Toby said. "But I've gleaned enough, both from you talking before we left our place for this insane trip, and what we've encountered ever since. This is a giant death trap, Jess, and we waltzed in here like it was some sort of crypto-zoological theme park. Like a dude wearing a Bigfoot costume was going to walk up and silently offer us a hug and a photo op. Like we could buy one of the Dead Sea Scrolls from the gift shop on the way out."

"Who's in the cell next to you?" Jessie asked. She was tired of arguing.

"What does it matter?" Toby replied dismissively.

"I'm taking stock of where we all are," Jessie explained. "So tell me who's next to you."

"No one, as far as I can tell," Toby said. "Is there someone on the other side of you?"

"Yeah," Jessie answered. "But I don't know him. It's not Walt or Alton. Whoever it is, I think he's sort of lost his mind. He's jabbering nonstop, but I can only make out a word here and there."

"What words are you making out?" Toby pressed.

"Nothing substantial," Jessie said. "And I might even be mishearing that, making his mumbles into something I want to hear."

"Like what?"

"A minute ago, he was repeating the same word over and over. *Symbols. Symbols. Symbols.*"

"SYMBOLS!" the man screamed suddenly, apparently having heard Jessie. But he quieted down immediately, returning to his constant stream of muttering.

Jessie listened to the low grumbles for a little while. "Why would they separate the group, but leave the two of us in adjoining cells?" Jessie wondered aloud. "It doesn't make sense."

"Maybe they don't care about us," Toby offered. "Maybe they're focusing on one of the others in the group. Like Alton. There's something about that dude that I can't quite suss out."

Jessie agreed, but didn't want to say it out loud. "I don't know, Tobes," she finally said. "I got a bad feeling about this."

"You're only getting that now?" Toby laughed softly.

"Does your bed leg unscrew?" Jessie asked.

"I'm sorry, what?"

"Check the leg of your bed," she said. "There are at least two types of bed frames the Collective uses in these cells. One has detachable legs so they can be used as clubs."

"What kind of weird-ass podcast talks about the differences in bed frames provided by a despotic world-dominating organization bent on terror and control?"

"Shut up and try to unscrew your bed," Jessie insisted.

"It's bolted," Toby said after a pause. "There, happy?"

"No," Jessie replied. "But thanks for checking."

Toby sighed. "How is it that I've known you for so long, and it took a podcast to bring out this tinfoil-hat side of you?"

"I don't know," Jessie admitted. "But haven't you ever thought to yourself that there's more to the world than we care to admit? That we're all stumbling around with these blinders on, choosing not to think about this or that? That the truth, as they say, is out there? Just waiting for someone to discover it, and change the way the world sees itself?"

"No," Toby admitted. "I want my mysteries to be small. Like whether or not Elvis is alive, or if Disney's head is cryogenically frozen and kept beneath the Haunted Mansion in California, or if David Bowie really predicted the rise of Kanye West."

"You lost me on that last one," Jessie moaned.

"Never mind. Google it if we ever get out of here," Toby said. "But my point is that the world's always been operating under an umbrella of ignorance. We live through it, we do our best, we find whatever joys we can, and we surround ourselves with people that make it all worthwhile. That's it. The actual nature of reality is just plainly too big for us to contemplate. And too much a headache to deal with too, especially since we can't do a damn thing about it."

Jessie took a deep breath. She could see what Toby was saying, but still . . . she decided to try another tack. Speak to Toby in a way he might better understand. "Okay, so you know how you love that old album by Arrested Development, the one with the title that I can't stand because it's too long?"

"*3 Years, 5 Months and 2 Days in the Life of* . . ." Toby said.

"Right, that one," Jessie said. "You've played that vinyl so often that I feel like I have it memorized."

"*Go ahead, Mr. Wendal,*" Toby half sang.

"Yeah, but not that song. 'Fishin' 4 Religion,'" she said. "Last song on Side A. There's this section that's always stuck with me. *What you pray for God will give / To be able to cope in this world we live / The word 'cope' and the word 'change' / Is directly opposite, not the same / She should have been praying to change her woes / But pastor said 'Pray to cope with those.'* He's talking about the importance of belief, but at the same time, about the damage caused by asking the wrong questions."

"Don't you throw the holy words of Speech at me, now," Toby laughed again.

"I'm serious, Tobes," Jessie said. "We have to be asking the right questions. That's what we're doing here. What *I'm* doing here. Figuring out the right questions."

They let the conversation drop for a bit, and silence fell around them both. Jessie was beyond tired, even if her eyes were wide open. She couldn't stop reliving their capture in her head, the feeling of the muzzle of a Kalashnikov in the small of her back, and another jammed against her neck. The way they were all led here through separate hallways, the way Carla yelled out when they realized they were being forced apart, and the sick thud that immediately followed. When Jessie was shoved into her cell, she didn't see Toby—he didn't arrive next door until sometime later, maybe more than an hour, presumably because of the paths the soldiers had to take to escort them individually. Toby had said they just kept him walking, blindfolded like the rest of them had been. The last thing Jessie recalled seeing before removing her blindfold in the cell in which she found herself was the placid face of the Archivist. If it was on any other face, Jessie would have thought he looked sad, distant, and resigned. But from the Archivist? It just seemed like disinterest.

"Toby?" Jessie said.

"Yeah?"

"I think I might sleep a little."

"Yeah."

"Think we'll wake up again?"

A pause. "I have no idea."

"Night, Tobes," Jessie said, choosing for the moment to imagine that she was back in her own bed, listening to the street noise outside the house and Toby's vinyl spinning out in the front room. Like it was any other night at their little rental house in Chicago.

---

Jessie woke to the sound of screaming. And not just any screaming. It was Carla.

"LET ME GO, YOU *HUELEBICHO PUTA*!" she shouted. Jessie could imagine her struggling mightily as a bunch of goons carried her down the hallway to God knew where.

"Carla!" Jessie cried out, but didn't know if her friend heard, because no response came as the sound of her struggling disappeared down the hallway. Then came more screaming, this time in sheer pain and panic, and Jessie was convinced that this, too, was Carla. Being tortured? For what? It went on for minutes that felt more like hours. In the end, Jessie wasn't certain if they'd stopped doing whatever they were doing to Carla, or if she'd finally, mercifully, passed out from the pain. At least Jessie hoped her friend's silence was just her losing consciousness.

"Toby!" Jessie whispered harshly. The way they'd been talking—almost casually, she chastened herself, as though they weren't prisoners with uncertain futures—was gone now, replaced by hushed, urgent tones. "*Toby!*"

No response. She didn't know what that meant, exactly, but it didn't fill her with confidence.

Over the next few hours, she heard the same thing happen

to Walt and Alton. Walt grunted as they took him down the hallway outside Jessie's cell, but wasn't as verbose as Carla had been. Still, his screams from whatever room they were using to torture them were gut-wrenching. He was calling out for his children. Apologizing to them.

And then, right on the heels of Walt, came Alton. He didn't make a sound as they passed, but it clearly took more soldiers to carry him. Maybe he was unconscious already. In some way, Jessie hoped so. That was probably the best-case scenario. She only knew it was Alton at all because she recognized the tone of his yells that came when they went to work on him. They were howls of a sort Jessie had never heard before. Almost like whale sounds, though nowhere near as soothing.

It took a while after they were done with Alton for them to finally bring out Toby. Jessie somehow knew it was him even before she had a chance to hear his voice. He was begging, the poor guy, begging for his life, to avoid the terrible pain he knew was coming.

"Please," Toby said plaintively. "Please, I don't know anything. I'm not even supposed to be here."

The muttering man in the cell next to Jessie's must have heard Toby too. It riled him for some reason, and the man screamed, "YOU ARE! OH, YOU ARE!" Then he seemed to collapse into a sort of weird giggle before returning to his stream-of-consciousness prattling.

"Not supposed to be here. You got that right," one of the soldiers said to Toby. "But we're going to have to find out what you've been up to. What you've all been up to."

"I don't know what to tell you," Toby whined. "I've seen some stuff, but I don't understand any of it. Monsters? I mean, what is that? Where do those come from? For all I know, you guys are the heroes, protecting the world from a Hellmouth spitting out killer beasts."

"Shut up," the same soldier said, and there was a wet crack that sounded like the butt of a rifle laying into someone's face. Toby's gargle of pain seemed to back up that presumption. "Get him to the room. This fat fucker is going to spill his guts."

"I don't think . . ." Toby burbled through what Jessie assumed was a bloody mouth, "that the fat-shaming is necessary . . ."

*Good old Tobes,* Jessie thought. But she was still worried about just how much he could take before he broke.

Seething with impotent rage, Jessie got to her feet and paced like a caged tiger, her fists clenched. Her bad knee was throbbing, and so was her head, but she ignored them both. They felt, compared to her anger, almost like a balm, something steady to help her focus. Her head wasn't swimmy in the least. She felt fully in control of her brain, perhaps for the first time. She felt like she could tear apart a team of soldiers with her bare fists, ignore bullet wounds and stray fists that might connect, and keep bulldozing through the whole complex if she had to. She went back to her bed frame and once again tried to extricate the leg, but it held fast. She wished for something, anything, to give her the power to change her situation. Where was the superstrength afforded to Sara in the podcast? Noah's healing? Alton's impenetrability? Anything. She'd take anything.

But there was nothing do to, no saving grace, no amazing and previously unknown powers that would reveal themselves. She was just who she was, here at what very well might be her end. Jessie stood there in the center of her cell, waiting for something to prove her wrong, but she was still Jessie, just a woman from Chicago, aimless and wandering even while standing stock-still, even when her cell door finally opened, and in came the men with guns, and they took her away too.

—

They were in a line, all of them, her friends on their knees and blindfolded with their hands tied behind their backs. Behind them, a row of soldiers held their rifles to the backs of their heads, and two soldiers on each end stood at attention with grim and deadly looks on their faces. Another soldier—this one unarmed but carrying a stick of some sort and wearing a beret—marched behind them all, back and forth, slapping the rod in his empty hand as he did so.

The room was utterly and probably purposefully nondescript. There was a table in one corner, but aside from that, the chair they'd tied Jessie to was the only other object in the room. Concrete floors, concrete walls. Undefined stains here and there that might have been blood, or perhaps something more benign. It was hard to tell.

Her companions were lined up left to right in the same order Jessie had heard them being dragged down the hall. Carla had been roughed up pretty seriously; her left eye was swollen and closed, and her lower lip split. There was blood on her T-shirt, and for some reason, they had taken her father's dog tags, too. Next to her was Walt, who'd clearly been crying at some point, the dirt and blood on his face—it looked like he'd had a bloody nose—streaked with clean lines of skin where the tears had flowed. Alton, however, looked exactly the same. He was wincing from some sort of inner pain, but his physical resilience had kept any of the blows he'd suffered from being evident. They did have him bound twice—aside from the wrist bindings, a cinch strap pulled his upper arms behind him so tight that his shoulders were likewise forced back.

*Maybe that's where some of the pain is coming from*, Jessie thought. *That shoulder might still be messed up from taking that bullet in the Domes.*

And then, at the end of the line, was Toby, sort of slobbering on himself as he whimpered and wept. Jessie had never seen him like this, but then again, it didn't surprise her either. Toby wasn't great with pain. He'd once stubbed his toe on their ottoman so badly that he'd broken it and had hobbled around with a boot cast for weeks beyond what the university medical center had prescribed. It got him out of vacuuming for over a month, and from then on, Toby referred to that ottoman as "that son of a bitch." They both had.

And now, Toby was on his knees because of her. This trip wasn't his thing. Hadn't been his choice. He'd made a series of decisions that led him here, yes, like they all had, but Toby had been making them on her behalf, not his own. Driving to Colorado because Jessie couldn't. Tagging along because Carla hadn't shown up. Investing in the process—to the degree that he did, anyway—because he knew it was important. Not to him. To her. She felt more than a pang of guilt. She wanted nothing more in that moment than to run over to Toby, hug him, and apologize.

But that wasn't on the menu of options. The soldier in the beret came around to the front, pacing now in front of her friends. Maybe for effect? Like there was an implicit threat?

"We're going to start this in a civilized manner," the man said with a smooth, low voice. He had something of a Southern accent, and his smile wasn't necessarily cruel. Jessie wondered why she was given the privilege of not being blindfolded like the rest of them. Why she was able to see where she was and who she was talking to. And then she realized with a sick feeling in her stomach: they wanted her to see what they were doing to her friends. Unless she talked.

"I'm not going to tell you anything," Jessie said. She was testing the waters, seeing if she was right about them threatening her friends to get to her. Did they know about her knowing Toby best? Would they make an example of him specifically because it would have more leverage? And what was Jessie supposed to know, anyway? She didn't even understand what she was meant to spill.

"I haven't asked any questions yet," he said. "But let's not get ahead of ourselves. I believe introductions are in order. You're Jessica Boyer. I'm Captain Vargas. And yes, I do need some information from you. It's my hope that we can be reasonable people."

"Then we're starting off badly," Jessie said, her voice sounding stronger than she felt. "Because my friends are tied up and have clearly been beaten. That's not exactly a way to build trust."

"Well said," Vargas replied with a cool air. "But this isn't about them. It's about you. Really only you. It's your responsibility that they're here, isn't it? Some"—and he looked pointedly over to Toby—"significantly more than others."

"Not true," Jessie said. "We're all here by our own volition. We owe nothing to each other."

"And so I'll get nothing from you by punishing them," Vargas smiled as he walked. "Yes, yes. I understand your position. Or at least the one you're attempting to present. But again, you're getting ahead of yourself, young Miss Boyer. Aren't you even the slightest bit interested in what questions I might have for you?"

"I have absolutely nothing to say to you," said Jessie.

"Come now," Vargas balked. "That can't be true, can it? You're a curious sort, after all. You want to know things. You said as much in the cell. That's why you're here. To ask the right questions, I believe you put it?"

"So you bugged the cells," Jessie said. "Exactly what we expected. Has it occurred to you that I knew we were being listened to? That you heard exactly what I wanted you to hear?" Jessie began to worry that she was saying more than she should, putting on too much of a show. She didn't have an endgame.

Didn't know what the Collective wanted, and other than absolute escape, what *she* wanted either.

"No," Vargas smiled. "No, I don't, miss. I don't think you knew you were being listened to. Or at least, you weren't speaking purposefully because of it. This place . . . this complex . . . it has a way of inuring one to the idea that they're under scrutiny. At first, one edits themselves scrupulously, being more than careful about what they say and what they do, knowing it's all potentially being seen, possibly recorded. But over time . . . that changes, doesn't it? It slowly becomes background noise in your head, something you only occasionally notice. Until it slips away completely, and it's just the way of the world in which you find yourself. Not even a thought any longer.

"But you and your friend here," Vargas again pointed to Toby, "you were talking like old friends in the cells, weren't you? Very old friends." He looked directly into Jessie's eyes. "So, let's not insult each other, yes?"

"Fine," Jessie said, meeting his gaze. "Then tell me what this situation is, exactly. What's gonna happen to us?"

"That's entirely up to you," Vargas responded slowly. "If you cooperate, possibly nothing. Release, well-wishes, fare-thee-wells. If you don't, well . . . then we can't work together, can we? We'll be on opposite sides. And I assure you, Miss Boyer: my side always wins. All of which is to say this—you don't want to know what the consequences of your lack of cooperation might be. I can promise you that."

"They're never letting us go," Alton said quickly, and loudly.

"Shut up, man," Toby retorted.

"He's right, Jessie," Walt called out.

"Fuck these guys," Carla added.

The soldiers looked at Vargas for direction—the captain calmed them with a single sharp shake of his head.

"Your friends are putting themselves in harm's way for you, Miss Boyer," Vargas said. "Might I suggest that you alleviate the risk to them by just agreeing to cooperate?"

"There's not even a question on the table," Jessie pointed out.

"You're absolutely right," Vargas agreed. "I was hoping to have your agreement before the questions started, so we'd have an easier time. But let me give you the first one, and perhaps the largest one on my list. We'd like to know what evidence you've recorded here, and what you think that evidence implies. We want to correct any misconceptions you may have before they can . . . fester."

"You confiscated all our equipment," Jessie said. "You have our memory cards in the case I had as well. It's all there. That's not even a question you need me to answer."

"Your *interpretation* of the data is what's vital," Vargas explained. "And it's only question one. As I said, a broad question, and one that would take considerable time to deal with, should you be a willing participant in that process. But there are far more questions we'll need to ask, it's true. Things having to do with your theories. Things like symbols drawn in sheds. Does that ring a bell? Does it seem like information that's worth the well-being of your friends?"

"Go fuck yourself," Jessie snarled.

"As I feared," Vargas said. "You may begin." The soldier behind Carla moved quickly and precisely, firing a single round into her right arm. Carla shrieked and fell face-first onto the ground. She wrestled her way back up to her knees quickly, cursing in Spanish and insulting the soldier's mother's size and nighttime proclivities.

Vargas looked intently into Jessie's widening eyes. "Next," he said a little more loudly, and the soldier behind Walt clubbed him in the back of the head. Like Carla, Walt toppled forward and fell hard, face-first. The zip tie holding his wrists together snapped somehow, but that only allowed him to crumple to the ground more like a cast-off rag doll. He didn't get up, didn't even move, and blood began flowing from his sparse hair on the back of his skull.

"NEXT!" Vargas yelled this time, still not taking his eyes off Jessie's, and the soldier behind Alton opened fire, a full burst of bullets into Alton's back. Scraps of T-shirt cotton went flying—Papa Smurf crumpled to the floor—but there was no blood. Alton lurched, but didn't fall forward. When the Kalashnikov stopped firing, smoke thick in the air, Alton was groaning, working to control the evident blunt-blow agony. But he was still up, defiant.

"PUT A BULLET INTO THE NEXT ONE," Vargas called out. "WE ARE DONE FUCKING AROUND."

The soldier put the muzzle of his AK to the back of Toby's head.

"FULL BURST, SOLDIER," Vargas ordered.

"Stop," Jessie said, maybe too softly, so she said it again, more loudly. "STOP!"

"Oh, are we talking now?" Vargas said, his voice abruptly soft. "Are we cooperating, Miss Boyer? How lovely. Wouldn't it have been so much easier to have done this from the start?"

"What do you really want to know?" Jessie seethed.

"Tell us about what you saw in your father's shed," Vargas demanded, all pretense gone. "Tell us everything he said to you the day he left."

"My father?" Jessie said, bewildered. She could feel tears streaming down her face, but she was too shocked to process her emotions.

"*Answer*," Vargas growled.

It was too much.

Jessie broke, and began saying everything she could think to say, even if she didn't understand the details or the importance of any of it. She recounted the story of finding the symbols on the wall of the shed, described them in as much detail as she could recall, admitted having a Polaroid of the sigils, copped to the fact that she'd never known what they meant or how to find out. Talked about the podcast until she felt too much like a gushing, panicked superfan. Mentioned how they found the shaft, how they got to Ward, what happened there, and how they managed to find their way into the mountains. She left out Patsy, innocently at first, but once she realized she could omit that detail, she kept at it, glossing over that part and focusing on how they descended into the complex, what they found first, how they lost Jace, and how they then lost Otomi. It all seemed like it had been so long ago, but the wounds, when she probed them, were still terribly fresh. She cried her way through describing their deaths, but kept going until the fateful meeting with the Archivist.

"You're leaving out what your father said to you before he left you and your mother," Vargas said with a pinched face. There was the cruelty Jessie had expected to see initially; she had just needed to dig a little.

"He told me to remember who I was," Jessie replied. "That I was special. That I was like no one else."

"No," came a woman's voice from behind Jessie. She couldn't see her, but the sound of her voice . . . was that her mother? It was similar, but somehow stronger, more commanding. "He said you *were* no one else. That you were only you."

"That I was me," Jessie said, trying to process, craning her neck in a fruitless attempt to see who was speaking. "That I was better."

"And that was it? I thought he'd have left you with more," the voice purred. "But like I've said before, child, you always did like all eyes on you."

"*Mom?*" Jessie croaked in a pained half whisper.

"Your ego . . ." the woman mocked, ". . . rivals the best of us. Unwarranted, certainly, but there it is." The voice paused, took a breath, as if considering something. "Do you believe her?"

Jessie assumed the question was directed at Vargas. But to her utter horror, and no small bit of absolute confusion, it was Toby who stood up from the line of her friends, brought a hand up that had clearly not been tightly tied behind his back, and removed his blindfold. He stood straight and tall, an unfamiliar posture for the friend she'd known for so many years, who slouched as a general rule, who would have done anything for her, anything in the world, or so Jessie would have sworn.

"Yes, ma'am," he said, and saluted.

"All right," the voice said softly, but with authority. "Fall in line."

Toby did, right next to the soldier that had just earlier had a gun to his head. He didn't look at Jessie, but she stared at him, her best friend, sudden proof that nothing, absolutely nothing in this whole insane world, actually made any sense at all.

# CHAPTER SIXTEEN

OUBLIETTE COMPLEX GAMMA

INTERROGATION ROOM

"How much of my life has been a lie?" Jessie finally gathered herself enough to ask. She wasn't sure if she was addressing Toby or the woman behind her or Vargas, or herself.

*Any of the above will do*, she thought.

"All of it," the woman said simply, and her heels clicked on the tile as she rounded Jessie and limped a little as she came into view, favoring her right knee. It *was* her mother—or at least her mother at a much younger age. Her mother when Jessie had been a girl. Change the hair just a bit, smooth out some of the wrinkles that Jessie sort of assumed had always been there? This was her mother. There was no joy in seeing her, though that was all too normal. But this . . . this was too much.

"Mother, I—"

"I hate it when you call me that," the woman said, but the blunt remark was almost casual. "Always have." With a snap of her fingers, Vargas had his men pick up Carla, Walt, and

Alton—none of whom were in any shape to walk unaided just yet—and they all evacuated the room. Including Toby, who didn't even look back.

Jessie was stunned all the way down to her toes, which were tingling for some reason she couldn't explain. Shock, maybe? She tried to play it off as though it didn't bother her, but she knew she wasn't that good of an actress.

"I guess . . . I guess I always knew," Jessie said, fighting back emotion. "Maybe that's why I called you by your first name when I was in high school for a while, but you didn't seem to like Margaret either."

"That's because Margaret isn't my name," the woman said. "It's just one of the many things we told you."

"All right. What else, Not-Margaret?" Jessie asked.

"What a strange thing to call me," the woman laughed.

"It's all I know of you," Jessie pointed out. "And I'm sure never calling you Mom again."

"Thank God for small favors," Not-Margaret laughed. "But to answer your question about what else we told you—simply everything, darling. You were an empty vessel when you first came out of the growth pods. We simply filled you up with what we wanted you to know. To be."

"The what? The growth pods?"

"Need-to-know basis, child. Need to know, and you don't. Especially now."

"What did you do to Toby?" Jessie pulled at the zip tie binding her wrists behind her back. There had to be some play she could make, something to save her, some hidden talent she had yet to unlock. Or maybe Toby been right when he said *Sometimes it's just game over.*

Not-Margaret scoffed. "Oh, my dear." She shook her head. "Are you still under the impression that he was really your friend?

That we didn't plant him like everything else in your sham of a life? There's nothing you've experienced that I didn't plan, have implemented, and approve."

"That's a lie," Jessie said. "I had a grandmother. We went to her funeral." It was one of the few good memories she had of her mother. They'd gone out for dinner afterward—burgers at Fuddruckers, which was a place Jessie never thought her mother would step foot in, but there they were, chowing down on cheeseburgers the size of their heads in a corner booth, talking about family stories and laughing, with music in the air and shells of free peanuts littering the floor.

"We had an actress who played your grandmother," Not-Margaret explained almost impatiently. "And the damn psychologists were pressing me to connect more with you, for all the good that did. But the lady we hired to play the role of dear, sweet Granny—she wanted out. Her heart had softened for you too much. I tried to reason with her, but she was adamant. Her name was Anne—that's all that was true about her. It took two full doses of the paralytic that eventually stopped her heart, I'll give her that."

"You . . . you fucking killed her?" Jessie almost spat.

"I've killed everyone," Not-Margaret said simply. "Everyone who got in my way. Everyone who became unusable for our purposes. It's what needed to be done. That's my job, really. Doing the things that need to be done. I've made myself indispensable, which is where you come in. My weakness, you see, is that I'm human. Mortal. I'll age out of this role within a few decades, at most, even with the science available to us. You were the potential answer to that problem. If I could grow a new, younger me, I could more or less live forever."

"That's insane," Jessie hissed. "I'm not you." Her father's words rang again in her head. *You're you. Not anyone else. You're better.* "What about my father?" she ventured, keeping her voice as steady as she could. "What, he was just an actor too?"

The woman's smile faltered a little. "No," she said. "He was a fool. He was supposed to be a man of science, but he betrayed himself. He and his pathetic little shed with his scratches on the wall. He grew a little too close to you, apparently. Began to care. But a scientist should never fall in love with their monkeys."

"I wasn't a lab rat to him," Jessie insisted.

"You were at first, dear. But yes, he deluded himself into thinking you were more than just a shadow of me. It really was touching, his last words to you. So weighty and potentially significant. Deliciously mysterious, no? Like it meant something . . . something more. But I assure you, it didn't. Like you, I thought he might have left you some sort of code, some sort of secret, some key for you and you alone to use to unlock this place. But apparently not. He fed you pablum, and then left you."

"Because you made him," Jessie snapped.

"Yes," Not-Margaret said with an evident irritation that Jessie recognized all too well. "Exactly." She paused, frustrated. "I so need a cigarette right now. Do you smoke?"

"Never picked it up," Jessie replied. Nicotine addiction wasn't much of a weakness to exploit, but it was something.

"Smart girl. But you don't know what you've been missing. And if you were avoiding it to prevent lung cancer? Well, let's just say that was a poor investment of your efforts, considering the way your death will go."

"What happened to your knee?" Jessie pressed. She needed to change the subject; didn't want to talk any more about the man she thought of as her father.

"Looking for an advantage, are we?" the woman smiled, and then glanced down at her right knee. "It's a reminder of what happens when I lose focus. I thanked the thing that did it by ending its miserable life a few seconds later."

"Sounds like you're bad at making friends," Jessie said.

"Apparently. But failure is always a part of discovery, yes? We fail and we learn so we can succeed the next time. Just like you, child—a failure from which we can learn. No great loss. We scrub our instruments clean, and we start again. And besides, over the years, other options have presented themselves. I don't know that we'll even start again with another one of you. You've frankly been far more trouble that you've been worth over the years, and that, my dear, is a significant understatement."

"I always knew you were a terrible mother," Jessie admitted. "I just didn't know you were also a fundamentally terrible human being."

"The hubris!" Not-Margaret barked with a mix of delight and impatience. "As if you were the arbiter of good and bad in this world. As I've said, you don't know anything about anything. Everything you've ever known is a construct. Your memories from childhood aren't even real. You didn't come into being as a baby. How worthless would that be? Ten or twelve years to wait for an infant to grow up into something even approaching utilitarian? No. You were postpubescent fresh from the pods. No one in their right mind wants to deal with adolescence in a test subject. So, we brought you about in your early teens, and gave you memories sufficient enough for you to believe that you'd lived a life."

"Another lie," Jessie said, but she heard the tremor in her voice. "I remember falling on the playground when I was three. We had Kool-Aid and cookies, and someone was pushing me on the swings and I fell off and got sick and threw up all over my coat. I had a dog named Rover who barked at everyone but me, and he died when he ate your philodendron. I had a friend, Lily, at Bottenfield Elementary. I slept over at her house many times.

We made chocolate cake as we watched old black-and-white *Son of Svengoolie* horror on Channel 32. I remember way too much of my childhood for it to be fake."

"Precious," the woman responded, smiling unnaturally at what she was hearing. "You have no frame of reference for this, I know, but you actually recall your 'childhood' far too much for it to have been real. Naturally born humans don't recall events from early in their life like you do, certainly not with that level of clarity. If you wanted to, you could write a near-perfect timeline of your life, even though it never happened. No one born to this world can do that. It is, in some ways, your only remarkable talent. Your brain works faster than most others too, for some reason. It's a shame we won't be able to study it more, but maybe in the lab, when your brain is all that's left of you."

"So . . . what? Toby is just an actor?" Jessie's head was getting that circular spin, the dizziness that she dreaded. "All this time, just a guy playing a role?"

"Yes and no," Not-Margaret said. "He's a clone just like you, literally crafted to be your companion."

"And a spy."

"Yes. But to be fair to him, he was never given a choice. We were able to block the part of his brain that would have felt conflict between serving us and being hopelessly devoted to you. Of the two of you, he's by far the more successful experiment. He did his work admirably. We'll have to dispose of him with some grace."

"So now Toby dies too, is that it?" Jessie said. Her head was really spinning now, and her instinct was to keep talking. As long as her mother—no, not her mother, this *bitch*—kept talking, there was hope. Hope for what, Jessie had no idea.

"Yes," the woman sighed. "He'll never work another shift at that drugstore near your adorable and somehow affordable bungalow in the city. If it means anything to you, I'm never returning to that awful little hovel where you assumed I lived, either. My god, I hated that place, with all its tiresome bric-a-brac. But no loose ends, darling. Both those houses—yours and what passed for mine—are slated to be demolished, new homes built and sold for a song to someone who'll never know what went on there. They'll disappear, just like I will, *finally*, from the book clubs and the coffee klatches I had to suffer through. Just like you will, and your sweet little Toby too. This chapter of our story is over, and I'd like to say I appreciate your participation, but honestly, you've been terribly awful to work with."

"Nothing's over, *Mom*," Jessie spat. Was her head literally spinning in small uncontrolled circles, or did it just feel like that?

"Remarkable, you still believing. Thinking you might somehow win," the woman smiled, but there was definite cruelty there, like the delight of a scientist watching a rat struggle under a scalpel. "I suppose I'd be doing the same thing in your situation. The apple might fall far from the tree—too far, for this little experiment to continue, I'm afraid—but there are certainly still vestiges of me in there, aren't there, child?"

"I'm not your child," Jessie said through gritted teeth, and a head so dizzied with confusion and sadness and anger that she was seeing white spots before her eyes.

"Oh, Jessica," Not-Margaret said. "You are more my child than any other child born to this godforsaken world. You aren't just from me, you *are* me. Which should make it difficult to terminate you, I understand. But then again . . ." She lifted a syringe full of a murky-looking fluid. "I've never been sentimental."

"I'm going to kill you, you know," Jessie threatened, but her words were slurring a bit. She tried to focus as best she could, but her consciousness was fading.

The woman smiled and brought the syringe up close to

Jessie's face. "Sorry, dear," she whispered softly into Jessie's ear. "That's *my* line."

There was a sudden swoop to the room, and the world went away as the seizure Jessie had felt coming took hold of her completely. She felt the cold, electric grip of her troubled brain, her eyes rolling back in her head, and the physical surrender to a power far greater than she was able to control anymore. She saw flashes of light inside her head, tiny crackling explosions like the fireworks she remembered seeing—but probably never actually happened, she now realized. Her mind dulled, made to retreat from the world. Inside her skull, Jessie took something like a deep breath, a preparation for diving beneath deep black water.

And then she submerged. And there was nothing.

---

"Jessie . . ." Someone was shaking her awake. "Jessie!"

She felt fingers on her neck, checking for a pulse. Hands on her, examining her for injuries.

"Is she dead?" came a voice a little farther away. Was that Carla?

"No," said someone. It was Alton. "I think she's coming to."

"We can't stick around here, Doc," Jessie heard Walt say, and she could hear his fingers tapping what she assumed was a rifle in his hands.

"Toby . . . ?" Jessie heard herself say, and a distant part of her brain screamed at herself. *Toby's gone. Toby never existed. Toby was a lie.*

"That fuckwit," Carla sneered. "He'll get his, chiquita, I promise you that. I'll feed his guts to a fucking chupacabra."

"Shhh . . ." Alton felt Jessie's forehead, and put a warm palm on the side of her face. "Jessie, we need you to wake up if you can. I can help carry you, but it'll be easier and safer if you can do it yourself."

"Needta sleep . . ." Jessie heard herself say. This was normal, post-seizure—the intense need to return to the unconscious, but the alert part of Jessie knew that wasn't a luxury they had time for.

"I know," Alton said. "And you will, as soon as we get you out of here."

"Big promises, Doc," Walt interjected. "We don't even know where to go."

"One thing at a time." Alton's voice was practiced, soothing.

"That's medical speak for shut up," Carla joked.

"Yeah, I got that," Walt said.

Jessie was happy to hear her friends' voices, alive if once again on the run, joking with each other. It meant they weren't in absolute and immediate danger. That there was still hope. There it was: the chance she'd been looking for earlier. The hope that there was a way out. And the feeling wasn't coming from within her. It was from the people she'd come down here with.

Her friends. Her *real* family.

The world lurched for Jessie, and her externalized perception reunited with her body with an almost physical jolt. She sat up suddenly, saw that she was in a bed, and they were all in a room. Not a cell—more of a medical suite? A recovery room of some sort?

"Whoa whoa whoa," Alton cautioned, hands on her shoulders. "Not too fast."

"I'm okay," Jessie said, and her voice sounded louder than she'd intended. She'd gotten used to the sound of her own voice inside her head. "I'm okay."

"Breathe," Alton ordered. "Just breathe for a minute. Deep one in, hold it, count to three—then out, count to three."

"She's looking a little more pink," Carla said. "That's good, right?"

"Very good," Alton nodded.

"You okay, sweetie?" Walt asked, and it occurred to Jessie that this moment might be the first time in her life someone had called her by a term of endearment and actually meant it.

"Yeah," she smiled at him. At all of them. "What happened? How are you guys even here?"

"Walt's a fucking Rambo is what happened," Carla said admiringly. She had a makeshift bandage on her upper arm—it was gray soldier camo with a bright bloodred center.

Alton nodded appreciatively. "It's true," he said. "They dragged us into another interrogation room, and they were waiting for the orders to kill us. At least, that's what that Vargas guy said the orders were going to be, but he didn't want to jump the gun. He told the soldiers to wait there while he took Toby to debriefing, that your mom was going to dispatch you, and then probably have them do the same to us three. But they didn't count on Walt here."

"They thought I was still knocked out," Walt demurred. "They weren't keeping an eye on me. But you don't teach high school for thirty-some years without developing eyes in the back of your head. When they weren't paying attention, I was able to pick up the Kalashnikov Toby had left behind."

"He mowed them down," Carla said. "It was a thing of beauty."

"It was six men getting shot at close range," Alton countered grimly. "It wasn't beautiful at all. But I have to admit, it was a relief."

"Are you all okay?" Jessie asked. "Your arm, Carla? Your head, Walt? Your . . . like, entire back, Alton?"

"Alton made himself useful," Carla teased. "No one's still bleeding."

"I still have one hell of a headache," Walt said. "But I'm okay."

"Don't look at my back," Alton added. "It still hurts. A lot."

"It's like totally purple, dude," Carla said. "That's some wicked tough skin you got, but wow, you do pay a price for it."

"Tell me about it," Alton said. Jessie noticed he was no longer shirtless, too, having apparently acceded to wearing a fatigues top, albeit with the arms ripped off, creating a makeshift vest.

"We really have to go," Walt repeated. "Are you okay to move, Jessie?"

"I think so," she said, but she felt those familiar waves of dizziness when she tried to get up. "Just give me a minute."

"We may not have a minute," Walt responded, "but take what you need. Either of these doors moves an inch, I'm opening fire."

"Where are we, anyway?" Jessie asked, leaning back against the wall. At least this room looked more like a room than a cell or interrogation room. It never occurred to Jessie just how reassuring plastered drywall could be.

"That's the thing," Carla said. "We're not positive, but we think . . ."

"We think we're near where we came in," Alton finished. "Not too far, anyway."

"That seems like a long way from where we were," Jessie said.

"Oddly enough, no," Walt explained. "So far as we've been able to figure out, we've been more or less going in circles, or at least loops on a few different levels. Between our meandering and following Toby on the run the way we did, we haven't made it that deep into the complex at all."

"But how did I get here?" Jessie held her head in her hands. It was still pounding with pressure, her body continuing to twitch slightly despite its exhaustion. Having a seizure was like running a marathon in your sleep, Jessie had always thought. You wake up dead tired. "And how did you guys find me?"

"Finding you was easy," Walt said. "We took a two-way radio off one of the soldiers, and all the chatter has been about you. Why they brought you here is anyone's guess, but the important thing is that we were able to find you."

"We had to take out a couple of guards at the door when we arrived," Carla said, "but that's why Walt's got ants in his pants. Reinforcements could show up any minute."

"Maybe," Alton countered. "And maybe not. I don't pretend to understand all their protocols, but they've been consistent in announcing their movements so far, and we haven't heard anything about a squad being deployed down here."

"Right before I seized out," Jessie said, "that woman—the woman I thought was my mother—was about to shoot me up with some drug. I'm assuming that was meant to kill me, so I'm guessing she didn't get the chance to do it?"

"I don't know. Possibly?" Alton admitted. "I mean, we weren't there, and we didn't see you again until just now, waking you up."

"Fuck," Jessie sighed. One more mystery to solve. If she survived.

"Can you walk?" Alton asked her.

Jessie nodded. "Guess I have to, right?" She gingerly stood up, and her legs supported her, weary as they felt. Jessie stretched, just to get the sense of her body back. She hurt all over, but she was alive. That was something.

---

"Remember the traps," Walt told everyone as they finally, after a few wrong turns, found their way back to the massive Wetlands Overflow chamber. They found the same door they'd exited, and stole a look inside before going back in. The room seemed darker, somehow—or maybe their eyes had gotten used to the fluorescent glow of the hallways.

Jessie felt a little more centered after the hurried hike back, a little more like herself again. And hopefully able enough to help get them home.

Home. Fucking Toby. Still, despite everything, him not being there would make it completely different. And the woman—her "mother" Not-Margaret—had said the house was going to be torn down. She had to get back before that happened. She didn't care about the house so much—she'd need a place to live, sure, but Walt had already offered her a place to stay if she needed one—but she had to get back to retrieve her stuff.

One thing in particular.

"Something's different here," Alton said. "I think we may have some new players in our midst."

"New players?" Walt replied, suddenly looking worried. "Soldiers?"

"No, but they're coming," Alton seemed to sniff at the air, and then lowered his voice slightly. "Follow me."

The group slowly trudged through the wetlands in Alton's footprints as best they could. With Alton's gift of near invulnerability, he had the best chance of surviving a trap like the one that had taken Jace. They could see the half-log platform of the trap silhouetted in the near distance.

"When I get up there, I'm checking Jace again to see if I missed the Pigeon," Alton said in a whisper. "Didn't he have a belt pouch or something?"

"Now that you mention it," Jessie replied, "I think he did."

"Okay," Alton said. "I'm going up there, but the rest of you stay put when I say so. Don't fan out. Don't even move."

"Works for me," Carla confirmed.

Crickets sounded throughout the room as they made their way through the shallow water. It still smelled like algae and stagnant pools, and there were indistinct shapes flying above.

Or maybe they were just shadows. Down here, Jessie knew, they could be anything. She wondered for a moment why they'd have imported crickets, thought how familiar it was, and then considered the creatures might each be the size of a loaf of bread, and have serrated knives for arms, for all she knew.

Alton held up one hand to motion them to stop, and approached the darkened trap where Jace had been skewered.

He turned back to the group. "He's gone."

"What?" Jessie hissed.

"There's still blood on the spikes, but even his backpack is gone. I dropped it into the water right here," he said, mucking around in the black swamp, coming up with nothing.

"Who would take him?" Walt asked.

"Who indeed?" a voice came from above, and tactical lights from dozens of rifles suddenly lit up their position.

"This might be bad," Walt said, shielding his eyes with one hand.

"You think?" Alton sighed, putting his hands up in surrender as a figure landed gracefully in the gloom, detached from a belay rope, and strode forward.

It was Vargas, holding not a gun or a baton, but a strange and wicked-looking blade. "The good doctor has the right idea. The rest of you," he said, showcasing that smug smile that made Jessie want to shoot it off, "put your hands up, just for good measure. This will be quick, I promise. It will all be over very, very soon."

# CHAPTER SEVENTEEN

BACK IN THE WETLANDS OVERFLOW

As her eyes adjusted to the tactical lights, Jessie counted at least five squads of six. Maybe more, if there were others in line behind those groups, not shining their beams directly at them.

*More than enough to kill us*, she thought. *Way too many for us to deal with and survive.*

As Jessie assessed the situation, the assault teams split in two, surrounding them in a pincer formation.

"I know this feels like victory," Alton said slowly, directly at Vargas. "But you don't have all the data. This room has changed. Can you smell it? There's something new here, something neither of us know about."

Jessie wondered what he was talking about. Was this just a ploy, a stall of some sort until they could come up with a plan? Shit, was *she* supposed to be planning something?

"I can't smell a thing," Vargas responded with that maddening grin. If anything, the smile splitting his face got even wider. "But good to know you can. That's one more reason to celebrate. And you stalling for time won't do a damn thing. Time, you see, isn't on your side. We're going to be taking you all into custody not because we have to, but because we *can*. Because we *want* to. Oh, I might have my troops kill the others. They're inconsequential. But you, we want to study. And Miss Boyer over there?" Vargas chuckled. "My boss very much wants to take her time with that one."

"Your cruelty will be the thing that kills you," Alton said, and using an accent Jessie didn't recognize. His voice was suddenly a little more sibilant, even more precisely pronounced than his norm. And he was . . . *clicking*? It was unlike any sound Jessie had ever heard.

"Tell your men to stop," Alton continued. It was almost casual, the way he said it, as if he knew nothing would come of it, but he felt the need to offer the warning anyway. "I'm serious."

Vargas began to respond, but it was cut short by the sound of all hell breaking loose, traps going off all around them. Jessie couldn't help but feel a bit of vindication on behalf of Jace when the traps caught the soldiers unawares just like he had been. The troops had been blithely maneuvering to either side of Jessie and her friends, and the team on the left had hit the pivot point of a nasty pit trap. The ground fell out from under them, and eight figures in the dim light disappeared almost comically into the sudden space beneath them. There were small bursts of gunfire as the soldiers panicked while they fell, and the screams of pain and confusion suggested more friendly fire casualties even before they had a chance to land on whatever was down there. Jessie couldn't be sure, but she thought she could hear the sound of flesh meeting sharpened sticks at the bottom of the dead drop.

The opposite happened to their right, as something odd and wriggling fell from the canopy of a tree, a netted ball of something that burst on impact. Dozens of ravenous death worms rained over two full squads of soldiers, who responded by firing their rifles indiscriminately in their sudden terror. But the gunfire stopped abruptly and was replaced with helpless human whimpering and the shudder-inducing sound of giant worms beginning to feed.

"Hit the deck!" cried Alton in that strange clicking voice, and Jessie complied instantly. She heard Walt and Carla do the same behind her. The rest of the soldiers opened fire at the only figure they could still make out in the half-light: Alton, who was wrestling with the half log that Jace had been crucified on, tearing it from its hinged foundation as though it was a cereal box top. At first, Jessie thought he was going to use it as a shield of some sort, but instead, he threw it with incredible speed and accuracy at a squad of soldiers still in tight formation. The log platform slammed into the group of them, impaling the first row on spikes and bowling over the back row, crushing them under the bloody weight of their former companions.

Vargas's eyes widened, but he looked no less thrilled. "Yes," he said. "You're going to do nicely. I've been waiting for one of you to come along. Once we splice you in me, I'll be fucking unstoppable."

"You're insane. *Chk*," Alton said. "You're all insane. Always have been."

"How old are you?" Vargas asked. "I'm curious to know just how old you can get. Will I inherit your resistance, your strength, your advanced lifespan? All of it?"

"I'll give you nothing—*chk*—but a broken neck," Alton responded. "I promise."

Vargas smiled and brought to bear the blade he had—it was a vicious thing, like a piece of raw metal that had been torn, and torn roughly, from the door of an old car, with a thick brass cross guard and a leather-wrapped hilt that ended in a simple thong around Vargas's wrist. "You'll give me everything," Vargas promised in turn, and whistled.

More troops appeared from the darkness.

But as the soldiers hit the ground and began to run, they jerked back on an invisible tether. The beams of tactical lights swerved drunkenly about the room as the troops were upended, disappearing one at a time. More gunfire, but Jessie couldn't see at what.

Until a giant spider emerged from the shadows and slowly approached a screaming soldier stuck fast to a waist-high web. In an instant, the spider started eating, starting with the hapless mercenary's head, perhaps to stop his screaming.

Now that Jessie had an idea of what she was looking for, she saw them everywhere, dark blobs with thin slits of yellow-orange eyes in the dim light of the room, spindly legs reaching for captured prey, huge toothy maws opening to engulf them.

"So you have backup," Vargas spat. "We'd heard someone was down here rounding up the J'ba FoFi, but we didn't know why."

"We're—*chk*—full of surprises," Alton said.

*Okay, now that*, Jessie thought, *is a bluff.*

"You're alone," Alton said. "And out of—*chk*—options. I suggest you turn tail and run while you can."

"I'm not alone," sneered Vargas. "Being in the Collective means we're never alone. We have troops stationed at bases all over the globe. Countless numbers of soldiers in countless numbers of strategic facilities. Meanwhile, you have scientific rejects and mutants." He shook his head in disgust. "You *had* this world, you idiot. You had it and refused to fight for it. Refused to stand up to us when you could. The cattle have become the ranchers now. We'll never be your livestock again."

"You were never our cattle," Alton said. "But you've—*chk*—allowed yourselves to become the one thing you most despised. You've such short spans of attention. As lovely as you are, you can't see beyond your own brief—*chk*—shining moment."

"You're personally going to ensure my shining moment is anything but brief," Vargas boasted. "I had this blade made specifically for you." He held the weapon up to eye level. "It's not pretty, I know. But it's made from the only shard we've been able to carve from one of your goddamn ships so far. We thought it might be something that could also hurt you. Worth a shot, right? You know, the old Kryptonite thing."

*Ships?* Jessie's mind raced. Did that mean Alton was . . . an *alien*? And what was that about Alton's people losing the world? Not fighting for it?

"We found your last rope in the shaft," Vargas taunted. "I lit it myself and watched it burn all the way up. You have nowhere to go from here."

"Neither do you," Alton challenged. "And you're not so much a—*chk*—*we* anymore." It was true—those few soldiers that had survived had mounted a quick retreat.

"I'm by nature a *we*," Vargas gloated. "I have bestial blood running through me that you can't comprehend. I'm faster than you, even if you're stronger. My nose might not be as tuned as yours, but I can still smell your fear from here, even over the stink of monkey and mermaid and quite frankly, your friends, who are in desperate need of a shower."

"That's just rude," Jessie heard Walt mutter behind her.

"*Chts'ksch?*" Alton said. Was that a word? An alien fucking *word*? "We have a saying where I'm from," Alton continued. "*Home is where the—chk—seeds of everything are planted, from—chk chk—life to death and beyond.*"

Vargas shook his head. "Good for you," he scowled. "Want that on your tombstone or something?"

Jessie saw a glint of light shine off of the brass name badge Vargas wore pinned to his fatigues. E. Vargas, it read. E?

"Elmo?" Jessie yelled out.

Vargas was startled and looked in her direction. "How—" he started to say, but Alton took the opportunity to bolt forward with near-impossible speed. He grabbed Vargas around the neck with both hands—hands that seemed somehow larger than just seconds earlier.

Vargas's face reddened instantly, but he brought up the wickedly torn blade and plunged it into Alton's stomach. It penetrated cloth and skin without any resistance, its vicious tip blossoming from Alton's back with a rush of impossibly blue ichor. The blade stuck fast, despite Vargas's efforts to pull it out.

Vargas's eyes widened, then bulged as Alton squeezed harder.

"Patsy says hi," Alton whispered.

Vargas tried to say something in response, but in the end, was only able to emit a small squeak. Jessie heard the bones in his neck snap, and even though his head lolled to one side, Alton kept squeezing. Finally, with a muted pop not unlike the cork of a cheap bottle of champagne, Elmo Vargas's head broke free of his body. Both crumpled to the ground, his mouth still curled in a strange, surprised smile.

Alton fell to his knees, the blade still in his stomach and poking through his back. It looked at first as though Alton was having a seizure himself, as his body began to convulse. But when Jessie rushed up and knelt over him, it was clear that this was no seizure.

"Take . . ." Alton gasped for air, ". . . the blade . . . *chk* . . . out."

"But you'll die," Jessie said, feeling Walt and Carla cautiously creeping up behind her. Jessie hoped they were watching for any remaining Collective forces, because she didn't intend on taking her eyes off Alton for even a moment.

"Yeah," Alton smiled, and coughed up some blue spittle that dribbled down his chiseled cheek. "That'll be—*chk*—interesting, won't it?"

Alton's whole body was thrumming when she put her hand to his chest and gripped the blade to pull it free. When she did, Alton grunted, and thick blue blood pooled instantly in the wound. But it didn't gush out—it almost seemed like it was somehow adhering to the wound. Filling it.

"Alton, what . . . ?" Jessie started, but stopped just as quickly. She had too many questions to ask just one.

"I—*chk*—don't have much time," Alton said. "I don't have enough bioenergy left to reconstitute. I'm going to have to let go here in just a—*chk*—minute."

"Let go?" Jessie asked.

"You mean die?" Carla whispered.

"If you've got any other options, Doc . . . or whatever you are," Walt added over Jessie's shoulder, "I know we'd all appreciate it."

"*Chk chk chk* . . ." was the only response Alton seemed able to make. Jessie considered all that he'd done in the last day or so: having been shot several times, exhibiting massive strength in moments of great need, all while possibly maintaining a form that was now slipping away.

"Take—*chk*—this . . ." Alton pressed something small and rectangular in her hand. It was an SSD, no bigger than a stick of gum. "It'll explain some things. From my limited—*chk*—perspective, at least . . ."

Jessie realized she was crying. Behind her, Carla was sniffling, too—or maybe that was Walt. "Can't we do something, Alton? Anything?"

"Keep—*chk*—fighting," Alton said, and his body stopped buzzing. It went completely still, and Jessie could feel him growing colder under the hand she still had placed on his chest. "Know that you—*chk chk*—have friends who have been here longer than you know, and will stand with you." Alton smiled, and his eyes darkened into black glass that still emanated a kindness and a hardness both. Blue blood stained his teeth, and then his teeth abruptly melted back into his mouth. "Pliss," he said, and his voice was completely different now that his mouth was just a hole. "Nonn *chk chk* yet em gyet yii body. And *chk chk* non't be afrain . . ."

And then the light that remained in his glossy eyes dulled.

Jessie rose to her feet, still holding the silvery knife in her hand, both entranced and aghast at what was happening to Alton. He was melting, or something close to it. At first, it looked as though he were sinking into the soil, but she quickly realized that he was just morphing into something else, something smaller than the six-five, broad-chested, well-toned, model-beautiful man he'd been. The malleable flesh of blue and green and gray shifted like waves and finally settled into a smallish form with spongy and translucent skin in whorls of cream and cerulean shades. The creature was human sized—shorter than Alton had been, but still almost six feet. *Was Alton a Firben?* Jessie marveled. *Is this what they look like?* Whatever he'd been, he was of a race that had a rounded torso the comparative size of a basketball with no neck to speak of, leading up to a noseless face with large eyes set widely apart. No hair, no ears, not really even a chin. And the arms and legs were gangly and long, and had elbows and knee-type joints in several places on each limb, apparently able to bend fully in any direction. Both hands and feet ended in a trio of delicate fingers, also long and multijointed.

"Damn, I wish we still had our cameras," Walt murmured.

Jessie stared at the SSD Alton had given her. It was the only evidence they had left, the only thing they still had the chance to carry out of there. And Jessie found herself determined all over again to do just that. For Alton. For Jace. For Otomi. Hell, for Noah and Sara and anyone who had been screwed over by this place.

And maybe even her mother, who was also sort of Jessie, she reminded herself. But she quickly shook that thought out of her head. *You're you,* her father had said. The man she knew as her father. The man who left her only one thing that Jessie was now certain held some sort of secret for her. The thing she hadn't said out loud to the others. The thing Vargas and her mother and even Toby hadn't known about. Caballo Morado. She just had to get it from her childhood bedroom in Champaign before the whole damn house came down.

"We have to carry him with us," Jessie decided.

"The fuck we do," Carla replied instantly.

"I'm not even sure how we could," Walt said. "He's . . . sort of gelatinous now. He's holding together, but I'm not sure how we'd carry him very far."

"Well, we can't just leave him here," Jessie protested.

"He wouldn't want us sacrificing ourselves just to get his remains out," Walt argued.

"He's right," Carla said. "Alton was all about helping people, remember?"

"It was tough to make out, but I think his last words were about us not letting the Collective get his body," Jessie insisted. "And after what Vargas said before he lost his head, I don't blame him. I don't want them getting Alton either."

"It's true that he risked himself for us," Carla sighed. "More than once. We owe him, I guess."

"Exactly," Jessie said.

"Okay," Walt sighed. "I know when I'm outvoted. So, what can we do with him? None of us can climb a rope out of here while carrying him."

"We don't have to carry him out," Jessie said, recalling that Vargas had claimed they'd cut the one remaining rope in the shaft. A problem for a few steps later, she decided. If they survived long enough to face that problem, they'd be doing well. "I have an idea, but you guys might not like it. It's not far to carry him, especially if we can jerry-rig a litter or something from the Bwana Hut."

"I don't think there's gonna be much left in the hut," Walt nodded into the gloom up ahead.

For the first time, Jessie noticed that the silhouette of the hut was only partially there—it looked like it had been torn down or set on fire. It was hard to tell from this distance. But it didn't look good.

"Time to fucking find out," Jessie said, and started back up the path back toward what was left of Roger's hut.

—

"This was your big idea?" Carla said, seeing the Piasa beast through the cracked open door. The ferocious bird monster was swooping around the room, looping around the catwalk. They could still see Otomi's blood on the rail. "Feeding Alton to that thing?"

"It was the only way I could think of to make sure the Collective couldn't farm his DNA," Jessie responded. "I promised him."

"You didn't, technically," Walt said. And following a glare from Jessie, added, "Well, you didn't. He died before you could respond at all."

"I thought you were in favor of this idea?" Jessie countered.

"That was before I heard the thing screeching again," Walt admitted.

They'd managed to scavenge enough from the ruins of the Bwana Hut to fashion a litter—just two sticks and a filthy blanket, but Alton was no longer in any shape to care. They'd backtracked carefully, using the bodies of the soldiers—still lying where Otomi had taken them out—as a marker of where to turn. They made it up the ladder—no small feat while lugging Alton behind. His remains were wobbly—Walt had been right when he used the word *gelatinous* to describe Alton's natural form. But they made it back up into the office and through the sundered trapdoor that something—they still wondered what—had bashed its way through. Whatever it had been, it wasn't still in the office, something Jessie was grateful for.

"You guys ready?" Jessie asked.

"I don't know," Carla said, a little taken aback. "What's the goddamn plan here?"

"This is as far as I've thought it through," Jessie admitted. "We just . . . put Alton out there, I guess?"

"*Hostia puta*, Jessie," Carla rolled her,eyes. "You gotta start thinking things all the way through. What are we supposed to do, just waltz out there like we're servers at Waffle House or something? What's to keep that *pinche* monster from just eating us first?"

"Plus, he just ate Otomi . . . what, yesterday?" Walt added. "How do you know the thing is still hungry?"

"I get the feeling that thing is always hungry. It's sort of the rule of monsters, isn't it? But Carla . . . you have a point." Jessie considered for a moment. "How far do you think you could throw him?"

Carla slumped and shook her head. "Are you kidding? This is the worst plan ever."

"I'm sorry!" Jessie threw up her hands. "I've never disposed of an alien friend's body by feeding him to a mythical beast before." Her mind drifted to Toby. It was the kind of thing he would have said. It was going to take a long time to get him out of her head, and anger welled up to match the frustration she felt. She took a deep breath to quell it all. "Okay. Okay.

We need a distraction. Something to draw the Piasa all the way to the other side of the catwalk. Then we can carry Alton out halfway before the thing starts back toward us."

"And then?" Walt asked.

"And then we run like hell."

"You're nuts," Carla said.

"If it's a distraction you need . . ." Walt said, "I have something that might actually do the trick." He put one hand down the front of his pants.

"Whoa!" Carla said. "What are you reaching for there, papi?"

Walt pulled out a small pack of what looked to be firecrackers.

"Where'd you get that?" Jessie asked.

"Duct-taped 'em to the inside waistband of my underpants," Walt said. "I got the idea from a zombie game I played with my kids. You use these to send the undead in one direction while you go the other."

"Well, that's perfect," Jessie said. "Other than the fact that they were in your pants. Okay, Carla, how about throwing these?"

"I'm not touching those things."

"C'mon," Walt said. "I'll unwrap them from the pack for you. Jeez." He did just that, and then offered them to Carla, along with some matches he'd taped to the side.

"Fine," Carla said.

"Think you can chuck them all the way across the room?" Jessie asked.

"Varsity softball player right here, *mamacita*," Carla said. "When you're ready, I'll light up these crotch rockets."

Jessie held one side of the litter, and Walt the other, and then Jessie nodded. Carla lit the fuse on the pack of fireworks—Jessie hoped it was long enough. They pushed open the door, and Carla threw her Hail Mary best.

The firecrackers landed near the door on the other end of the catwalk and almost immediately began exploding. The Piasa screeched again and flew in that direction too quickly for Jessie's comfort, but she and Walt had Alton's body nearly halfway into the room already. The fireworks continued to go off, rattling the room with tiny percussions, and Jessie and Walt started running back.

But the Piasa was faster; maybe it was the scent of fresh meat, but the firecrackers quickly ceased to have an effect on the monstrous bird creature. It turned around in a blazingly fast arc to home in on Jessie and Walt, running for their lives.

"Faster!" Carla cried from the open doorway, reaching out with her hand as though she could actually reach either one of her friends.

The Piasa bird swooped in and grabbed Walt in one taloned claw. He grunted as ragged nails dug into his shoulder, but brought up the Kalashnikov he still had slung around his neck, found the trigger through his pain, and fired upward blindly, spraying in a short arc. It was enough for the Piasa to think twice about carrying Walt. It dropped him, and Walt had to grab the railing with his free hand to prevent a long fall.

It was enough time for Jessie and Carla to grab him—Carla went low to grab his waist and steady him so he wouldn't plummet, while Jessie took his hand to help him get himself back up and over the rail, through the door, and to the relative safety of the office. Walt collapsed back onto the shag carpeting, breathing hard and bleeding from his shoulder.

Over on the catwalk, the Piasa was busy ripping off jiggly pieces of Alton and eating them like a pelican might swallow a fish. "I guess it was still hungry after all," Jessie murmured.

"*Ay bendito*," Carla crossed herself.

"I guess it really is true what they say," Walt said, grinning as he propped himself up on his elbows. "*There's always room for Jell-O.*"

"Jesus, Walt!" Jessie exclaimed.

"That is so not funny, man," Carla said. "That was our friend in there."

"I think Alton would have thought it was funny," Walt countered. "Also, my shoulder hurts, so don't yell at me."

Jessie smiled despite herself while she and Carla wrapped Walt's shoulder with scraps of what had been Alton's makeshift vest. Walt was probably right. Alton had always appreciated a good joke, even when it didn't necessarily match his own dry sense of humor.

"See, Jessie thought it was funny," Walt gestured while Carla helped him to his feet.

"If I die and you make some stupid joke," Carla growled in mock fury, "I'm gonna come back and haunt your ass."

"Well, I'll be glad for the company then," Walt winked.

"We gotta get out of here," Jessie said. "Think we still have to watch out for traps?"

"And giant spiders now, too," Walt added, rolling his shoulder to test out the joint. "Don't forget them."

"I'm sort of done with the new and exciting ways to die," Carla sighed.

"Me too," Jessie agreed. "Let's head back and see if Elmo was lying about the rope."

"And if he wasn't?" Walt asked.

"Let's burn that bridge when we come to it," Jessie said. It was something Toby used to say. She wondered if the pain of remembering stuff like that, repeating it autonomically, would ever stop hurting, or if it was just another souvenir of this place, like Jace. Like Otomi. Like Alton.

Like, apparently, her whole damn life.

# CHAPTER EIGHTEEN

SECTOR 616-M

Running. Again. Or at least they had been, until they heard the telltale sounds of someone or something coming down the hallway in the direction they needed to go in order to get back to the wetlands.

Jessie was tired beyond anything she'd ever experienced. She felt like she could sleep for weeks, given the chance. In that moment, she so wanted to have that chance.

Not only that, but if she never saw another eggshell-white hallway or fluorescent overhead light? That would be just fine by her. Oh, and no more soldiers wanting to kill her. That would also be nice.

"I can hear a little Ukrainian," she said softly. They were crouched behind a corner, peering around occasionally to see how close anyone came. "I think that's Ukrainian anyway, which probably means more soldiers. So that's one thing we know, at least."

"Is it?" Carla whispered. "My science guy had an accent I couldn't place, too."

"Shit," Jessie said. "So we're back to knowing zero?"

"Feels familiar," Walt muttered.

"We could just take them by surprise," Carla shrugged. "I mean, Walt still has the gun."

"I'd really like to stop killing people," Walt said. "I know they're the bad guys, but still. You want the rifle?"

"I'm good," Carla shook her head.

"Yeah," Jesse said. "I think we're all sort of sick of the indiscriminate killing. That's probably a good thing."

"Though maybe not great timing at this minute," Carla countered. "And don't tell yourself it was indiscriminate, either. It was totally fucking discriminate. What the Collective is doing, what the monsters might do—*that's* indiscriminate. What we do is survival, chiquita."

"Noted," Jessie said. "And thanks. But in order to do that, we have to get through this bunch first. Assuming we're not going SEAL Team Six on them, what other ideas do we have here?"

"We could head back to that locker room," Walt suggested. "Get some fatigues, maybe try to blend in?"

"We'd have to go through not only the Piasa room again," Jessie said, "but the Domes cavern too. It's a big trek, and there's no guarantee we won't run into more of these guys on the way."

"Or get lost," Carla added.

"Or that," Jessie agreed.

"What about trying to find a locker room in this hall?" Walt countered. "They must exist all over this complex."

"I'm sure they do," Jessie reasoned. "But finding one nearby would just be luck. And we might end up opening a door to something worse. At least they don't seem to be coming this way anymore. They're just hanging out in the hallway up there." *Probably guarding the hall and waiting for us.*

"Okay," Carla said. "So that leaves us . . . what?"

"Sneaking around?" Jessie shrugged. "Not that I have any idea how we'd actually do that."

"Is there an option that doesn't involve one of us shrugging helplessly?" Walt asked. "I really don't want to die down here."

"Same," Carla said.

Jessie sighed and glanced down in frustration. She noticed a red mark in the bare skin just under the hem of her shorts and above her knee—a perfect crimson circle. It looked almost like a mosquito bite, but then she recognized what it was—a needle mark.

Her mother had injected her with *something.*

She touched the dime-sized spot cautiously. She couldn't feel anything beneath the skin, and it didn't appear that there was anything wrong. No heat, no itch, no raised welt. It seemed innocuous, so much so that Jessie began trying to convince herself that maybe she was wrong. That maybe it had happened running from the Piasa, or during any other of the recent events they'd been through. But none of it seemed likely. *Occam's razor,* she thought. *My mother was holding a syringe when I seized out. Ipso facto: she did what she'd intended.*

Her mind raced.

Maybe this was something that could help them out of this situation. Some power, maybe, like Noah and Sara had received? Invulnerability had been pretty nice, if still painful for Alton. Invisibility would be great, but probably too much to ask. Maybe some ghostlike power to be able to walk through walls? Flight? Super speed? Probably too convenient. But something. The more she thought about it, the more she considered it a real possibility. Maybe their *only* hope.

She turned from the corner with her back against the wall. "Okay, guys, I think I have an idea . . ." She explained the whole thing—the syringe, her mother, the idea that maybe she'd been injected with something that could help.

"How do you know it'll be something worthwhile though?" Walt asked. "I'm just being realistic. We don't know the range of possibilities, but there was that other guy from the podcast—he got telescopic sight. I mean, if you end up with something like that . . . how would that help us?"

"How do you know it's not a tracker or something?" Carla countered.

"I don't," Jessie conceded. "But I don't think so. There's no lump under the skin, and the syringe was full of liquid."

"Couldn't it be . . . nanobots?" Walt asked. "Wait, is that a real thing, or a comic book thing?"

"I think if you have to ask that question," Carla said flatly, "then it's probably not worth tossing out there, you know?"

"If we have any other ideas, I'm all for it," Jessie said. "But other than trying to take on a whole group of them with one AK . . . I think we've hit something of a wall in terms of options."

"What exactly is your idea here, Jessie?" Carla asked with an edge to the question. "That you're going to head out there and put yourself in harm's way and hope that you Hulk out or something?"

"I don't know, you guys . . ." Jessie started her sentence without a strong concept of where she was going with it. After all, she wasn't in any way sure that she could pull any effective rabbit out of her own depleted hat. But it was a chance, and one she was willing to take for her friends.

But something else filled the silence of Jessie's hesitation: a nightmarish screech, far down the hall. Something was rumbling toward them. And if Jessie's hearing was accurate, the group of Collective soldiers were right between them and whatever that thing was.

"Fuck, fuck, fuck," Carla said. "Another one? This place has too many goddamn monsters for its own good."

"Is that another Piasa bird?" Walt asked, peering around the corner.

"Different sort of screech," Jessie said. She was a little surprised that she could tell the two apart. "And the Piasa wouldn't be thundering down the hall. Those are footsteps, heavy enough for us to feel all the way down here. Whatever's coming, it's big."

The creature lumbered into view with a surprising suddenness considering its bulk. It filled the hallway, top to bottom and left to right, with wide shoulders and powerful arms . . . and the head of an owl.

Jessie immediately went to the idea of an owl bear, but that was just a gaming construct, not something from cryptid lore. Still, it bore a strong resemblance to the fantasy beast—huge, owl head, feathers—but it was also bipedal, with talons the size of butcher knives on all four appendages.

The soldiers were, as expected, shooting at it. And, also as expected, the bullets weren't doing much but making the monster even more pissed off.

"Move up behind them," Walt ordered. "While they're distracted. This may be our only shot, no matter who wins."

"I have a pretty good idea who's going to win," Jessie said. "And I don't want to look like a barn mouse for that particular predator." But they moved, all three in concert. Walt had brought to bear the gun he didn't want to use. Carla was steeled for battle, her fists clenched, looking wide-eyed at the melee before them, now coming more precisely into view.

It was the kind of fight that belonged in a fantasy novel, Jessie thought, the kind she and Toby had read obsessively over the years. Giant beast rampaging? Check. Picking up a hapless human foot soldier? Check. Ripping that guy nearly in half and beating the guy next to him with the bloody half corpse of his comrade? Check and check. The bursts of gunfire were constant, but the owl thing just seemed to absorb it all—bullets were falling to the ground uselessly with as much speed as the Kalashnikovs could fire them. And still, the beast tore through the line of soldiers. It raked open the stomach of one soldier with a vicious slash from its right winged arm while pinning another to the wall with a taloned bird foot that looked like the chicken feet that Jessie remembered trying once in a Chicago Chinatown dim sum joint—only here, each clawed toe was as big around as her wrist. The owl monster kept that soldier pinned to the wall in agony—it hadn't been cautious about where those talons landed, and one had gone right through the man's abdomen—until it dispatched two others nearby, at which point it turned back to the skewered soldier on the wall and put a claw through his right eye socket. The soldier slid down the wall to the ground, already dead.

There was only one soldier left, and he managed to turn away from the beast with his walkie-talkie out. He was panicking and saying *Ishkitini, Ishkitini*, over and over again . . . until he caught sight of Jessie, Carla, and Walt just down the hallway. His eyes opened wide, and it looked like he was about to say something more into the radio. But he only got out a single word: *Dochka*. And then talons closed around his head, the nails curling over his skull and penetrating his eyes. The soldier dropped the radio, which smashed on the floor, and then was flung backward as the beast turned, its heaving and impossibly muscled back now facing the group.

The hallway was awash in blood, suddenly silent once the thrown soldier had landed with a wet, meaty thud some twenty feet away. The monster just stood for a moment, its back still to the group, perhaps catching its breath.

And then its head swiveled around, 180 degrees, and gazed with menace at the three of them.

"Oh shit," Carla said, and took a step back.

"Hang on," Jessie cautioned, putting out an arm to hold everyone in place. "If it wanted us dead, I don't think it would have stopped when it did. It knew we were here. Walt, put the gun down. Put it down *now*."

Walt not only lowered the weapon, he threw it on the floor in front of them, almost as an offering.

The owl beast continued to stare at them for a long minute, cocking its head to one side slowly. And then, with a single heavy-lidded blink of its softball-sized eyes, it rotated its head back around to the front, let out a bellowing roar, and then took off lumbering down the hall the other way.

"Too many monsters," Carla repeated. "Just too many goddamn monsters."

"This place does tend to chew through soldiers," Walt said. "Good thing they can clone folks, I guess, right?"

"We gotta move," Jessie ordered, and started running, glad to ignore the question. She still didn't completely buy the idea that she was a clone. *Couldn't* buy it. Not yet.

Which was the problem, at least one of them, with this whole foray into the unknown. Far from finding answers, they'd found nothing but more questions, and didn't even have most of the evidence they'd worked to gather. What was the deal with Alton? How was he connected to the Firbens, and . . . well, *everything*? At least that answer might be on the drive he'd given her. Maybe more than that, too. Alton had come into this wanting more than what the rest of them had. He'd known far more than he shared. He wasn't even human. But he was, or had been, her friend.

Which made it all the more guilt inducing that she'd surreptitiously saved just a bit of the . . . stuff . . . that made up Alton's body. She didn't know why, but when a small piece came off in her hand when they were putting his body on the litter they'd fashioned, she'd slipped it into her backpack. She expected it to get all over everything, much like the gelatin it resembled, but when she went back to check when she'd had a spare minute, it had somehow solidified and desiccated a bit, even though it didn't really reduce noticeably in size. When she transferred it to the best container she had available—the clamshell case previously holding her sunglasses—the piece of alien flesh felt more like a normal cut of dry meat. Which explained why she now wore her Oakleys on her forehead like a yoga-panted mom with a jogging stroller.

Jessie half expected to run into another squad of soldiers, or worse, the owl beast, but the former never showed, and the latter had run in a straight line, according to the trail of bloody giant chicken tracks that kept going forward when they needed to turn right.

They made it back to the doors to the swampy area, and paused to catch their breaths before plunging back into the soup again.

"Do you think Woodsy Owl back there was what banged through the trapdoor back in the office?" Walt asked. "Right before we lost Otomi, I mean?"

"I didn't even think of that," Jessie admitted. "Definitely looked like it had enough strength to do it. But why would it try to get us at that point, and then take one look at us now and decide we weren't worth it?"

"Maybe we just look like crap," Walt suggested.

"Speak for yourself, papi," Carla snapped back playfully.

It was still surprising to Jessie how fast she and her friends were able to recover from witnessing cryptid abominations and the death they brought with them. She found it both endearing and somewhat worrisome. This level of horror wasn't something she wanted to get used to. "You guys ready?" she checked in.

"We haven't had a lot of luck in there," Walt said warily. "First Jace, and then Alton."

"We gotta get through, though," Carla insisted.

"I'm just saying we have to be careful," Walt responded, holding up his hands.

"Yeah," Jessie nodded. "We do."

They opened the door, ready for the immediate smell of stagnant water. Instead, they saw nothing but thickly corded webs.

Carla swore. Jessie sighed. Walt just murmured something about this maybe being a bad time to mention that he was "just the slightest bit incredibly arachnophobic." As if in answer, Jessie took out the jagged blade of alien ship metal, and started cutting through the webs. The impossibly sharp edge parted the webs as though they were water.

Jessie decided to consider this a good omen.

---

The positive thinking didn't last long.

It was hard to keep a stiff upper lip in what had become a chamber of spidery horrors. The trees that had once drooped with moss now sat laden with webbing. The walls, formerly that strange rock that seemed to grow on its own, were now invisible behind layers of the fiber, and dotted within it were the corpses of soldiers splayed at random angles, some fully cocooned, others not.

"You okay, Walt?" Jessie asked. She still wasn't sure how serious he'd been about the phobia.

"Yeah," he said, looking around warily. "I'm okay, I'm okay, I'm okay."

"He doesn't look so great," Carla observed.

*And she doesn't look a whole lot better,* Jessie thought. *Spiders do weird things to people.*

"I once moved out of a house I was renting," Walt murmured, "because I killed two spiders the night before I woke up to find one crawling out of my shoe once I put it on. That was it for me. I burned the shoes and got the hell out. Didn't even live there a week."

"That's wackadoodle, man," Carla said, letting loose a long, nervous sigh. "Can we just finally get to this shaft, please? I'm starting to think you're all lying to me about it, and I'm still in my cell dreaming or something."

"This is maybe the only place in the world where that would actually be possible," Jessie admitted. "But it's real."

"Do we just head back straight through?" Walt asked. "Or do we perimeter everything, and risk running into a trap?"

"I don't like either of those options," Carla said. "But if I had to choose, I'd probably try to retrace your steps as best we can."

Jessie nodded. "Agreed. Anyone see any of those giant spiders? What did Vargas call them?"

"Jabba Foofee or something," Walt recalled.

"One more thing to read up on once we're out of here," Jessie said.

"*If* we get out of—" Walt started.

"No," Carla cut him off. "Don't say it." She turned to Jessie. "And no, I don't see any of them."

"Just because we don't see them doesn't mean . . ." Walt tried again.

"How about you stop talking," Carla snapped. "How about you don't get to say anything else until we're safely through this goddamn room?"

Walt nodded.

They crept forward, keeping a low profile. They didn't see anything, didn't hear anything. It was preternaturally quiet, other than the sound of their cautious footfalls in shallow water.

They passed what was left of the trap that had taken Jace, and then past the site where Alton had fallen. Vargas's corpse was nowhere to be found, but they readily found his head when they approached the ruins of the Bwana Hut—it had been placed onto a stake right in front of what had been the hut's door. The eyes were still wide open, bulging out of the dirty, bloodied head. It was a warning, that much was evident—but they weren't sure who it was from, or to.

*Another mystery*, Jessie thought. *And sort of a disgusting one.*

Still, once they passed the hut, Jessie started feeling a little better. If they were going to be attacked, she assumed it would have happened already. They'd also seen a number of the traps that had been sprung—pits, snares, all of which now sat in plain view and more or less harmless.

They kept moving, and finally, after minutes of crouched and careful walking that felt more like hours, they came within sight of the door through which they'd come back when they'd started. It seemed like forever ago, Jessie thought. She took a breath. Even through the smell of the brackish water, she felt a sense of peace. She savored that for a moment, and kept moving the final fifty yards to the shaft door.

When the trio arrived, they looked back. The room was as dark as it always had been, but now that darkness was full of a sea of amber eyes, those same arachnid eyes that had flashed with an intelligent joy when they took out the Collective soldiers and hung them on the walls like slabs of meat. They weren't moving forward. They were just . . . *watching*.

"Can we go through the door now and not stand here and wave bye-bye to the giant spiders?" Walt asked with controlled panic in his voice.

They opened the door and backed out and onto the platform. The air smelled sweeter than Jessie remembered. She shut the door, and then heard something from the shadows behind her.

"Hey, roomie," came the all-too-familiar voice.

---

"Toby," Jessie said. "I seriously need you to stop being a fucking asshole."

"That's a relative term," Toby said. He was out of his usual clothes and dressed in fatigues, wearing a beret and holding an AK. "I could say the same thing to you."

"How do you figure that I'm being an asshole, asshole?" Jessie barked. "I'm not the one holding the gun on someone who was supposed to be their best friend. For ten years, Toby. Ten fucking years. And that was all . . . what, just bullshit?"

"Of course it wasn't," Toby said, and looked genuinely hurt. "It was deep cover. I couldn't have kept it up if I didn't also feel it. But it's not about not feeling the thing—it's about being willing and able to give it up immediately when duty calls. Besides, bestie, no offense, but you're a clone. Eminently replaceable, as the Boyar liked to say."

"The what?" Jessie scowled.

"Your mom or whatever," Toby answered. "The Boyar. It's her title, and why your last name is Boyer. You needed a last name despite you having no real family tree, I guess. But that's above my pay grade."

"What the fuck is a Bo-yaaar?" Jessie snorted.

"Russian feudal nobility," Walt murmured. "Part of the peerage for centuries, right under royalty. Military leaders and civil authority."

"Thanks, teach," Toby smiled at Walt with no kindness. "Now shut the fuck up."

"What are you doing, Toby?" Jessie pleaded, and didn't like

the exhaustion she could hear in her own voice. "Seriously. What, you're going to kill me now?"

Toby shrugged. "I assumed I'd have to kill you someday. But I swear, Jess, I would have been kind about it. No violence, no terror. I owed you that much."

"I . . . I don't even know what to say to that," Jessie stuttered. "Are you actually trying to comfort me by telling me that if the termination order came down, you would have killed me *quickly*?"

"And painlessly," Toby added. "And probably without you even knowing. I had any number of ways to do it. I kept a whole list, because I wanted to be ready, just in case."

"You kept a list. Of ways to murder me."

"Murder you *nicely*," Toby corrected. "There's an important distinction. And also, not for nothing, but I'm not even sure you can define the elimination of a clone as murder. It's not like killing a person."

"You're insane," Jessie said, aghast.

"No, no," Toby replied. "You're not getting it. It's like that scene on the Ferris wheel from *The Third Man*, right? Harry says to look down at the ground from way up high, so high the people walking below are dots. And he asks his friend how much money it would take for him to agree that one of those dots stopped moving. Or more than one? How many dots would he give up—just dots, remember—before it made any real difference to him? That's what I'm talking about, Jess."

"So I'm a dot," Jessie said. *We have no way out of this*, she thought, and then remembered her earlier idea. The syringe—what had it potentially done to her, and what could she do to trigger it? "And now you're going to stop me from moving?"

"I mean, yeah," Toby admitted. "You and Carla and Walt. Sorry, guys. Collateral damage is sort of part of the gig."

"You still have a choice, son," Walt said. "Just put down the gun and join back up with us. This is a complicated place, and you've just gotten a little lost, is all."

Toby smiled. "It's nice that you think I have that option, or that I'd be willing to take it even if I did. I appreciate that, I really do."

"You're a piece of shit," Carla growled.

"There we go," Toby said. "Now I feel less bad about making you dots stop moving."

"Toby, I hate . . . well, no I actually *love* to be the one to break this to you," Jessie smiled. "But according to my mother—your Boyar? You're a clone too."

Toby scowled. "No, Jess. I *was* cloned. Or at least they were going to clone me, once I joined up. I remember it distinctly."

"You would, you moron," Jessie said. "Why would she lie to me about something as inconsequential as that? Assuming what she told me about my own memories is true, then you've been implanted with the same bullshit backstory that I was. It's how we work best, I imagine. How they keep us happy. How they mold us into the good little dots they want us to be. Why no matter what you do here—if you go back to the Collective, even bearing our corpses as trophies? You're a dot they're going to stop from moving too."

"You're stalling," Toby said, shaking the thought from his head. "You're just trying to delay the inevitable."

"With the inevitable," Jessie countered, "that's pretty much all you can do, right?" She closed her eyes and reached down inside as deep as she could go. She saw lights in her mind's eye, something swirling, a light that was blue but also not blue at the same time, and it swooshed up suddenly and turned into a bird, or something that looked like a bird. Jessie felt that lurching sensation all the way down to her toes, and in her gut too, and she felt lighter than she had in a long time, and wondered if it was due to endorphins or something else—*please let it be something else!*—and she opened herself up, or imagined herself opening up anyway, to whatever fantastic power her mother and that chemical in her knee might have planned for her, for whatever experimental reason, it didn't matter why anymore, just so long as she could do something in this moment of sheer powerlessness, something grand and effective and maybe even the smallest bit vengeful toward her former best friend and confidante, the guy who knew every detail about her, even false and implanted memories, and Jessie wondered in that moment what was about to happen, and when, and had she ever in her whole life ever really had a real friend?

But nothing happened. Nothing at all. The Collective's complex under Denver International Airport was never designed to be that kind.

"What was that?" Toby scoffed.

Jessie opened her eyes and dismissed the self-induced moment. If nothing was happening, maybe a bluff would work. "My mother injected me with some serum," Jessie said. "You can shoot me. But you can't hurt me."

"No she didn't," Toby said.

"She did," Jessie insisted with a smile.

"No," Toby protested. "She wouldn't have had the chance. You both seized out at the same time, idiot. Haven't you ever noticed that you do that seizing thing whenever you've been around the Boyar too long? It's something the scientists haven't figured out—can't be too near your double for very long, or your brains start to do some weird uplink shit, and you go offline."

Jessie felt her whole body go cold. She searched her memories for a time when the seizures hadn't happened with her mother around. It explained so much: why her mother was never around above all else. Aside from the fact that she didn't give a shit about Jessie. She was, after all, just a dot.

But someone *had* injected her, she thought. With *something*.

Not that it was apparently going to do any good now, or—once Toby opened fire—anytime in the future. She wondered what death for clones might feel like. Did clones get an afterlife?

"Bye, bestie," Toby lifted the Kalashnikov. "It's been real."

"Hey Toby! Want a Coke?" Walt suddenly shouted, and threw something as hard as he could. It was small, cylindrical, and red.

"Wha—" Toby stepped back, surprised, and swung the AK around as the can bounced off Toby's chest and plunked onto the ground, busting open where it hit and spitting a hissing stream of cola.

In that moment of distraction, Carla surged forward and pushed the rifle to one side. Toby tried to bring it back around, but he was no match for Carla's corded muscle, and she had the advantage of leverage. Toby fired a few bursts from the AK in a panic, but Carla moved up and, in a single smooth motion, brought Toby's right arm down over her knee. The crack that came from his elbow, now turned at the wrong angle, echoed throughout the shaft.

Carla took the AK from Toby's useless hand, and pushed him to the ground. Toby fell hard, only scant feet from the edge of the platform.

*It's a long way down*, Jessie thought. *Too bad he didn't fall a little farther.*

But it was a thought she immediately regretted. That wasn't her. As much as she wanted Toby to suffer, she didn't want his blood on her hands.

"Well, well, well, you traitorous *bitch*," Carla taunted. "*Estás jodido.*"

"You broke my fucking *arm*," Toby screamed through gritted teeth, and rose to his knees.

"You broke my girl's fucking heart, *puta*," Carla said, and handed the rifle to Jessie. "And now she's going to do to you what you were planning to do to her." She turned to her friend. "Shoot him in the face."

"I . . . I don't know," Jessie said, but reluctantly took the gun. "Wouldn't it be better if, like, we left him to the Collective? Isn't that more poetic justice than just shooting him while he's helpless on the floor? I don't want to be that person. And the Collective might make me a lot of things, but they're not going to make me that."

"I get it," Walt said softly. "You do what you need to do."

"Absolutely," Carla agreed.

Toby was still kneeling, cradling his broken arm. He looked up at them with something approaching sorrow in his eyes. "Jess, I—" he started.

But he'd never finish. Carla took one step toward Toby and kicked with a powerful blow that struck him hard in his sternum. He fell helplessly, and was plummeting from the platform before anyone realized what was happening. His scream as he disappeared into the darkness slowly vanished as the three survivors stood in shocked silence.

Jessie couldn't find it in herself to feel bad for him. "So long," she said, and thought of bouzouki music and better times.

"Well, that dick got what was coming to him. Great job with the soda, Walt," Carla slapped him on the shoulder. "I was looking for the right moment to charge his stupid ass, and then you made it happen."

"I was hoping to get it home so I could try to figure out the formula," Walt mourned. "But I didn't have anything else to throw. Plus, Toby said he liked it, so . . ."

"Okay," Jessie said, still a little stunned. "We're alive. That's good."

"But no rope," Walt said, pointing up. "So, that's bad."

"Wasn't one of these shafts supposed to have ladders?" Carla asked.

"This apparently isn't one of those," Jessie said. "Let's think. What's back in there that we could use to fashion a rope or something?"

"We're not going back in there," Walt insisted. "Did you not see the millions of spider eyes in the darkness? That was not a come-on-back-and-see-us-sometime look."

"I don't see that we have a choice," Jessie pointed out. "After all—" She stopped as a sound came from the door leading back into the swamp area. A scratching.

"Do spiders have claws?" Carla asked.

"Oh god, probably," Walt said with terror in his voice.

"Did they?" Jessie tried to remember.

And then they heard more scratching, and—was that whining?

"That sounds like a dog," Walt said. He went over to the door and put his ear against it. "Hello?" he said. "Spider?"

"It's not going to answer you, Walt," Carla rolled her eyes. "Stand back."

Walt did, and Carla opened the door just a bit. Immediately, a yellow snout with a black, wet nose popped through the slim opening.

Carla opened it wider, and the dog came trundling through happily. It was a yellow lab like Roger had described in his video.

"Baldr?" Jessie said, and the dog barked with joy and jumped up to lick her face. He had a fanny pack cinched around his belly. While Jessie was busy giving Baldr pets, Walt took the pack off the dog and unzipped it.

He held out the Pigeon, Patsy's little emergency drone. It

was Jace's pack. "There's a note here too," Walt told them. "It just says *Go*, and then its signed with like a symbol or something."

Jessie managed to extricate herself from the engulfing embrace of the yellow lab long enough to take the note from Walt, who was already separating the small drone from its controller. The symbol was the same one that she'd seen in the center of the wall of her father's shed. What that meant, she had no idea. But she was determined to get out of there and find out.

They wrote a short note and tied it to the Pigeon with some fishing line from Jace's fanny pack. Walt was happily testing the small drone to make sure he was proficient enough with the controls that he could manage to maneuver it without hitting a wall.

"Ready?" Walt said, as the drone hung in the air.

Jessie took a deep breath. There were still too many questions lingering. What was on Alton's drive. What the injection on her leg might have been. What her mother, Not-Margaret, the Boyar, whatever—had planned for her next. She was sure this wasn't over. But survival—extrication—had to come first. Jessie took a deep breath. The scent of the surface world filled her, and the pinprick of light coming from above held more promise than anything she'd felt in a long while.

"Ready," she replied. And she was.

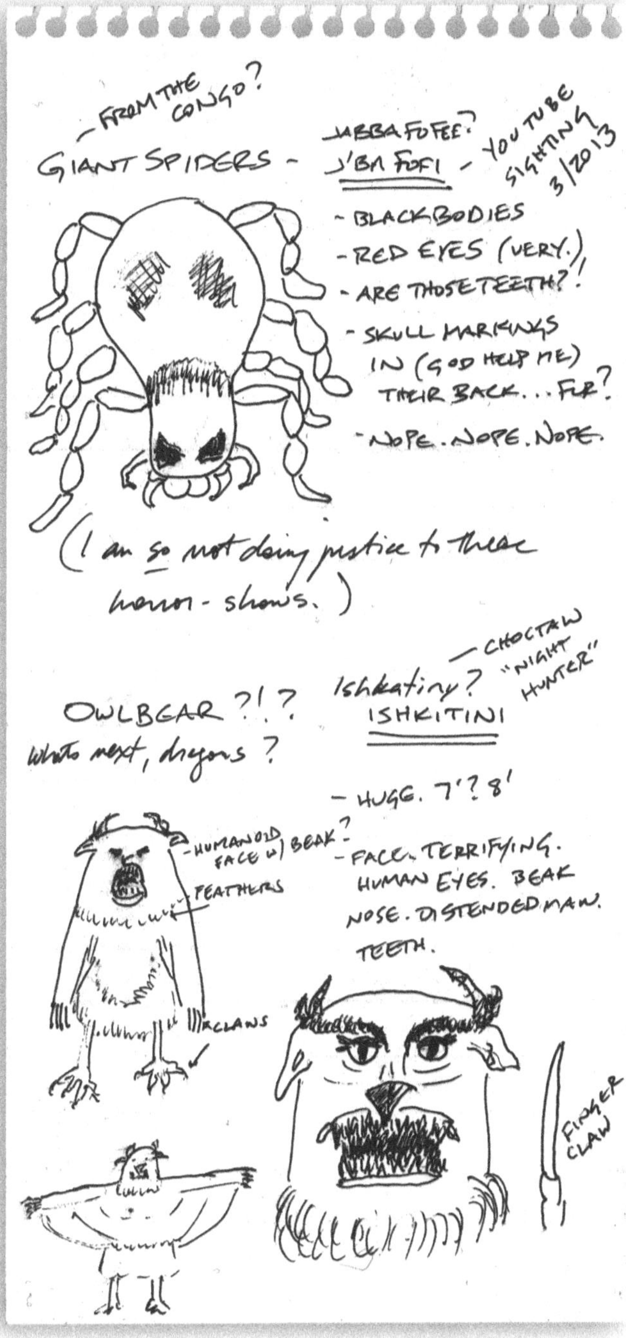


Walt's Field Journal, page 31

# EPILOGUE A

TOPSIDE, SHAFT 69

Patsy wondered if today was the day. It felt like it would be, or at least that's what she sensed, and her senses rarely failed her. It was midday, a beautiful early afternoon with the sun almost directly overhead, warming the mountain air in welcome. She munched on a peanut butter sandwich on white bread. It was the little things, she thought, as she sat against a tree and felt her muscles relax into a thatch of tall grass.

She was surrounded by something approaching carnage; the small clearing had seen a number of battles in the days she'd been waiting for her temporary charges. Drones, certainly, more than a dozen wrecked all over the grounds, but the occasional beast as well. There was a small pyramid of needle beaks across the way where she'd stacked up their corpses once she was done dispatching them. There was the carcass of the hairy alligator that had come through—she wasn't sure if that was sent, or had just gotten loose, and this was its hunting ground. But no matter. It hadn't been much of a challenge. She'd been a little disappointed, frankly, but then again, the loin cuts she'd enjoyed after butchering it last night had been divine.

She heard a buzz—another drone. She knew she had to blow this one out of the sky as quickly as she had all the others, so it wouldn't have time to send back any messages. Or such was the hope. Always tough to tell with these little machines. She never trusted any of them, personally. In fact, she got a little extra satisfaction every time she popped another one into oblivion.

She brought out her .308 Winchester and shouldered it—but then stopped. It was her Pigeon. She chuckled. Looks like at least one of the explorers had survived after all.

Patsy went over to where the drone landed clumsily, and plucked it up before it could take off again. She read the note.

THROW DOWN A SHITLOAD OF ROPE. WE'RE READY TO GO HOME.

# EPILOGUE
# B

IN THE HEART OF THE COLLECTIVE

The Boyar sits before more monitors than one might easily count. She has her shoes off and feet up, an ice pack covering one knee. She has a remote control for the screens, each showing different angles of her meddling daughter—her *alternate*, as the scientists keep correcting her—in various parts of the complex. Some showcase security footage. Some were taken from the memory cards in the Pelican case they'd recovered when they captured her—at least temporarily.

Her Jessica. Her own little girl was trapped in a hole. She almost admired the girl's tenacity. It was annoying, yes, but like a mosquito in your room at night when you're trying to sleep. Just a nuisance. Easily dealt with, and barring that, easy to dismiss as having absolutely no long-term importance.

The Boyar stops her search and focuses on one monitor in particular. It shows the girl in a cell, talking to her friend, the mole. The woman hits a few buttons on the remote, and another screen lights up with video of the cell next door—a man, sitting in the middle of the room on an overturned bucket, rocking back and forth. He's sweating, even though the air is dry and cool. He has a crazed look to his eyes, and he's muttering to himself. He sometimes erupts into screams, and then returns to the sublimated murmur that seems to be his baseline state.

The Boyar picks up her phone and makes a call. "I need transcripts on anything said in B-21 while the girl was in B-23." A pause. "Yes, immediately. Eliminate the background noise, clean up the audio, do whatever you need to, but get me a translation of exactly what was said, and what that girl might have been able to make out."

The woman glares at the screen and zooms in on the man sitting on the bucket, chewing his nails and moving in ways that he didn't seem to notice or even intend. *More trouble than he was ever worth*, the woman thought.

"Keep me posted," she orders with menace in her voice. "I need to know what her father may have told her."

# EPILOGUE

# C

CHAMPAIGN, ILLINOIS

If anyone were there to witness it, they'd see a young woman dressed in cargo fatigue BDU pants and a tank top under a frame backpack that seems too large both for her and for its appearance on a quiet neighborhood street in a Midwest college town. The woman has impossibly brown hair—an unnaturally consistent chestnut—tied back in a short ponytail, and she's wearing mirrored sunglasses despite the overcast skies. She's exiting a modest clapboard house of blue siding and black shingle with no apparent urgency to her pace.

This might strike an onlooker as strange since the house behind her is on fire, flames slowly building from somewhere within, consuming the drapes, the wall-to-wall carpet, and the bone-white furniture. A window explodes from the growing conflagration—the house is too small to contain its consumption for long.

Neighbors start to poke out from their own small homes like ground squirrels emerging from their burrows, full of inquisitively wide eyes and sharp jerks of their heads as they take in what's happening and who else is watching. But primarily they watch the flames as they grow higher—sad in the abstract for an oft-absent neighbor in that blue house with its dark windows and professional landscapers and housekeeping that are most times its only visitors. But grateful, too, that it's not their houses, that they've been spared this tragic happenstance, that the side yards in this development from the 1960s offered enough space that the homes to either side won't be likewise threatened and burn.

There are sirens in the distance. Help, such as it is, is already on the way.

And no one pays much attention to the young woman, walking away as though finding her car in a supermarket parking lot. It's an exaggerated casualness, some might say, if they were paying attention to her at all as she walks to the end of the block where a dark-windowed Lincoln Navigator sits idling. She opens the rear door to put in her backpack, then enters the SUV on the passenger side. There's a man at the wheel. Older. Paunchy. Sporting a mustache. There's someone in the back seat, too, at least one person, because the woman looks back, says something, and nods as she puts on her seat belt and glances at the house one more time. Her face is stoic as she shuts the door.

But unknown to her, to any of them, there is a witness. A neighbor who isn't a neighbor. Someone there on purpose. Someone at their post. Someone doing their duty.

Because someone—somewhere—is always watching.

# MANUAL OF MONSTERS

THESE ARE ALPHABETIZED AS WELL AS I COULD, BASED ON THEIR "OFFICIAL" NAMES—ANY NICKNAMES, ETC., ARE NOTED IN THE ENTRIES. NEED TO DO MORE RESEARCH ON MOST OF THESE WHEN I HAVE TIME, BECAUSE I ONLY KNEW A FEW OF THEM OFF THE TOP OF MY HEAD. A TASK FOR LATER, ASSUMING THERE IS A LATER.

—WALT

**BIGFOOT**: This dude needs no introduction. Call him whatever you want: Sasquatch, Yeti, Skunk Ape (they probably hate that last one; it's rude!), but he's not just a him, he's a them. Full race of these guys. Mainly from North American legend, but have been seen in various forms worldwide. We didn't see any of these big guys, but we know from the *ED* podcast that they exist in the tunnels. I'm including things we only heard of—or saw obliquely—just for the sake of the record. From the sound of it, this is no *Harry and the Hendersons* shit, but more like a vicious Wookiee that you don't want to beat in space chess. (Also: is "Bigfeet" the proper plural of "Bigfoot?" Seems like something we'd want to get right.)

**CHUPACABRA**: Traditionally, these "chupes" are Mexican demons of a sort. Their name means "goat sucker" in Spanish due to their original chosen prey. I remember hearing about these as a kid growing up in the American Midwest, but they weren't dogs, as I recall. More like smallish lizard people? But the chupes we've seen (too many) are definitely more canine than anything, both in look and behavior. Pack mentality, all fours, the whole nine. Scaly skin, spikes on the neck, vicious jaws, and what I think are multiple rows of teeth. (Didn't get close enough to be sure.) Jessie, Alton, and I went back and forth on how to spell the abbreviation for these guys—I liked the simple "chup," which in Spanish would be pronounced correctly (like "choop"), but I got overruled. By the way: as Carla demonstrated, these guys can be controlled with a whistle, so they might be scary, but they're also useful if you know what you're doing.

**FIRBEN**: Pronounced like "fear-bean." There is no way in hell I'm going to be able to explain what these guys are. Not really. Not that I even know. They're an alien race, that much is clear, and they've been here a long time. Lots of abilities, including shape-shifting, some form of invulnerability to physical harm, great strength, and perhaps a greater intellect than humans. There's some suggestion that there's a caste system of some sort that relates to physiology; Alton mentioned some being of an academic caste, but didn't elaborate. As such, abilities could differ within the race. We're only scratching the surface of them, but they've clearly been living among us for decades, if not centuries.

**FIVE-LINED CONSTELLATION FISH**: Man, I wanted to see one of these. Read about them a long time back—a hypothetical aquatic species called *Bathysidus pentagrammus* supposedly found by an explorer in the 1930s off the coast of Bermuda. Supposedly they live in the canals lining the Domes.

**FLYING MONKEY**: How to explain these things without pissing off the Baum estate? Well, these guys are even more terrifying than in the movie. No hats or bellhop uniforms, of course, but literal winged chimpanzees that you can smell coming before you see them, by which time it's too late, if they're after you. On the bright side, they don't seem aggressive by nature—just territorial.

**GIANT STRIX**: I'm just connecting these bloodsuckers to the ancient Greek myth of Lake Stymphalia in southern Greece. For all I know, they could just be modified giant hummingbirds, which is more or less what they look like. Pretty sure their needle beaks have been reinforced somehow with steel, but maybe that's just a trick of the eye, the metallic sheen. Still: they hover, they puncture, and they feed. No thank you.

**HAIRY ALLIGATOR**: There has to be a better name for these things, but if there is, I'm not familiar with it. We never saw one, but I'm pretty sure we saw some of the damage it could do. From the descriptions, it's essentially a monstrosity composed of an extra-large gator with its scales covered in a mat of coarse hair. Why? No idea yet.

**ISHKITINI**: The horned owl beast from Choctaw legend. Heard about this supposedly roaming the plains of Oklahoma, and never thought I'd see one. Sort of looks like an owl–bear hybrid in a way. Huge pile of feathers and claws and a head that can rotate all the way around.

**J'BA FOFI**: Giant spiders from the Congo. Six-foot legs at least, no shit. Skull-like markings in the black fur—FUR!—on their backs. Clearly intelligent, from the gaze of their very red eyes. Based on the effects we saw, some fast-acting poison too.

Webs its prey to consume later. Nightmare fuel. I hate them.

**JACKALOPE**: Remember the killer rabbit at the end of that Monty Python movie? Yeah, these things would have that little guy for breakfast. Cute chubby little bunnies that have sharp antlers and know how to use them. Teeth, too; carnivorous as hell. Consider them land piranhas. Meet them in a group, and you're toast.

**JERSEY DEVIL**: Known by a lot of names: Wozzle Bug, the Hoodle-Doodle Bird, etc. We only saw them from a distance, but they seemed to be a sort of little dragon, maybe, with a horselike head? Scaly, so possibly dinosaur in origin. Their bodies and method of attack are very similar to kangaroos, too—they attack with punches and kicks to take a foe to the ground, at which point they eat them alive by virtue of the gnashing teeth in those horse jaws.

**MERMAIDS**: Alton swears he saw one of these in the canals, but I only saw shapes in the water. From his description, they definitely don't sound like the beauties of legend—instead, they're more of an abomination. They're huge fish, essentially, up to the armpits. No breasts of which to speak, apparently, and a head that resembles that of a waterlogged crone more than a young maiden. Spoilers of adolescent dreams everywhere. Definitely don't want to "kiss dis girl."

**MONGOLIAN DEATH WORM**: A terrifyingly giant bloodred worm with a mouthlike terminus at one end that looks like the Sarlacc pit gone mobile. Probably the fastest-acting poison we've seen. Not sure about standard size; some were no more than a couple of feet in length, but I'm sure I saw a few that had to be five to six feet or more. The big ones weren't wider—just longer?

**PIASA:** (Pronounced PIE-a-saw) A great bird, possibly related to the Native American thunderbird myths? Known previously only as cliff art along the Mississippi River. Iridescent crimson wings on a multicolored body the size of a large cow. Horned, with a humanish face somehow—maybe it's the awareness in the giant red eyes. Sharp beak with razor teeth and bird talons on the feet. That's the one we saw. Other depictions suggest a more feathery body and an almost skull-like face behind the killer beak. Not sure if that's indicative of there being more of these. Hope not.

**TIDDALIK**: Again, we may be ascribing myth to something that's essentially an overgrown example of something more mundane—in this case, a mammoth frog. In Aboriginal legend, Tiddalik was the frog that drank all the waters of the land, causing a drought . . . until he's tickled, and the water returns as he laughs. What we saw wasn't big enough to do that, but it did swallow some soldiers whole.

**TOM BRADY**: I include this here so I remember Alton's vague comment about there being more to this football legend than meets the eye. Not sure what to make of it, other than I trust Alton.

**YA-TE-VEO**: Also known as the Man-Eating Tree of Madagascar, this willowlike tree is something out of a *Poltergeist*ian nightmare. A hungry tree that's all too happy to pluck you from the ground and consume you in big crunchy bites. It does seem to have a variable appetite—it didn't like the taste of some of us, or at least left us un-snatched? Gotta be a reason, but what it is still remains a mystery.

## *ESCAPING DENVER* SOUNDTRACK

"Straight into Darkness" by Tom Petty and the Heartbreakers
(Chapter 1, Jessie running in Chicago)

"Conspiracy" by Paramore
(Chapter 2, when the group gathers for their Zoom meetup)

"Rocky Mountain Way" by Joe Walsh
(Chapter 3, while driving to Ward)

"I Washed My Hands in Muddy Water" by Stonewall Jackson
(Chapter 4, as Patsy eludes those in chase in her War Rig)

"Time Is Time" by Andy Gibb
(Chapter 5, as they climb up from the dude ranch)

"Black Ops" by They Might Be Giants
(Chapter 6, as they enter the complex)

"Stranger in a Strange Land" by Leon Russell
(Chapter 7, fleeing from soldiers)

"Scary Monsters (and Super Creeps)" by David Bowie
(Chapter 8, on seeing the Piasa)

"There's No Way Out of Here" by David Gilmour
(Chapter 9, traversing the Domes)

"Meet Me in the Woods" by Lord Huron
(Chapter 10, in Bio-Dome 466)

"The Conspiracy Song" by The Dead Milkmen
(Chapter 11, in the control tower)

"The Happening" by the Pixies
(Chapter 12, on the run again)

"Man on the Moon" by R.E.M.
(Chapter 13, in the studio)

"Books About UFOs" by Hüsker Dü
(Chapter 14, in the Archives)

"Fishin' 4 Religion" by Arrested Development
(Chapter 15, in captivity)

"No Children" by The Mountain Goats
(Chapter 16, talking with Mom)

"Goodbye Stranger" by Supertramp
(Chapter 17, after the melee)

"Kiss Off" by Violent Femmes
(Chapter 18, in the fight back to the shaft)

"All the Way Down" by The Felice Brothers
(Chapter 18, at the end)

"Burning Down the House" by Talking Heads
(Epilogue C, Jessie moves out and moves on)

# ACKNOWLEDGMENTS

First and foremost, I want to recognize the passion and perseverance of Mike Howorun, Brady Roberts, and Matthew Hall, the builders of the world of *Escaping Denver*, who were kind enough to extend me an invitation to play along. To David Slayton for letting me know the opportunity existed. And to Brendan Deneen and the team from Blackstone who trusted me with the gig. Special thanks to my two readers, my daughter Teagan and her friend Beth Briggs, who read an early draft to make sure that it made any sense at all.

But I wouldn't be writing this without the opportunity afforded me by my years working with the Denver alt-weekly *Westword* and its fearless leader Patty Calhoun, who assigned me—twice!—to write about the *Escaping Denver* podcast. Long live the free press, independent journalism, and doors that open even when you don't realize it.

I'd like to thank my friends from my undergrad days at the University of Arizona (Bear Down!) and my cohort and professors in my MFA years at Arizona State, who set me on the writing path. Thanks too to my colleagues and students at CU Denver who walk it with me now. Likewise, recognition to the literary championing done by Lighthouse Writers Workshop in Denver. All these institutions are vital to the arts, to learning, and to the provision of colleagues that so enrich the writing life.

Heartfelt gratitude also to those who supported me through the creation of this book: my brilliant and beautiful lady friend Stephanie, my friends who shared all the nerd pursuits over the years and always had a place for me at the table, and my children Teagan and Thomas, who are the sweetest of mysteries, worlds within worlds. I love you all.

And finally, a salute to all the lurkers above and dwellers below, the denizens of unknown lairs and the delvers into the unknown recesses of whatever underworld might be handy on the search for tales and treasure. The truth is indeed out there, even if it sometimes has jaws that bite and claws that catch and come whiffling through the tulgey wood, perhaps burbling with eyes of flame, but nonetheless utterly frabjous.

—Teague Bohlen, April 2025